Mystic Man

TOREN CHENAULT

DEDICATION

This book is dedicated to all people facing racism, sexism, classism, and all other prejudices in the world.

TABLE OF CONTENTS

ACKNOWLEDGMENTS

To my other half, my support system, and the one who helped me through all of this. I love you and thank you.

Part One

HUMBLE BEGINNINGS

CHAPTER 1

Most people who have any common sense would tell you that the city of San Francisco is a beautiful place to live. From the bevy of sights to see, along with some of the most immaculate people, the majority enjoy the lively city. The only person who would rise against popular opinion would be Isaac Martin Eckspo. He had lived in the Bay area for thirteen years now. He was sitting at his desk one afternoon when there was a soft knock at his door. His body became jittery at the thought of it being someone who could help save his business. When his daughter Alisha walked in, he focused on his beautiful six-year-old and not the financial quagmire he was in.

"Hey Daddy," Alisha said. She grabbed her father's notes from the week and began flipping through them. She was always grabbing things that she shouldn't be grabbing. Isaac knew she had no idea what she was looking at, but he found it necessary to teach his daughter a lesson in respect.

"Baby Girl, what have I told you about looking at other people's things?"

"Don't do it," Alisha said.

"So why are you looking through Daddy's things?"

"Mommy told me too. Says you hide things from us," Alisha said. She smiled as hard as she could, trying to be as cute as she could be too.

"Is that right? Well you tell Mommy that going through people's things isn't nice." As Isaac finished his sentence he picked up his daughter and began to run around the room making airplane noises. Alisha began to laugh uncontrollably, and the two shared a couple of minutes of playful airplanes, tickling, and silly name calling. They were both on his office couch when his wife, Cynthia, walked in. For a moment, Isaac had to appreciate his breath-taking Mexican wife. The outfit she was wearing showed off her voluptuous curves. Her long dark hair always looked as if she had come straight from a salon, even though she constantly reminded Isaac of how disgusting her hair was. What Isaac loved most about his wife though was her eyes. He never thought brown could look so majestic. Whenever he stared into her eyes, he felt a sensation he knew that most men have never felt, and he felt it every time he looked at her. It didn't matter if they were dressed up for a banquet, or if she was laying in their bed on Saturday morning, her beauty was something that Isaac could not describe. She looked mad right now though. No, not mad, Isaac thought, more like frustrated. It tended to be the main emotion in the Eckspo household recently. Still, Isaac couldn't get over how gorgeous his wife looked.

"So, this is you hard at work, huh?" Cynthia asked as she walked into his office.

Isaac and Alisha abruptly stopped their tickling session to give Cynthia their full attention. Cynthia had that ability. No matter what someone was doing, when she spoke, people listened.

"Go play with your toys, Baby Girl," Isaac said.

Alisha shrugged her shoulders and ran off, making more airplane noises.

"How was shopping?" Isaac asked.

"You are supposed to be trying to find a solution to our problem, but you're just in here playing," Cynthia said.

After Isaac and Cynthia left college, they decided to move out to San Francisco. The couple wanted to open a business that helped people learn the wonders of science. Neither of them knew what they could do to achieve their outlandish dreams, but one day Isaac had an idea. He planned on opening a business that was focused on increasing children's and teen's knowledge of science by letting them directly interact with it. He named the program Science Supreme. Isaac didn't consider himself much of a scientist, that was Cynthia, but he was very crafty and invented tools all of the time. Isaac's dream was to show his inventions to youth all over the country and explain to them how science was used to make the invention. He'd even let the children explore his and Cynthia's lab.

Over the years, while Cynthia was doing research, she came across a unique element called Immobulum. She first discovered the element during a research trip she went on with her colleagues to China. Once she harvested the majority of the Immobulum, she was able to use it for Science Supreme. This element could be molded into almost anything, and the possibilities of its uses were endless. For five years, Isaac and Cynthia used it to power their Science Supreme Center and to shape the majority of Isaac's crafty inventions.

"I'm trying. Trust me, I have been contacting every person we know about Immobulum. Nothing is coming up," Isaac said.

Cynthia sighed and then tried to put a smile on her face. Isaac tried to remember the last time his wife smiled and actually meant it.

"I'm sorry, I guess this is all getting to me now. Our bank accounts are still frozen, and the government is always calling here asking for money," she said.

Isaac sat up from his chair to console his wife. He didn't know what to say to her, so he decided to embrace her as tightly as he could. She shook a bit when he first grabbed her. There was no way to tell if the shaking was from fear or because his office was always cold. Either way, the feeling of his wife's body made him feel safe.

The couple shared a kiss. Then, Cynthia ran her hands across Isaac's face.

"Some of the scars seemed to have healed," she said.

Three years ago, while working on an experiment, Isaac severely injured his face when acid from an invention spilled directly onto him. For months, he thought his face would never look the same. To hear his wife say he looked somewhat normal made him feel good.

Once they separated, Isaac went back to his computer. There was a long moment of silence before he talked again.

"Who's been calling from the government?" he asked.

"He doesn't say his name. He says the Pinnacle is going to keep taking money from us, unless we give them more Immobulum," Cynthia said.

"Why don't those idiots get it through their thick skulls that we don't have any more!" Isaac ran his hand across the table and threw whatever papers and folders were on his desk, onto the ground. The noise prompted Alisha to come into the room with a worried look on her face.

"Daddy's fine, Baby Girl. Now go play."

Alisha left the room slowly.

"Calm down, Isaac. We don't need you going into cardiac arrest," Cynthia said.

"Sorry."

He picked up the papers he had thrown off his desk and neatly placed them back.

"So, this man is from the Pinnacle, huh?" Isaac asked.

Cynthia nodded.

"I'm going to pay them a visit. Hopefully I can get some answers on why they are harassing us," he said.

"Do you need me to come?" Cynthia inquired.

"No. You need to stay here so you can watch Alisha. I won't be gone long."

For the next hour, Isaac packed his bags for the trip. He didn't plan on being gone for longer than a couple of days, but he wasn't sure the Pinnacle would take a meeting with him so soon. The Pinnacle was a place that could eat a man alive, so he knew he was going to have to be stern and not take no for an answer.

While he was washing his face in the bathroom later that evening, he realized that he could be making a mistake. He knew the Pinnacle wouldn't care to listen to a failed inventor, let alone a black one, but he knew he had to try something to save his family. Isaac laid down in bed next to his wife. Her warmth comforted him. He embraced her as his thoughts began to race. Cynthia, without saying a word, curled her body up against her husband's and let out a deep sigh. For the next couple of minutes, Isaac wasn't worried about going to the Pinnacle at all.

"I love you," he whispered. Cynthia didn't say anything, but he knew she heard him. He always talked to her while she slept. Whether it was about his day, their financial situation, or what to get Alisha for her birthday, he always talked to her. He kissed her forehead softly before relaxing the muscles in his body. His head sank into the pillow. Within seconds, Isaac felt his eyes welling with tears. Images of him, Cynthia, and Alisha becoming homeless entered his mind. Alisha would still be playing with her toys as she always did. But he knew she wasn't completely naïve. Questions of why they weren't at their home would become frequent. Isaac could hardly contain his tears. Cynthia, as if she sensed his pain, turned to face him and kissed him on the cheek. But she didn't say a word.

"I'll fix this Cynthia. I will," Isaac whispered. "I won't let anything happen to you or Alisha. Without you two, I am nothing."

— ·· — ·· — ·· — ·· — ·· — ·· — ··

The next morning was filled with anxiety for the Eckspo family. It was June and Alisha didn't have school. Every morning she'd wake up at about 9 am to watch her favorite television shows. The anxiety began with her anticipating what SpongeBob was going to do about Patrick struggling in boating school. Alisha loved SpongeBob. She wasn't a big fan of Patrick though.

Cynthia's anxiety came later, around noon, when she was trying to decide her outfit for the day. Typically, she didn't give a damn about what she wore, but today she wanted to be sexy for her husband. He was leaving in a few hours, and the family was going out to an early lunch with Isaac's mother. She wanted her husband to know that she was all his and that she'd be waiting for him when he returned from the Pinnacle.

The last member of the Eckspo family was dealing with the greatest amount of anxiety. Isaac awoke refreshed and feeling healed from last night's pain. As he brushed his teeth, the music from outside made him start to dance. He was preparing to dance around all the crap the Pinnacle was going to throw at him today. The music continued, and Isaac continued to dance. He looked out his window to see two of his favorite people standing near his front door. Isaac didn't have a clue what their names were, but every day they played some of the best jazz music Isaac had ever heard. One man had a saxophone, the other, had drums. They noticed Isaac looking out of the window and waved. He waved back.

Isaac headed downstairs, and when he reached his wife, he noticed how dolled up she was.

9

"What's this?" he asked. "The Pinnacle is only about four hours away, and only about an hour by plane. I should be back tomorrow night if everything goes well, maybe even tonight."

"And I'll miss you every second," Cynthia said as she hugged her husband. They passionately began to kiss but were forced to stop when Alisha started watching.

"Yuck," she said. Isaac laughed.

"Are you ready to go see Grandma Rose?" Isaac asked Alisha as he picked her up. She screamed joyfully, so Isaac could only assume that meant yes. SpongeBob had been interrupted for a special news report. The newscaster was talking about a shooting that had happened recently. A black male had been shot ten times by police officers. Reports said that it wasn't yet known if the black male had a gun. All that was truly known was that the man was dead. Isaac moved over to the television and turned it off. He sighed deeply because he realized the shooting had taken place in San Francisco. The main reason he moved out here with Cynthia was to avoid that sort of stuff. But he knew that this wasn't something you could outrun. Today though, he didn't want to think about it.

"You know your mother has heard about it by now," Cynthia said.

"I know. My dad is probably talking to her too," Isaac said.

"Where is he anyway? I haven't seen him since the family reunion few years back."

"Probably off saving the world. You know him. He won't rest until injustice dies. He wants to be the one to shoot the final shot," Isaac said.

"It's a hard job for any man to do."

"Yeah, I couldn't do it," Isaac said. He opened the door of their house and stared across the street. Science Supreme was still standing strong. They rented out an old bakery right across from their own home. A few renovations later, and they had their dream lab. It had plenty of room for kids, media, and whoever else wanted to join, but they also made a special area that no one else could enter. It was where they did most of their work. Isaac loved living right next to his work, even though his home had been turned into an office ever since they had lost most of their money. He always talked to Cynthia about the importance of cash. The only reason his family wasn't on the street right now was because of the cash Isaac had saved up during Science Supreme's peak viewership. Another deep sigh came from him as he made his way onto the street.

"My mother's down the street. We should walk, it's good exercise," he said.

Cynthia nodded. The walk didn't take too long; ten minutes tops. The restaurant the Eckspo family went to was one of Isaac's favorites. His mother was sitting in her favorite seat outside next to the door. Rain or shine, she was in that spot. Isaac loved that about his mother; she never changed for anyone, not even mother nature. She looked good for her age, and her age didn't stop her from dressing flashy. Her long hair was braided beautifully. The bright grey of her hair made her dark skin shine in the San Francisco sun. That smile too. Isaac loved his mother's smile. Always smiling no matter what. As they walked up, she opened her arms so wide the entire family could've fit. Alisha ran into Grandma Rose's arms first. They always enjoyed a full thirty seconds of screaming and yelling whenever they saw each other. Isaac's mother loved having a grandchild. Alisha loved having a grandmother. They enjoyed each other's company to no end. Isaac made sure Alisha could spend as much time with her, no matter the circumstance. It warmed his heart to see them so happy.

After Alisha made her way to their table, Cynthia went into Rose's arms next. Isaac's family loved Cynthia. It wasn't hard to love a beautiful, well-mannered, Mexican scientist, but the Eckspo family was especially fond of her. His mother always bragged to her friends about Cynthia. The "Mexican Michelle Obama," is what she called her. Isaac always told his mother not to compare his wife to another woman, but Momma Rose didn't care. She said what she wanted. Isaac admired that about her, honestly.

Last, but not least, Isaac went into his mother's arms. They embraced for a bit and then sat down at their table. The waitress took their orders. There was a bit of an awkward silence for a while. Alisha began blowing bubbles in her lemonade. One bubble too many caused her drink to overflow out of her cup and onto her clothes. Cynthia said she'd take Alisha to clean up.

"You all need a place stay yet, son?" Rose asked.

"No Momma, we're making it right now. I'm headed to the Pinnacle today, in a few hours actually," Isaac said.

She looked up from the table. Isaac didn't like when his mother disagreed with him. He knew going to the Pinnacle was risky, but he didn't see another way.

"I'm sure you've thought about this long and hard," Rose said.

Isaac nodded. He put his hand on his chin; his thoughts were running wild. Cynthia came back with Alisha. Isaac noticed them and put his hand up signaling for them to hold on. He motioned to the arcade area in the restaurant. Cynthia was able to pick up on his signals and nodded. She took Alisha to the play area. He looked up and noticed the Golden Gate bridge in the distance. The breeze from the water off the coast washed over his face. Isaac had learned to find comfort in moments like this. Moments where you feel insignificant in a world that is about something bigger. Isaac felt more alive in these moments because knew he was lucky to be alive. Money didn't matter. Immobulum didn't matter. Nothing did. When he opened his eyes, his mother was staring at him.

"Sorry," he said.

She smiled a wide smile.

"I get it. Sometimes you just need to close your eyes, visualize, and take a deep breath," she said.

"Yeah, exactly," Isaac said.

"You be safe going there, son," Rose said.

"I will, Momma," Isaac said.

"These men already considered you a threat. A black man coming into their city, soaking up all the money, attracting attention? They wanted to make an example out of you when you ran out of the stuff."

"I know Momma. I go through them to get the contract and then they pull this mess," Isaac said.

"You couldn't have just set it up yourself?" Rose asked.

"No. Immobulum is a new element. We had to report that. Any profit we earned from its use had to be government regulated. Standard business stuff, but the Pinnacle is a bit tricky."

"Still doesn't explain those men taking all your money," Rose said.

"They didn't take it. The Pinnacle froze my accounts because they claim I breached some clause in my contract regarding my knowledge of Immobulum. They say I know where more is. I don't. The actual government agrees with them too, so not much I can do," Isaac said.

"Look at this," Rose said. She pulled a piece of paper from her purse. As she put it in front of Isaac, Cynthia returned with Alisha, and their food was right behind them. Immediately, Alisha began to stuff her face with French fries and chicken tenders.

Isaac looked over the article. His mother didn't have a smart phone, but she loved her computer. Whenever Isaac called her, she was surfing the web looking for interesting stories to read. This one was interesting. The headline read: "Government Lies: What They Aren't Telling Us About Immobulum." As he read the article, he noticed it talked about secret deposits of the element all over the world. It stated that the United States government has been working to cover up the whereabouts of these deposits mainly to keep the money for themselves. Other countries are reported to have stakes in these deposits as well. Nigeria was one, Columbia was another. These countries, along with the United States, have been reportedly shipping Immobulum across the world for almost a full year. The end of the article talked about some billionaire responsible for the shipments. Isaac didn't need to read anymore though. He felt his heart thumping.

"I don't see a CNN or Fox News logo on top of this, Momma. Where'd you get this?" he asked quietly.

"Some guy sent it to me. I've been talking with him in some political chat room. I told him about your situation. He wanted to help," Rose said.

Isaac wanted to yell at her. He wanted to tell her that not only was this stupid, but it could've put her in danger. He wanted to snap, but he didn't. Mainly because he knew that his mother in fact *knew* what she was doing. When Isaac let his mind calm down, he realized that even in her elder years, his mother was willing to risk her life for his. She didn't have any stake in him finding the Immobulum. He knew she just wanted him to be happy. That's all.

"You've got to be careful though Momma. People are crazy," Isaac said. "And besides, they can ship all the Immobulum they want. It is worth a bunch, but honestly, only Cynthia and I know how to maximize it. If they could, they would be broadcasting it to the world."

"You think I don't know that? I made the man give me his name and everything before I began to talk to him about you," Rose said.

"Well, what's his name?" Isaac asked.

"Stanley. The last name is escaping me right now, but that isn't important," Rose said.

Isaac handed the article to Cynthia. She eyed it for a second.

"What are you thinking, Honey?" Isaac asked.

"It wouldn't be the first time the government would be hiding something from people. We came across something very valuable to them. I can give it to one of my contacts in the Pinnacle. She can tell me whether this is legit or not," Cynthia said.

"What if it is?" Rose asked.

There was a silence among them. Isaac could hear the chatter of people outside. One lady was talking about picking up her kid. She was mad at her husband because he was always out doing something. Another person was talking about her food. Apparently, it was cold. Isaac refocused. Alisha was the only thing he heard. She was continuing her dominance against her food. Isaac smiled a bit.

"I don't know yet," he finally said. He touched his daughter's head. She looked up with a giant smile. He began twirling her hair around his finger.

"We'll figure it out."

"I'm sure you will son. By the way, have you talked to your father recently?" Rose asked.

Isaac shook his head no.

"He'd love it if you'd join one of his rallies, Isaac" she said. "Or attend one of his talks."

"Yeah, I know. Where is he anyways?" Isaac asked.

"Ferguson."

"I saw him on the news last night. More protests," Cynthia said.

Isaac was embarrassed he didn't read about this in the news. He didn't like keeping up with many things, but cases involving the black community always caught his attention. Even when he turned off the news this morning about the shooting, he felt bad. As he had gotten older, Isaac had gotten somewhat out of touch with his people. He didn't like to admit it, but he knew it was true. He always wanted to give back to his community. He wanted to empower all children, especially black children, with science. He wanted to show them that science was ten times more powerful than sports or music. Ever since Science Supreme closed though, he had lost motivation.

"What happened?" he asked. His mother gave him a weird look.

Cynthia placed her hand on Isaac's hand.

"Another black man was killed yesterday. He was thirty-five. There was a video released but it's really hard to tell what happened," Cynthia said.

"It's easy to tell what happened. They murdered that man!" Rose yelled. A couple of people looked at the family weirdly. Isaac could even hear a man whisper "Dumb black people" to his friend, but that didn't bother them. Alisha was looking up wide-eyed. She didn't really know what Grandma Rose was talking about, but now, she was interested. Isaac didn't want her to know anything about this. Not only was she only six, but he didn't want her life to start off fearful. He knew these conversations needed to be had with Alisha someday, but not now, not yet. She just needed to worry about being a kid. Isaac knew children were smarter than adults gave them credit for.

The anger in Isaac's eyes must have been obvious. Rose retreated in her seat a bit.

"Sorry," she said. "It's just getting worse."

"No, I agree," Isaac said. "Does Dad know about the shooting that happened here in San Francisco?"

"I'm sure he does, but I didn't talk to him this morning," Rose said.

"Well, I promise I'll go see him if he ends up coming here," Isaac said.

"Good. He'll be happy to see you. I think you should get going though, Son" Rose said.

He looked down at his watch. She was right. His flight was leaving in a couple hours. The family sat in silence for the next fifteen minutes to finish their food. The waitress came up to take their money. She was black. Isaac didn't like his ability to see the most obscure things on people. He noticed bruises on the girl's neck. Scars too, on her upper cheek by her ear. She was attempting to cover it up with her hair. Isaac could see that she'd been crying too. He didn't notice it before, due to the conversation with his mom, but now she was all he could focus on, and all he could think about. He wanted to help her out in some way. The black community across America needed to unify. Isaac had no idea how that was going to happen. The shootings played over and over in his brain. News casts of reporters providing "solutions" even though they didn't give a damn about black people. Isaac also began to think about black athletes condemning the black community; taking a soft stance on issues so they won't get in trouble. This girl was struggling, and no one cared. Isaac wanted to show her that she could count on someone, especially her fellow black man. When everyone got up to leave, Isaac told Cynthia to go ahead. He wanted to give the waitress her tip.

"Don't be flirting with her," Cynthia said smiling.

"Never that," Isaac said. The two of them shared a quick kiss.

Isaac walked inside to the front where the host was standing.

"Hey! Where's the waitress who was at our table," he asked the receptionist.

"Oh, you mean Kamayra? I'll go get her!" she said with a smile, then skipped between the tables. Isaac laughed.

"That girl is happy," he muttered.

Kamayra returned with the receptionist. She looked confused.

"Hey, how's it going?" Isaac asked. He tried his best to smile. but Kamayra's confused frown made him feel awkward.

"Hi?" she said.

"Your service was really great. I just wanted to thank you personally," Isaac said.

"Thanks," Kamayra said. She started to walk off, but Isaac grabbed her by the arm. She jumped, and her eyes widened. He could see the fear in her eyes.

"I'm sorry," he said. "I didn't mean to startle you. I just—I just wanted to tell you I'm here for you."

"What?" she asked.

"Your bruises, your scars. You do a good job of hiding them, but I can tell you're struggling. But I see that you're working your butt off, and you do a good job," Isaac said.

Kamayra smiled, but she still looked confused.

"There you go, there's a smile. Here, take this," Isaac handed her a fifty-dollar bill.

"I can't take this. Sir, seriously I can't."

Isaac laughed again.

"Sir? I'm only thirty-five. But I guess that's like seventy to you. How old are you?" he asked.

"Twenty-one," Kamayra said.

"Going to school?"

"Georgia State. I live here though. I work in the summer to help pay tuition," Kamayra said.

"Very admirable. Keep working. If you ever need a reference, or anything, let me know," Isaac said. He handed her a card with his contact information.

"You're the guy who used to run that Science place aren't you?" she asked.

"Yeah. I'm working on starting it up again. Stay in school. It was nice to meet you Kamayra," Isaac said.

"You too, Mr. Eckspo," Kamayra said.

"Sheesh! Call me Isaac. Have a good one," he said. As he walked out of the restaurant, Cynthia greeted him with another kiss. His mother hugged him one last time before they went their separate ways. As they were walking home, Alisha almost ran out into the street. Isaac grabbed her hand and scolded her about the dangers of the street. She dropped her head in sadness. Isaac picked her up on his shoulders, and instantly her sadness was gone. Isaac didn't want to punish her for a child's mistake, there weren't any cars in the street anyway. She seemed to completely understand her error. So, he rewarded her. When they returned to their home, Alisha hugged Isaac and went upstairs to her room. A taxi was waiting for Isaac across the street. Cynthia had called it.

"You're always prepared," Isaac said.

"I know," she said smiling. He grabbed her again, this time they kissed much longer.

"I love you," she said.

"I know," Isaac replied laughing. "I love you too." They shared one final kiss before departing. As he got into the taxi, Cynthia waved at him. On his ride to the airport, Isaac thought about the valuable time he had spent with his family. His mother, his daughter, and, most importantly, his wife.

I really need a son, Isaac joked. He wouldn't trade the three women in his life away for anything. Meeting Kamayra was a positive too. It was one step towards helping the black community more. He didn't give her much, but she needed to know someone like him supported her. All this positivity, and he had to go to the Pinnacle. It made him sick. There was only one person who he needed to talk to at the Pinnacle. The man responsible for the government siding with them in the first place.

"Richard Walkman," he whispered.

CHAPTER 2

T he Pinnacle was clean. Too damn clean in Isaac's eyes. As he stepped off the plane, the shine from the buildings almost blinded him. Every building was basically the same, and they reflected light the same as well. The city was so clean, it literally looked white to Isaac. It made him stick out like a sore thumb. It was obvious that comfort for minorities wasn't something they were going for when the city was built. He had made his way through the airport, and as he stood and waited on a taxi, two young white men were behind him. Isaac saw them only for a second as he passed them. He could hear them whispering. He wasn't trying to hear them, but they were so loud. Finally, their words started to become clear, just like the buildings in the city.

"What do you think he's going here?"

"No idea. Hopefully he's not going to beat up my cousin. He got into some dispute last week at his financial planners meeting, and one of his coworkers threatened him. Said he was going to hire help to beat his ass. Well, here's help."

"Matt, you can't be serious."

"Crazier things have happened here."

"No Matt, nothing ever crazy happens here. Ever. Except outside of town, but I wouldn't dare go out there."

"That's my point. This guy must be from the outskirts. Sometimes they slip through the cracks."

Isaac had heard enough. He turned to face the two men. They instantly walked away from him, acting as if they were on the phone.

Slip through the cracks? Those idiots do know this is still a free country, right?

Still, he couldn't help but feel uneasy in the gargantuan city. His taxi arrived.

"Walkman & Johnson," Isaac said. The taxi driver gave him a funny look.

"You got money?" the driver asked. He parked the car and continued to stare at Isaac.

"Seriously?" Isaac asked. He dug into his pockets. He didn't want to throw the money at the driver, but his body didn't listen. "Drive, asshole," came out of his mouth next. The driver took the money hesitantly. Isaac had been in this city for five minutes, and people were already starting to piss him off. He knew he had to stay calm talking to Walkman though. Walkman was an asshole that didn't respond well to people being an asshole back to him. Sucking up was the only thing he responded to. Isaac had to figure out a way to communicate with him in some other way though. Sucking up wasn't an option.

The drive through the city was peaceful. The buildings took Isaac's breath away once he got used to the blinding light. He couldn't remember the last time he was in the Pinnacle, but he was sure that at least five of these buildings were new. They passed through the center of the city. It still looked the same to him. At the heart of the Pinnacle, Facebook's new headquarters lied. Directly next to them, Amazon. ESPN was across the street. The ESPN building was the most extravagant and breath-taking. It was ESPN, ABC, and Marvel all combined into one. Each section was marked with a bright, luminescent sign. Isaac had to appreciate the architects that thought of that design. Coca-Cola was a little further down the road along with McDonald's. There were other businesses in the city as well. Isaac had stopped looking around though. His destination was located next to the national headquarters of the IRS. The sign for the firm was daunting. A larger than life W and J hung halfway up the building. They had golden arches, real golden arches, over the entrance. It cast a shadow over the front door. The arches were inscribed with Walkman & Johnson's slogan: "Greatness Personified". Isaac always thought it was a bit cheesy. The building stood over 2,900 feet tall. It was the largest building in the world.

The driver drove up to the curb. Isaac wasted no time getting out. Once he exited the taxi, a group of people walking past gave him glaring looks. Isaac took a deep breath.

It must be what I'm wearing, he joked. However, he was actually wearing one of his favorite outfits. A blue dress shirt with a nice black tie with diagonal white stripes. His pants were pressed, and his shoes almost mirrored the shine of the buildings. His hair was a bit nappy, but he didn't mind. He loved having long, thick hair. He combed it of course, but if one thing made him look like he was an outsider, rather than an everyday working man, that was it. The watch he decided to wear was a special one Cynthia got him for his birthday five years ago. Confident, Isaac stepped up to the entrance. The arches hid the sunlight immediately. When he opened the front door, he was greeted by security.

"Hold on, Sir," the guard said. He put his hand up. Isaac almost fainted at the massiveness of the building. The emptiness too. He only counted three people in the lobby with two more heading up the escalator. The security guard touched his ear piece. He mumbled something to himself. Then he waved Isaac through.

"58th floor. Walkman is expecting you," the guard said.

"Expecting me?" Isaac asked. "I didn't set up an appointment."

The security guard pointed to the cameras. Then he pointed to the outside of the building. Isaac understood.

He's been watching me on the cameras. He probably has connections lined up throughout the city. He even probably saw me get off my plane. Uncomfortable wasn't even the word to describe Isaac's feelings about being watched that closely. Isaac went to the nearest elevator and pressed the button for the 58th floor. The music that started to play reminded him of the two men outside of his home, and he couldn't help but tap his foot. He wanted to enjoy every second before speaking to Walkman. As the elevator door opened, and Isaac was immediately staring down the extremely long hallway. No offices on either side of the hallway, just one at the end. Isaac could see the golden "W" on the door. In seconds, he was at the door. It opened without him having to knock. Richard Walkman stood smiling an annoying smile. He greeted Isaac with a tight hug. Isaac wanted to punch him. The office wasn't necessarily a luxurious one. A simple desk, a simple computer, and your normal bookshelf that was comprised of nothing more than reference and law books. Two of the chairs in the office looked uncomfortable though. That's where Walkman showed his money. The two chairs in front of his desk were extremely small. They looked nice, but the width was laughable. Isaac wasn't a small man. His legs were mainly muscle. His hips weren't small either. His lower body would scream the entire time he was in those chairs. He glanced at Walkman's chair. An enormous brown, leather office chair. Isaac couldn't tell but he thought he noticed gold "W's" engraved on the handles on the seat. Walkman's suit was nice too. Isaac had only seen suits like these in movies. Walkman stood just as tall as Isaac. They both towered over most. Isaac was six feet three inches. Walkman's hair was balding, but he didn't cut off the rest. His wrinkles showed age. Isaac had no idea how old he was. He didn't care either. All he wanted was for Walkman to let go of him.

"Okay, enough, Richard," Isaac said.

Walkman made a strange face. He let go and sat down on his throne of a chair.

"Please, sit down Mr. Eckspo," Walkman said.

Isaac looked at the chair.

"I think I'll pass," Isaac said.

"Suit yourself. You've been here for less than one minute and have shown no respect for me or my company," Walkman said with a sly smile. He talked so slowly. Isaac knew he wanted anyone who stepped into this office to feel his power. Hear every word he spoke.

"Let's get right to it. Why have my accounts been frozen?" Isaac asked.

"It clearly stated in your contract you signed through us," Walkman said slowly.

"It isn't though," Isaac had a briefcase with him. He put the contract on the table.

"There. Section 46. Paragraph 17. It clearly states you must relinquish all knowledge of any deposits of Immobulum. That you must share all knowledge with us here at the Pinnacle," Walkman said.

"I did that. Your office has shown no proof that I knew where any deposits were," Isaac said.

"We also received knowledge of your usage of funds from your program, money that was used for illegal activities," Walkman said.

"What are you talking about? I only used money for my life. Bills, groceries, my program, nothing illegal," Isaac said.

"Exactly. Illegal activity. You didn't notice that your contract states all of your profits from the program should have gone directly to us."

Walkman pulled up his own version of the contract. Isaac felt uneasy at how prepared he was for this. He pointed to an extra paragraph that Isaac hadn't noticed before. Isaac had two lawyers look over the contract. They both approved of the deal and said that no funny business would happen. Isaac looked over the contract too. He did not remember this section. They must have added it after Science Supreme began.

"Why don't I have that extra section on my original copy?" Isaac said.

"We contacted you about the update," Walkman said. His smile came across his face slowly. Isaac knew exactly what this was. He threw the papers on the ground in frustration. Walkman backed up.

"Why are you doing this?" Isaac asked.

"You're the one who breached the contract, Sir. We're just following protocol at this point," Walkman said. "If you don't calm your tone, I'll have to call security."

Isaac felt his face getting hot. He looked down and noticed his hand had balled up into a fist.

"Watch my tone? Look Walkman, this is my family you're putting out on the street. And for what? Because I pissed off a few suits here at the top? You guys really don't know how to share. You're always thinking someone is doing something for their own benefit."

"You really don't get it do you?" Walkman asked. His face tightened.

"Finally, that smile leaves your face. You don't have to hide your feelings," Isaac said.

"You were getting irresponsible with the Immobulum. So, we had to intervene," Walkman said.

"I was educating children. About science! And they were enjoying it. The only purpose for the Immobulum was to power my most high-profile experiments. It kept the lab running too," Isaac said.

"You just weren't cut out for it, Isaac. It's in better hands now," Walkman said.

"Is that so?" Isaac asked. He took out the folded paper from his pocket. It was the article from his mother. Walkman's eyes widened. He snatched the paper from Isaac quickly.

"Where did you get this?"

"A little something called the internet," Isaac said. "If this is true, you really have taken it up another notch. It must really hurt that I beat you there first. That I developed it quicker than you could. That I made discoveries your people could only dream of. How does that make you feel? A black man from the Bay is smarter than every hired suit you could find," Isaac said. "I'm guessing you still haven't even figured out how to use it. Or better yet, I'm guessing you haven't even found more yet."

Walkman didn't say anything. He didn't even look at Isaac immediately. The enormous chair caught Isaac's eye again. Walkman walked over to the chair. He stroked it slowly. The golden engravings shined bright as he turned it.

"You shouldn't be so naïve to bring race into this Isaac. You can't believe everything you read on the internet."

That was it. Isaac didn't need to hear anymore. This man didn't want to reason. He had no intention of making a compromise today. All he wanted to do was show Isaac how much control he had over him. Isaac made his way to the door.

"Before you go, I need you to know one thing," Walkman said.

Isaac stopped. He sighed and then opened the door. Two security guards were waiting outside of the door.

"I control all of your assets right now," Walkman said. "They only unfreeze when you pay the amount listed. Until you pay that money, I own your ass. Own it! The next time you come into this office, you'll be on the street, begging me for a handout. Just like the rest of your people out there do," Walkman pointed outside. Isaac didn't need to look to see what Walkman was pointing at. The struggling city outside of the Pinnacle was filled with Blacks and Hispanics struggling to live. The security guard motioned for Isaac to leave. He resisted a bit at first.

"Hold on. Let me say something before I go."

"Let him talk," Walkman said.

"There's going to be a time where you're down on your luck. You're going to need and ask for help, but there will be no one willing to help you. Don't judge people you don't know anything about. Because I'm going to be alright no matter how much you think you own me. Money doesn't equate to happiness. My will to feed my family is all I need. That will keep me and them alive. You remember that," Isaac said.

Walkman smiled that slow, wide smile.

"Get out of my office. I expect an apology the next time you're here." Isaac left without a problem. Within minutes, he was in a taxi, headed to the airport to return to the most important people in his life.

— ·· — ·· — ·· — ·· — ·· —

Cynthia prepared a nice big meal for Isaac when he got home: spaghetti and meatballs. It was his, and Alisha's, favorite. He texted her about the meeting while he was waiting for his flight home to take off. It was agreed between the two of them to not speak about Walkman for the rest of the night. All he wanted to do was spend quality time with his girls and to rest his feet a bit. Plans about the future would come tomorrow. As he walked through the door, the place smelled like heaven. Alisha ran up to her father quickly. He picked her up and gave her a kiss.

"How's my baby girl?" Isaac asked.

"Mad," Alisha said.

"Why is that?"

"Patrick was being stupid again today," she said.

"Well, Patrick tends to be a bit slow," Isaac said, with a slight chuckle.

He put her down and she ran into the kitchen. He followed her. Cynthia was a sight for sore eyes. He walked up behind his wife, kissed her on the neck and embraced her. She reached up to grab his arm.

"Food's almost ready," Cynthia said. "Afterwards, I was thinking we could all watch a movie."

Isaac kissed Cynthia. Her lips always tasted sweet to him. He stroked her hair.

"Sounds good to me, nothing serious though," Isaac said. "Let's have a laugh tonight."

"Okay," Cynthia said.

"Let's go to the park tomorrow too," Isaac said.

"I have a job interview tomorrow. After that, we can," Cynthia said.

"Where at? How much are they paying? Where is it?" Isaac realized he was talking way too fast. Everyone started laughing, even Alisha.

"You're talking funny, Daddy," she said.

"Hush little girl before I buy you a Patrick Star shirt for Christmas," Isaac said. Alisha, sitting at the table, slid her finger across her mouth. She was done talking. Both Isaac and Cynthia laughed.

"Some local university needs help with some lab experiments. They contacted me, and the interview is just a formality. They want me, but they just have to put the interview on paper. I would start this week actually," she said.

"That's amazing!" Isaac said. Instantly, he thought of what he said to Walkman. He said his will would keep his family alive. Not only did he fail to mention his wife, but he felt ashamed for not doing so. He admired Cynthia because the last thing she needed in life was a man. Her independence and intelligence were off the charts. She had a brilliant opinion on everything, but never voiced it unless necessary. She shared Isaac's love for science, so that was a plus, but her will would keep them alive too.

"Food's done!" Cynthia yelled.

"No need to yell," Isaac said. "We're both right here."

"Right!" Alisha said.

"I thought you weren't talking," Isaac said.

"Not talking's hard!" Alisha said.

The rest of the night was filled with joy for the Eckspo family. Dinner consisted of Isaac and Cynthia discussing something she had read about in a scientific journal. One of her friends from college made a breakthrough in cancer research. One of the biggest in twenty years in fact. They talked about that for a while before Alisha talked about her day. Cynthia took her shopping, and they got some coloring books and paint for her to have a craft day. She showed Isaac her paintings in between slurps of spaghetti. Sauce dripping down her shirt and all. Isaac knew that every parent thought their kid was funny, but he genuinely thought Alisha was hilarious. When she was older, he would have no problems supporting her career in stand-up comedy.

After dinner, the movie was an animated film Alisha picked out. Isaac couldn't remember the title. In fact, after a few laughs, he fell asleep. The entire family did. Cynthia's food had a way of doing that to all of them. Each meal felt like Thanksgiving to him. It was all full of love and flavor, each and every bite. Alisha was in their arms when they fell asleep but made her way to the floor by the end of the movie. Isaac helped his little girl up to her room. Cynthia wanted to sleep on the couch, but Isaac talked her into coming upstairs. When they got upstairs, he double checked on Alisha. If he was awake when she went to sleep, Isaac usually checked on her about five times a night. Once they were in bed, Isaac felt the emotions of today invade his brain. The great time he had seeing his mother, helping the waitress out, and a family dinner. Then Walkman entered his brain. The suits of the Pinnacle entered his brain.

As soon as that happened, the only thing he could think about was systematic racism and how powerless it made him feel. Isaac could understand if he was a crook. Selling Immobulum overseas, using it for profit. He could understand if any of his activity with the element had been questionable. But it wasn't. Isaac prided himself on being honest. More than honest, especially when children looked up to him. He lived for the sparkle in children's eyes when he showed them his levitation boots, or his state of the art gaming system powered by Immobulum. He loved it. The last thing he wanted to do was jeopardize his family's well-being just to make a quick buck. It angered him. His mother was right. They saw him as a threat from the moment Science Supreme opened. Then he realized, it probably wasn't just Science Supreme, but what Isaac told Walkman earlier. Without Isaac and Cynthia, Immobulum was useless. It was just a pretty purple rock that could be used for simple things in its raw form. And the possibilities of it were endless, Isaac and Cynthia were just starting to figure out what it could do. Now they couldn't do anything.

They've played their hand, Isaac thought. I must fight through this. There's nothing else to do. After a while, he was finally able to fall asleep next to his beautiful wife.

─ ·· ─ ·· ─ ·· ─ ·· ─ ·· ─ ··

The next morning, despite the lack of sleep, Isaac woke up early. He didn't have any plans on being up so early, but he enjoyed the mornings. He walked over to his window. The two men were playing a slow jazz tune. He opened the window a crack to hear the song better. Sadness was the only word Isaac could think of. The drummer was tapping his cymbal softly while the saxophonist blared his soul for the streets of San Francisco to hear. Isaac sat at the window for almost thirty minutes. When Cynthia asked him to shut the window, he went downstairs. He decided to go outside and watch the men. There was a group of people outside that Isaac didn't notice before. He counted at least fifteen people. Each of them watching in silence. The entire street was silent. The saxophone sang a song of betrayal, anger, and sadness. The mix of the drums provided a chilling sensation on the ears when combined with the melody from the saxophone. The drummer noticed Isaac. He nodded slowly. Isaac had lost track of time. Soon, he was the only one standing there. People were walking past dropping money into the saxophone case. He wanted to talk to them, but their somber song continued. Isaac was amazed at their endurance. He waved a goodbye to them as he walked back into his house.

Alisha was up now. Cynthia was making everyone breakfast.

"You don't have to do that. I would've made breakfast before your interview," Isaac said.

"And force us all to endure your burnt bacon again? No thanks," Cynthia said.

"Not my fault you can't handle a little black on your food," Isaac said.

"Daddy, your bacon is black everywhere!" Alisha remarked.

"Just like me," Isaac said, as he broke out into a dance. Alisha began laughing uncontrollably. Cynthia chuckled as she finished up making breakfast. They ate, and Isaac helped her pick out her clothes for her interview. She was wearing a black dress that showcased her body, but still made her look professional. She had curled her hair too. Isaac was always amazed at her beauty. She was rubbing lotion on her body before she left. Her light brown skin shined usually, but Isaac loved it when his wife dressed up. Those brown eyes twinkled. She looked twenty-one again in his eyes. The last thing he wanted right now was to be apart from her for a couple of hours, but he knew this job could help his family avoid a life on the street. They both walked downstairs. He handed Cynthia her purse. They kissed, and she was out the door. Alisha was standing behind Isaac with an empty look on her face.

"Just me and you, Baby Girl," Isaac said. "What do you want to do?"

Alisha shrugged her shoulders. Isaac ran his hands through her hair.

"Let's do your hair," he said.

Alisha ran off quickly. Isaac knew exactly where she was going. She returned with her two favorite dolls. She always played with her dolls whenever Isaac did her hair. He got the comb, grease, and told Alisha to go by the couch. He started working on her hair shortly after. The local news was already on, so he decided to keep it on that channel. Developments were coming from the shooting of the black man killed by police. The city released footage of the shooting. Well, not really the city. The man's wife recorded the entire incident in the car. The cop shot the man because he thought the man was going for his gun.

Philando Castile all over again, he thought.

The news continued to tell the story. The man's name was Lonnie Smith. People had spent the night protesting throughout the streets in San Francisco. Isaac continued to watch as the local news said that none of the protests had turned violent. He thought Alisha was going to stay occupied with her dolls, but she looked up quickly and saw the people walking down the street.

"What are they doing Daddy?" Alisha asked.

"They're marching," Isaac said.

"For what?" Alisha asked.

"Something they believe in," Isaac said. "They want people to listen."

"Listen to what?" Alisha asked.

Isaac didn't say anything. Thankfully, Alisha had lost interest.

Isaac didn't join in on protests himself, but he saw the need for them. Without them, White people around the country may not even hear about Lonnie Smith. It's when they turned violent that Isaac turned against them. At the same time, however, he understood people's frustration. Blacks in America have been oppressed since the days of slavery. Isaac wasn't ignorant to the fact that subtle was the key word now. Every time he turned on the TV, they showcased little black girls with uncontrollable, wild hair. Athletes and rappers dominated the news feeds. Authors, scientists, journalists, and black politicians were getting their recognition, but the media didn't paint them in the same light. And that wasn't the fault of black children. Schools didn't do a good job teaching students how important science and literature were. Isaac was conflicted to a degree because artists and athletes like Tupac and Muhammad Ali were needed in society. But he noticed a saturation of arrogance taking over as well. His mind was running wild when there was a knock at his door.

He didn't recognize the woman at the door. She was a white woman with blonde hair. She looked harmless, but Isaac didn't trust anybody as of late. He opened the door slowly.

"Hi. You're Isaac Eckspo, right?" the woman asked.

"Yes."

"Okay, good. Is Cynthia around? My name is Ashley. I'm her friend from the Pinnacle."

"Yeah, she's mentioned you before," Isaac said. "But she's not here. What do you need to talk to her about?"

Ashley pulled a manila folder from her purse. Isaac knew what this was about.

"Come in," he said. "I'm doing my daughters hair. Follow me."

Alisha waved to Ashley when she saw her.

"You're a cutie. What's your name?" Ashley asked her. Alisha smiled and put her head down in embarrassment.

"Alisha," she said quietly.

Isaac laughed.

"Come on Baby Girl, sit back. So, Ashley, I think I know why you're here. What's in the folder?" he asked.

"Cynthia asked me to do some digging regarding that article she found. I did, and I found some things you two definitely need to see," Ashley said.

Isaac opened the folder. Before he even read the first word, he noticed the emblem in the top right corner. It was the Pinnacle's emblem. An emblem that only showed up on their official files. The files that no one was supposed to look at. Only workers with special clearance got access to these files. Isaac didn't want to judge, but he doubted she had that clearance. Instantly, he dropped the folder in fear.

"W—Where did you get this?" Isaac asked.

"I knew this would be difficult," Ashley said.

"Difficult is what I'm trying to do to Alisha's hair. You have an entirely different definition of the word," Isaac said. He must've pulled Alisha's hair the wrong way. She yelped in pain for a moment. He apologized to her.

"Baby Girl, go play with your dolls. When Ms. Ashley leaves I'll finish your hair," Isaac said. Alisha had run off before he said "hair".

"Listen," Isaac said. "I'm sure you know about our situation already. But I don't need them tracking you here with documents you obtained illegally," Isaac said.

"I'm sorry," Ashley said.

"I can't risk my family's safety. That's one thing I won't do."

"Just look at the file. Please," she begged.

He sighed. The local news was still talking about Lonnie.

He knew that this file could contain life-saving information about extra Immobulum deposits around the world. But then what? He damn sure didn't want to go to the deposits. Even if he found them and tried to use them for Science Supreme, the Pinnacle would just continue to suck money out of him. They'd claim he knew where they were the whole time. The only other options Isaac saw didn't provide much hope either. Sue the Pinnacle for their concealing information or harvest the Immobulum at these sites and sell it on the black market. The first option circulated in his head.

Sue the Pinnacle? The more he thought it, the more ridiculous it sounded. Executive cabinet members could have private email servers and get away with it, Isaac knew suing the Pinnacle would earn him a spot on a blacklist. But selling it on the black market could cost people their lives. There was no way to know what someone wanted it for. This was one of the most powerful, durable, elements in the world. Every country was in a tailspin over it, so Isaac knew a profit was possible, but he wasn't sure if that risk outweighed the benefits. On the other hand, if he failed to act soon, his family would struggle, even with Cynthia's new job. His head began to hurt.

"Excuse me," Isaac said. "I need to get some water." He attempted to catch his breath. Ashley followed him into the kitchen.

"You used to work with Cynthia?" Isaac asked, as he drank a water from the fridge in 3 giant gulps. "She's talked about you before, but never how you know each other."

Ashley laughed a bit.

"We actually met at a wedding. Her sister's wedding two years ago," Ashley said.

"Oh, you're the new bitch friend Cynthia was complaining about?" Isaac asked. Ashley's face tightened. "I'm joking! Yeah, I remember now. You are tight with Lydia. I'm guessing you guys kept in contact ever since?"

"Your guess is right. Look, I'm sorry if I'm overstepping. I wanted to help you guys, and this was the only way I knew how," Ashley said.

Isaac grabbed another water bottle from the fridge. His breathing was normal now.

"So, you hacked into the Pinnacle's server? How'd you learn to do that?" Isaac asked.

"I took a couple of courses, but mainly self-taught. Some people watch Netflix at their desk jobs, I read Pinnacle files," she said laughing. Isaac wanted to laugh, but he couldn't get behind her way of life.

"You're crazy," he said playing along with her joke. "Alright, let me see that file." She handed it to him. The file was a bunch of financial stuff. Money owed to other countries. Immobulum prices and rates for every country. Isaac found what he was looking for when he reached the end of the file. There was a map that folded out. He unfolded it and laid it out on the table. There were a bunch of purple markings in areas of Australia, China, and Russia. Pink markings all around South America. Red markings were all over the US. An enormous "I" was marked near the purple markings.

"The purple is where the Immobulum deposits are?" Isaac asked.

Ashley nodded.

"What are these other colors? What do those stand for?" he asked.

"I wasn't able to find out. Probably some other type of element deposits," Ashley said.

Impossible, Isaac thought. He was deeply involved in the discovery of Immobulum, and the development of how to utilize the new element. When he and Cynthia became overnight sensations in the science community, a bunch of their colleagues came to them seeing if some obscure elements were Immobulum. Isaac doubted that there were any deposits in the States. But he was happy that Ashley gave this to him. He took out his phone to take a picture of the map.

"Keep it," Ashley said. "Keep all of it. You can make sense of all of it better than I can," Ashley said.

"Thank you," Isaac said. "Sorry I freaked out earlier."

"It's okay. It was understandable. Well, I better get going," she gave Isaac a quick hug and left. He called Alisha back into the living room to finish her hair. He had no idea what he was going to do, or even wanted to do, with all this information.

Thank God my wife is smarter than me, he thought.

CHAPTER 3

It was Isaac's turn to make dinner that night. Cynthia had gotten home from her interview a few hours after she had left. She told him it went well, and then the Eckspo family had headed to a nearby park. Alisha played on the swings with a neighborhood girl, while Cynthia talked with the girl's mother. After a while, she walked back to the bench where Isaac sat.

"What did you want to eat tonight?" he asked.

Cynthia shrugged. "No idea," she said.

There was a silence between them for a few minutes. Isaac didn't like being quiet around Cynthia. He was still trying to digest the information from that file. He had no idea what he wanted to do. He also didn't want to put it on Cynthia's plate right now either. There was no doubt in his mind that she could handle it, but he just wanted to enjoy his time with his wife. Shortly after that thought crossed Isaac's mind, Cynthia ruined that hope.

"Ashley called me after she left our place," Cynthia said.

Isaac felt his heart drop.

"I'm not mad or anything," Cynthia said. "But we do need to talk about it."

"I was trying to figure out what to say. I'm sorry," Isaac said.

"We're in this together. We'll figure it out," Cynthia said.

He smiled. Alisha was waving at them with a smile on her face as well. Isaac loved watching his little girl play. He could watch her for hours. Some days he did. The kids in the neighborhood loved Alisha. She was extremely smart and funny. She always made up games for the other kids to play. Isaac would take her to the park as long as she wanted. It was great for her to be around other children, and nothing gave him more joy. He turned back to face Cynthia. She put her hands on his face.

"I love you, Isaac," she said.

"I know," he said, chuckling. She hit him in the arm. They embraced in a hug for a few seconds. When, they pulled apart, Isaac left his arm around Cynthia's shoulder, and she left hers around his back. They sat there in each other's arm for nearly two hours, watching their daughter play. Alisha was playing hide and seek with three other kids on the playground. She always frustrated with them because they could never find her. More frustrating than that, she found them in a matter of seconds. When the sun started to set, the Eckspo family headed home. Isaac didn't feel like cooking, so he talked Cynthia into getting food on the walk home. They got burgers and fries. Alisha got an extra serving of fries after she begged Isaac for them. She claimed all that running around merited more food. Isaac explained to her that more junk food was just that, more junk. But he gave in because it was his Baby Girl. Alisha didn't know it, but she had earned extra vegetables the next time Isaac did make food.

As they approached their house, Isaac immediately noticed their front door had been messed with. Once he got closer, he realized the lock had been broken.

"Hold on," he said to Cynthia.

One of their neighbors was walking her dog.

"Hey, Mary," Isaac said as she past them. "Did you see anybody messing with our door?"

The lady took her earbuds out. Her dog didn't want to stop.

"No, but there were a bunch of men in suits walking up and down the street earlier." Isaac barely understood her she was talking so fast. Mary sped off with her dog. Isaac approached the door with caution. He could see the fear on Alisha's face. He wasn't going to let anything happen to her. He'd die before that happened. As he opened the door, he handed his bag to Cynthia. Isaac walked in slowly, gesturing for them to stay put.

Everything was trashed. Papers were thrown everywhere. Their television was broken too.

Assholes think they're funny, he thought.

After a couple of minutes of searching, he realized no one was in their house. He told Cynthia it was okay for them to go in. Alisha was horrified. Isaac told her to go into the kitchen and start eating her food. As smart as she was, food was still her weakness. It bought him some time to talk with Cynthia.

"What were they looking for?" she asked.

"That file Ashley gave me. She didn't cover her tracks as well as she thought," Isaac said. He was trying to stay calm.

"Where is it?" Cynthia asked.

"Our safe with all of our money. There's no way they found that," Isaac said.

"You sure?" They went into his office. Sure enough, the money and file were there. He opened it and showed it to Cynthia. They went into the kitchen to check on Alisha. She was stuffing her face.

"The purple areas are the Immobulum deposits," Isaac said.

"I figured," Cynthia said.

He began pacing in the kitchen. His mind was racing, but he knew what had to be done now. The Pinnacle wasn't going to stop until Isaac was finished. After this, he guessed they were probably charging Ashley as soon as they could find proof that she was the one who hacked their servers. They probably had surveillance on her, which is why they knew the file was here. Isaac figured they would charge him as well. He knew he shouldn't had done this. Now though, he had no choice. His family needed him more than ever.

"We're going to Australia," he said.

"What?" Cynthia said.

"We're going to harvest the Immobulum before they even know we're there. We're leaving tonight. They won't be expecting us to go after the Immobulum," Isaac said.

"What exactly are we going to do with it?" Cynthia said.

"I'm not sure yet. But they don't own it. Maybe we can get there, harvest it, and start Science Supreme again. I can talk to Ashley about this file later. Maybe they don't know it was her."

"How so?" Cynthia asked. "They came here. There's no doubt they know she was here."

"Not necessarily. They might be in a scramble searching for that file. Who is prime suspect number one?" Isaac pointed to himself. "They came here thinking I took it but didn't find it. So now they're searching through their computers to see if someone misplaced it."

"I think you're right," Cynthia said. She showed Isaac her phone.

It was a text from Ashley. She was fine. Still at work in fact. She told Cynthia that no one had questioned her or even looked at her funny today.

"They don't know," Isaac said. "We get that Immobulum first, we can end this mess. Especially if it's deep in a mountain somewhere. They can't claim it until it's harvested and back on US soil."

"Exactly," Cynthia said.

Alisha was still eating. Cynthia's eyes got wide for a moment. She pointed to the living room. She walked there, and Isaac followed. She lowered her voice to a whisper.

"We can't go out in the world experimenting with Alisha," Cynthia said.

Isaac was ashamed. Of course, he agreed with his wife. He just forgot about Alisha momentarily and that made him mad. Everything he had done since she was born was for her. He thought about her constantly. Every penny he saved was going to her college fund. Any extra time he had was spent with her. The love Isaac had for his daughter was endless. He'd kill for Alisha if it came to that. He was ashamed for forgetting about her safety while discussing his plan with Cynthia. She must've noticed the pain on his face. Cynthia grabbed her husband's arm softly.

"It's okay, Isaac," she said.

"I don't want to leave her," Isaac said.

"But do we really have any other option right now?" Cynthia said. "What are we going to do with the Immobulum once we harvest it?"

"Sell it to someone. I don't care who honestly. All the Pinnacle wants is their money. Once I give them that money, we'll be free to do what we want. I didn't want to go down that path at first, but it's like you said, we don't have much choice," Isaac said.

"It won't take long to harvest it. Depending on the quality, location, and the time we do it, I can get it done in a day or two," Cynthia said.

"My mother might be able to watch her for that time," Isaac said.

Cynthia smiled.

"Alisha loves her time with Grandma Rose. And your mother will no doubt welcome a sleepover for a couple of days," Cynthia said.

Isaac's was still wrapping his brain around everything that had happened. He was starting to believe this was a possibility.

"I'll call her now," he said. He pulled out his phone and fifteen minutes later, he was off the phone.

"Well?" Cynthia asked.

"She went through the entire 'stay safe' speech, but she wants Alisha over as soon as possible," Isaac said.

"This is going to work," Cynthia said. They kissed, and Cynthia went into the kitchen to tell Alisha the good news. Alisha instantly began jumping up and down. Isaac couldn't help but join in on the fun. Alisha jumped into his arms and the two danced around the kitchen. Cynthia joined in.

As night came, the Eckspo family packed to be gone for a few days; Alisha for grandma's place, and Isaac and Cynthia for Australia. They had bought airline tickets and a hotel for the area closest to a deposit. The deposit looked like it was in a mountainous region, but that worked perfectly for Cynthia. She didn't need much to harvest it out a mountain. She packed the pieces of her machine she could bring. They were going to buy the other parts in Australia. Alisha packed her favorite toys. Isaac helped her pick out her favorite pairs of pajamas too. She took her pajamas seriously, so the process took a while. After everyone was packed, the family loaded their car. On the ride to grandma's house, they sang along to the radio. For the life of him, Isaac didn't know the artist, but the song was catchy. Whenever it came on, it became Alisha's favorite thing of all time, so he always joined in. The pure joy on her face when he did stuff with her was indescribable. No matter what it was, Isaac did it with her. Cynthia joined in where she could too. Isaac always made fun of her, because she never knew words to songs, no matter how much she listened to them. They were at grandma's house soon after. Everyone got out of the car, while Rose stood at her front door and waved. Alisha first hugged Cynthia. Cynthia squeezed her daughter tightly, kissed her on the forehead and got back in the car. Alisha then ran to Isaac.

"You're going to be good for me, right?" Isaac asked.

"Yes, Daddy. I'm going to miss you," Alisha said.

Isaac's heart dropped for a second.

Is there something else I can do? Do I really need to go all the way to Australia for some damn Immobulum? Is there another way? He hugged Alisha tightly.

"I'm going to miss you too, Baby Girl. But you'll be safe, because look who I brought," Isaac pulled out Alisha's favorite toy. She had drawn a picture of a superhero last year, so Isaac had it made into a toy. Alisha lost the toy a couple of months ago, but while cleaning up tonight, he found it underneath their bed.

"Mystic Man!" Alisha yelled. "Where was he?"

"Underneath Mommy and Daddy's bed. I told you about playing in our room," Isaac said.

"I know," she said. She put her head down.

"Hey," Isaac said. He picked her head up by her chin. He was smiling, so she began to smile.

"Your friend here will protect you while we're gone," Isaac said.

"Mystic Man can do anything!" Alisha said. Isaac laughed and gave her one more hug. She ran off and into Rose's arms. Isaac could feel a tear rolling down his face. He didn't even wipe it. He got back into the car.

"What's wrong?" Cynthia asked.

Isaac chuckled slightly.

"Absolutely nothing," he said. "I love our family." She grabbed his hand and they drove off, headed for the airport.

CHAPTER 4

17 Years Ago: Northwestern University

Isaac never got nervous, but this was college. His first day on campus, and he was busy looking around, trying to find his classes. His roommate was with him, but he wasn't interested in his classes at the moment. Isaac wasn't too fond of his roommate. The second their parents left, he pulled out a bottle of alcohol. He asked Isaac if he drank. Isaac wasn't a genius, but he knew his roommate wouldn't be around long. They were walking around exploring campus. Every campus group was out and about telling all the wide-eyed freshmen about their programs. Wooing them with promises of a better future. Everything from fraternities to chess club. All their speeches were the same. Isaac wasn't sure what he was looking for, but it wasn't any of this nonsense.

The school was amazing. It was everything he thought it would be. Going to one of the best schools in the country. Majoring in mechanical engineering. This was everything he wanted. He had come across one of the buildings his classes were in. His roommate didn't want to stop though.

"Hey, I'll catch up with you later," Isaac said.

"Sounds good bro. Go Wildcats. Whoo!" his roommate yelled. He ran off with another group of freshmen. Isaac didn't want to judge, but he was almost positive he wouldn't see his roommate around next year screaming "Go Wildcats". He went into the building to check out his morning class.

Isaac looked down at his schedule and realized this was his chemistry class. This is what Isaac came to school for, knowledge. This was the only thing he wanted out of college. Everything else was irrelevant. He walked down the hallways and noticed the alumni on the walls. Their achievements were endless. Isaac wanted to be on that wall someday. He wanted to be remembered for great discoveries. He made his way into his classroom. The sheer size of

it almost made him faint. He wasn't used to a classroom like that.
him faint. He wasn't used to a classroom like that. He didn't want to
be a nerd on the first day by showing up almost an hour early, sitting
in the front, but that's exactly what he was going to do. Hand up on
every question, impeccable notes, Isaac didn't care if he was judged.
If he was lucky, he'd pick up on the material early enough and
could tutor anyone struggling. Then, he'd charge people by the hour
to help them with their work. He'd have his own little business going
in his first year of college. He didn't care how people saw him. His
father taught him that. His mother too. They went down their own
path in life, but Isaac noticed even they fell to the pressure of society
sometimes. He learned from them, aspired to be like them, but he
realized what they did wrong too. By the time Isaac had determined
he was going to Northwestern, he was also determined to live life the
only way he knew how. Whenever something came to his mind, he
did it. Of course, he tried to resist the urge to be impulsive, but
Isaac did what made him comfortable. He also did what made him
uncomfortable. Life was all about changes. Whenever an
opportunity presented itself, Isaac sucked up that nervous energy he
had growing in his stomach and took it. His life, his rules. If people
laughed at him, or called him a nerd in college, then so be it.
Because Isaac didn't want to die with regrets. Death was something
he didn't think about too much, but it was everywhere. Death was all
over television, movies, books, and even video games. Isaac wanted
a legacy before he died. Whether it was a Nobel Prize at age 78 or
his accomplishments as "that guy who's good in Chem," at age 18,
he didn't care. Life was too short to ride the social wave.

His butt was getting sore. Isaac looked down at his watch. He
didn't really have anywhere to be, but he wanted to find the rest of
his classes before sunset. He promised his roommate they would go
to some freshmen festival tonight.

All this talk about not riding the social wave, and I'm going to
some meaningless festival. Of course, he could tell his roommate he
was doing something else. Which is exactly what he was going to do.
There was a book that had eluded him for too long. As he stood up,
he saw something, no, rather someone. Isaac didn't necessarily
come to college for girls, but his male instincts couldn't ignore what
he was looking at. She was beautiful. The girl was shorter than him,

but not too much shorter. Her long, dark hair complemented her brown skin perfectly. Isaac thought of that cheesy glove on the cheek line from Romeo and Juliet. This girl was something special. He could hardly see her eyes, but they had a sparkle to them. She was with about five other girls and they were getting ready to leave. They took one last look around the classroom. Isaac was guessing there was a good chance he had a class with her. Then the thought of never seeing this girl again popped into his head. He almost screamed. That feeling was unbearable. Isaac decided to put himself into an uncomfortable position. They were almost out the door when he yelled.

"Hey! Hold up," is what he meant to say. Isaac couldn't really understand what he said. The looks on the girl's faces said they didn't understand it either. As he was running up the stairs, Isaac tripped and almost fell. All the girls, including the one he wanted to talk to, laughed. They were laughing uncontrollably.

Compose yourself, Isaac. At least you have their attention.

Isaac walked up to the girls. He stared directly into the girl's eyes. Her friends were still laughing a bit.

"My name's Isaac Eckspo. The reason I fell is because I noticed you and wanted to get a chance to talk to you before you left. As you can tell, I'm a bit nervous," he said. He extended his hand between the girls. They backed away.

"My name's Cynthia. And at least you didn't fall on your face. Then you probably would've lost your chance," she said. As she smiled, Isaac couldn't help but smile.

"You're beautiful," he said. "I saw a really cool restaurant down the street. Could I take you out there sometime?" Cynthia put her head down in embarrassment. She began twirling her hair.

"You're bold," Cynthia said.

"Not really. But I figured if I asked you now, the embarrassment won't be that bad when I ask the next girl out," Isaac said.

"Hopefully there isn't a next girl," Cynthia said. "Here's my phone number. Text me."

Cynthia left with her friends. Some of them were still laughing. Cynthia was smiling still. The classroom was empty again.

This is going to be a good year, Isaac thought.

— · · — · · — · · — · · — · · — · · — · ·

Present Day

Because of the time change and the length of the flight, Isaac and Cynthia arrived a day and a half later in Australia. It was early evening when they arrived, and there wasn't much they could do that night. They took the time to explore for a few hours and enjoy themselves before they headed to their hotel. Australia was amazing, and the hotel the Eckspo's were staying in was nice too.

Several days were spent to make sure harvesting the Immobulum went perfectly. Parts were gathered, machinery was built, and research was completed. Isaac woke up early the morning before they were planning to go to the deposit in order to run some final calculations on it. He wanted to make sure that everything with the harvest went well. He wasn't too worried. Cynthia knew what she was doing. Isaac was standing on the balcony of their hotel room when she finally woke up. She came outside to join him.

"You're up early," Cynthia said.

Isaac smiled.

"I'm always up early," he said.

"That's true." She put her hands around his waist. Isaac forgot how small her hands were sometimes. She struggled to reach around his body. They moved closer to the edge of the balcony.

"What's on your mind?" Cynthia asked.

"How much I hate Richard Walkman," Isaac said.

Cynthia didn't say anything.

"We'll get all of this figured out soon though," Isaac said. "And when we do figure all of this out, I want to do something."

"Do what?" she asked.

"Selling Immobulum on the black market will make us extremely rich. More money than we'd both know what to do with. We should give it all back," Isaac said.

"All of it?" Cynthia asked.

"Well, not all of it. We should keep some of it for our family obviously. But I'm talking about helping our community. San Francisco is struggling right now. It's a city divided. The news is filled with police killings. Filled with hate and suffering. That football player who took a knee for the anthem, you remember that?"

"The quarterback, right?" Cynthia asked.

"Yes. Everyone refused to talk about the reason why he was kneeling. They focused more on the kneel itself. That tells me something," Isaac said.

Cynthia didn't say anything. She just stared at her husband.

"It tells me that Americans aren't concerned with people of color. Well, they are when a new rap song takes over the radio waves, or a new dance trend takes them by storm. But overall, they don't care. I don't know if they ever will. I want to use that money to start rebuilding the black community. San Francisco first, but then we'll go across the country," Isaac said.

"We won't be able to do it by ourselves," Cynthia said.

"Of course not. But we have a ton of friends who would love to help," Isaac said.

"We do," Cynthia said. "Why is all of this on your mind right now?"

Isaac shrugged his shoulders.

"Why not? I haven't been doing my best job at helping the community. Even when we had money with Science Supreme, all we did was write checks to fancy charities. I'm sick and tired of the way black people are looked at in this country. Walkman is the personification of that hate white people still have towards black people. Walkman was a child during the civil rights movement. I've read stories about his father. A legendary member of the KKK. Walkman's father had killed over fifteen Blacks during his time with the group. There's a picture online of a little Walkman attending a lynching with his proud father. Now Walkman is all grown up. He studied hard, worked hard, and achieved great success. Now, he's a wealthy businessman who controls our country's money, essentially. There's no reason for him to turn his back on Daddy's values. No matter how many black security guards he has, no matter how many apartment complexes he builds, at the end of the day, he's a Walkman. A man of the Whites. Too many of those men run our country right now. This money and our education is our chance to help," Isaac said.

Cynthia gave Isaac another hug.

"We'll do our part," Cynthia said.

"I know we will," Isaac said. "But first, let's hurry home back to Alisha. Are we ready to leave soon?"

"We are. We can leave tomorrow if you want," Cynthia said.

"Good," Isaac said.

"Another thing, Isaac," Cynthia said. "Don't be so hard on yourself. You've done a lot more than write fancy checks. I can't count the number of children you inspired during our time with Science Supreme. All those parents that come up to you talking about programs their kids can get into? That's change. All the kids whose grades improved in Science class because you helped them understand it? That's change. Don't let guilt lead you to give back. I know you want to do it because it's right, but just know, that you've done a lot already."

Isaac smiled.

He pulled Cynthia in for a kiss. They made their way back into their room. Their television was on. They both laid down on the bed. As the day went on, Isaac felt that the harvest was going to go well. Cynthia's impromptu machines had been made and his numbers looked good. All that was left now, was to wait. They passed the time watching movies. Isaac cherished any moment with his family, but he hadn't had true alone time with Cynthia in a while. Nothing could come close to the love he felt for Alisha, but the love he felt for Cynthia was special too, in its own way. When he was alone with her, he felt like a nervous kid again. It was everything he ever wanted. Cynthia gave him the chance to forget about all the mess in his life. No Walkman, no Immobulum, no racist country, no guilt, just love. That's all. He looked at his wife's beautiful eyes.

"Why are you staring at me like that?" she asked.

"Because I love you," Isaac said. They kissed, and she pressed her forehead up against his chest. She had started to talk in a whisper.

"It's night time, Isaac," she said. "We stayed in bed all day. When's the last time we did that?"

"Not since college," Isaac said. "I still remember that night. It was our one-year anniversary."

"Yeah," Cynthia said.

"I made you breakfast, you made lunch, and we ordered pizza for dinner. One of the best days in my life," Isaac said.

"Well, that's in my top four, three other days top it though," Cynthia said.

"What days?" Isaac asked.

"If you must know, the day Alisha was born, the day we left for our honeymoon, and the day you proposed to me," Cynthia said.

Isaac laughed a bit. He kissed her forehead.

"Those are all pretty great days," he said.

About twenty minutes went by, and Cynthia had fallen asleep. Tomorrow was the big day. Isaac was still in bed, but he couldn't sleep. He wasn't nervous, but he wanted to savor this moment for all it was worth. If everything went well tomorrow, his family was going to prosper. Sure, it meant doing something illegal, but the government had forced his hand. Isaac thought about the decision to sell the Immobulum on the black market. He thought about it as a possibility since the Pinnacle froze his accounts. Now that the moment was getting closer, he was thinking about who to sell it to. Isaac knew that if the wrong people got their hands on it, it could be weaponized. It was unlikely, but it could happen. He easily could've used it to make weapons for the government, but he refused to do so. He also knew he wasn't the only scientist in the world. Someone else could unlock its true potential. Maybe that's why he was up, why he couldn't sleep. He looked at Cynthia. She was peacefully asleep. He needed to go to bed too. He finally laid his head down on his pillow. As he began to drift off, Walkman entered his mind. Isaac didn't let him win this time though. Alisha came into his mind. Cynthia followed. They were at the world's biggest park. All the swings and toys Alisha could ask for, and the comfiest benches for Cynthia and Isaac to sit on. That was what sent him into a deep sleep, and he couldn't have been happier.

— · ·· — · ·· — · ·· — · · — · ·· — · ·· — ··

16 Years Ago: Northwestern University

"Isaac, you better put your phone down," Cynthia said.

"I'm sorry. I was just looking at this story. Did you hear about that reporter from our school? Apparently, he was doing some research on some conspiracy theory, and now he got kicked out of the country," Isaac said.

"Really? What's his name?" Cynthia said.

"Doesn't say. Oh, here it is. Walter Daniels. This article doesn't say what he was investigating though. I can't find one that seems to talk about what he was doing. But now, he's being exiled to Russia or something," Isaac said.

"That's all cute, but it's your turn to make dinner."

"My turn? I made breakfast. I think you should make it, since lunch was only some sub sandwiches," Isaac said.

"But they were tasty sub sandwiches, right?" Cynthia asked.

"I've had better," Isaac said laughing. Cynthia hit him on the arm.

"But back to the issue at hand, I'm not making dinner. Let's just eat pizza," Isaac said.

"We decide to stay in bed all day, make meals for each other, and you want to get a pizza?"

"We can get whatever kind of pizza you want," Isaac said.

Cynthia laughed a bit.

"That's why I love you," Cynthia said, but the second she said it, she looked down. "Sorry," she said.

"Sorry for what?" Isaac said laughing. "I love you too, my little Mexican Princess," Isaac said. They hugged each other.

"So, if I order the pizza, will you get it?" Cynthia asked.

"Deal," Isaac said. "But first, let's take a little nap. It's not like we have anything to do today."

CHAPTER 5

The mountains were beautiful; Isaac had never seen this part of Australia before. They had left the city about two hours ago, and Cynthia's scanner was going crazy. It said the Immobulum was close. They decided to get out of their rental car and walk the rest of the way. Isaac expected to walk, but when he saw the hill they had to walk, his heart dropped a bit.

"You ready for this?" he asked Cynthia.

"You only ask me that because you're nervous?" she asked.

"Pretty much. I'm guessing the Immobulum is going to be inside one of these caves. It flourishes in colder temperatures. It's winter here, but still too hot. Where's the nearest cave entrance?" he asked.

"I see one there. The scanner isn't telling us to go there though," Cynthia said.

"We can't let technology tell us everything," Isaac said. "We have nothing but time, so let's go."

They entered the first cave, and sure enough, there was Immobulum. It wasn't much, but enough to harvest. Isaac got his gloves on, Cynthia prepped the machines, and the process began. Immobulum in its pure form, wasn't usable. A special type of saw was needed that could shave the protective crystals to get to the Immobulum itself. That was tricky too, because after the saw shaved the outsides of the crystals, the element was reduced to a liquid, an extremely cool liquid that would burn the hands of any human. Isaac had created special mechanical gloves laced with Immobulum, so he could handle the liquid if any spilled on him. The machines Cynthia made included the saw, and a special type of container to hold the liquid. Everything went well with that first deposit. Isaac carried the machine once they exited the cave. The mountain was becoming steeper. He could see the fatigue setting in on Cynthia's face. Both had the special containers attached to their backpacks too. Isaac assumed he could carry maybe 50 pounds of liquid Immobulum. He didn't want Cynthia carrying more than 20. From the research he'd done, Isaac knew that 5 pounds would sell for almost 20 million dollars.

The next four caves they checked didn't have anything in them. They both were extremely tired. Isaac found a flat surface for them to sit down for a while. He checked his watch; they had already been out for more than five hours and they only were able to collect less than a pound. Cynthia was exhausted, and Isaac was getting there, but he was determined. After five minutes, they got up to check the next cave. The scanner said huge deposits should've been there, but they didn't find anything.

Three hours later. The sun was starting to set. Isaac's back was extremely tight. Cynthia couldn't hide her exhaustion any more. Isaac noticed that every step she took brought her closer to passing out. He didn't want his wife to suffer anymore.

"We can leave," Isaac said.

Cynthia tried to respond, but instead, she dropped to her knees. Her mouth opened but words didn't come out. Isaac took off his backpack. Cynthia was dehydrated, and she couldn't speak. There was a water bottle in his backpack. Isaac gave her some water, then Cynthia laid on her back for a couple of minutes. Isaac looked up at the sky. Not only was the sun gone, but it had been shielded by the darkest clouds he had ever seen.

"Jesus," he said. "Come on Cynthia. We have to get inside. There's a storm coming," he said.

"Okay," she said weakly. Isaac didn't wait for her to stand up. He couldn't bear seeing his wife in pain. He picked her up and continued up the mountain. Thunder began to rumble. Lightning soon followed. Isaac could hardly breathe. Cynthia was now unconscious. He knew he couldn't stop, not yet. The entrance to the cave was close. All he had to do was push through it. Push through the pain. Push through the fear of losing his home. Push through the fear of his family going hungry. Isaac knew if he stopped, even if it was for a second, his life would be over. Everything he had worked for would crumble if he rested for one second. Cynthia was counting on him. That was all he needed. He finally made it to the entrance of the cave.

He gently sat her down on the ground. Now it was his turn to fall on his back. Everything hurt. His lungs were on fire, his back was beyond repair, muscles were all screaming, and his head was pounding. He slowly worked his way to his feet though. His hands were shaking. Cynthia had woken up.

"Where are we?" she asked quietly.

"Some cave," Isaac said. "Look outside," he pointed to the entrance. Rain was pouring down. The cold breeze was giving him and Cynthia chills.

"Did you---carry me?" Cynthia asked.

"I had to. We would've been trapped in the storm," Isaac said.

Cynthia put her head in between her legs. She was crying.

"What's wrong?" Isaac asked.

"I don't know," Cynthia said. She continued to cry.

"C'mon, it's me," Isaac said. "Talk to me." He tried to lower his voice to a whisper. The last thing he wanted was for Cynthia to feel like he was attacking her.

"I guess I'm just embarrassed," Cynthia said. "I let you down."

Isaac laughed a bit.

"No, you didn't. I'll always take care you, my Mexican Princess," Isaac said.

Cynthia smiled.

"You haven't called me that since college," she said.

"There's my girl. There's that beautiful smile."

Isaac sat down next to her. They ate some apples and talked about the Immobulum.

"Isaac, look at this. My scanner says there are enormous deposits in this cave," Cynthia said.

"I'm guessing they're deep in the cave. Because I don't see anything right now," Isaac said.

"I would assume so. Not like we can leave anytime soon," Cynthia said. "Help me up."

Within minutes, they were up, exploring the cave. They walked around for about twenty minutes before they came to a drop off. There was water at the bottom of the cave. On the edges on the cave though, purple light shined bright. Isaac couldn't believe his eyes.

"Damn," he said. "Cynthia, I don't think we need the scanner anymore."

The Immobulum was plentiful. The entire cave was so well lit, they didn't need their flashlight. Cynthia screamed. Isaac followed. They ran on the edges of the cave screaming and laughing. All that pain he had felt went away. They had accomplished their goal. There was more Immobulum in here than they knew what to do with. He decided to conserve his energy. Isaac stopped Cynthia and they immediately got to work on the deposits. During the process, Isaac couldn't help but feel giddy about what the future held for them. Isaac loved seeing her smile. They harvested over 60 pounds of Immobulum. It ended up that Isaac's container could hold it all, so he decided to carry it. He didn't want to put any more strain on Cynthia's body. They were high up on one of the edges of the cave. Isaac decided they should make their way down to the bottom.

"We need to be careful going back down," Isaac said.

"I know," Cynthia said.

They eventually got down to the entrance.

"Look at it all," Isaac said. "We didn't even scratch the surface."

"What if Walkman and the Pinnacle find this?" Cynthia asked.

"I don't know," Isaac said.

"Immobulum is one of the most useful and powerful elements in the world," he said to Cynthia.

"I think we're thinking the same thing," Cynthia said. "People are going to kill over this."

"Exactly. Innocent people are going to die, and this beautiful land will be turned into a warzone as companies and billionaires scramble for control of Australia," Isaac said.

"I can see it so vividly in my head," Cynthia said. "What can we do it about it?"

"I'm not sure. My first thought was to blow this place to hell, but that'd be irresponsible," Isaac said.

"So many people could benefit from this element," Cynthia said. "We just have to make sure it gets into the right hands."

"Is there any way to actually do that?" Isaac asked.

"I'm not sure. Let's just get out of here. Then we'll figure something out," Cynthia said.

"Good idea," Isaac said. Before he even finished his sentence, the ground began to shake underneath his feet. Cynthia could hardly stand. Isaac could tell she was still fatigued. The ground continued to shake fiercely. The Immobulum crystals on the wall began to fall. Isaac and Cynthia ran to the entrance. The violent shaking slowed them down drastically. Cynthia fell to the ground. Isaac wasn't going to leave his wife behind. Just as he tried to pick her up, rocks from the top of the cave fell and blocked his path.

"What's happening?" Cynthia yelled.

"I don't know!" Isaac yelled back. He hurried and moved the rocks out the way. More rocks fell from the cave. Cynthia let out a loud scream.

"My leg!" she screamed. Isaac could see the blood. Her leg was completely shattered. He knew he'd have to carry her the whole way now. He finally moved the rest of the rocks from around her. Tears were streaming down her face.

It's okay. Just breathe," he said. "We're not dying here today." He smiled, and Cynthia smiled, but he could tell she was in immense pain. Isaac didn't have time to wait. He picked her up quickly. Nothing was worse than seeing his wife in pain. Once he had her on his shoulders, Isaac ran as fast as he could towards the entrance. With every step, breathing was becoming a task. The rocks were falling rapidly around him. All Isaac wanted to do was get out alive. All he wanted was to see his wife healthy again. Walking, laughing, and being the beautiful woman that he knew and loved. Except that Isaac knew that if he let his mind wander anymore that both he and his wife would be dead. So, he took one more deep breath and gained speed.

"I'm sorry if I'm hurting you," he said. She didn't respond.

The rocks continued to fall as Isaac exited the cave. He knew that was the easy part. What was going to be extremely hard was going down the mountain. Isaac didn't have time to pace his steps or to even watch where he was going. The entire mountain was crumbling. Not only did he have to get down it fast, but he had to make sure he didn't drop Cynthia.

A burning sensation in his chest caused him to pause for a moment, then he started running down the side of the mountain. Rocks and Immobulum shards approaching him behind. Isaac didn't pay it much mind though. Within minutes, he was at the bottom of the hill. He sidestepped the falling rocks and ran to a dirt road that was near their car. He tried to slow his heartbeat so that it didn't beat out of his chest. One problem down, now another one presented itself.

Cynthia was weak. The run down the mountain caused her to go unconscious. Or maybe she went out before that, he didn't know. Isaac wasn't a trained medical professional, but he knew his wife needed care, and soon. Their drive to the hills had taken at least two hours. If Isaac didn't think of something fast, he knew he'd lose his wife. Blood loss, shock, and fatigue would be her downfall. Isaac finally got them back to their car. He tried his best to wake Cynthia up.

"Cynthia," he said. "Come on Baby, wake up." He lightly hit her body and face. After a while, he noticed she wasn't responding. He could feel his face becoming hot. Isaac looked around the terrain of the hills. It was pitch black. This wasn't a good time to be outside in the middle of nowhere. He took another deep breath. Once he regathered his thoughts, Isaac opened the first aid kit. There were some ice packs, gauze pads, bandages, everything he needed. Cynthia still had a pulse, so Isaac figured he could administer some type of aid to her before they got back to the city. First, stop the bleeding. Isaac wiped her leg clean of most of the blood. Her leg was contorted in a way that almost made him vomit. No doubt it was broken. For a moment, Isaac wondered if she'd ever walk again. He dismissed the idea because it was ridiculous, all that mattered right now was making sure she stayed alive. Her leg had swelled up severely. Isaac found some disinfectant to clean her wound with. After he cleaned her wounds the best he could, he positioned her in the car laying down in the backseat. Gently, Isaac laid the ice packs on her leg and began to wrap them up in the bandages.

Once that was done, he felt like she'd survive the drive into the city. Only one more thing needed to be done.

She's going to hate me for this, he thought. Isaac got a bottle of water from the first aid kit. He poured most it on Cynthia's face hoping she'd wake up. Almost instantly, she woke up coughing and wheezing, then she grabbed her leg and screamed in pain.

"I'm sorry," he said. "I did the best I could with your wounds, but we have to get you to a hospital. We have a long drive, so you have to stay awake for me, you understand?"

Cynthia had a lost look on her face.

After what felt like forever she spoke.

"When we get home, I'm pouring water on you," she said forcing a smile.

He smiled back, then started the car.

"We've got about two hours. Let's talk about something to keep us occupied until then," Isaac said.

"Sounds good to me," she said.

There was a long silence.

"You're the one who suggest we talk," Cynthia said. "But nothing's being said."

"Shut up," Isaac said laughing. Cynthia laughed too.

"So, you carried me all the way when I hurt my leg?" her voice was serious now.

"Yeah," Isaac said. "Couldn't let my queen down. So, I acted," Isaac said smiling. He knew she couldn't see him, but it didn't matter.

"Thanks," Cynthia said.

"You're my wife. Why wouldn't I save you?" Isaac asked.

"It just amazes me sometimes," she said.

There was another long pause.

"What does?" Isaac finally asked her.

"Your will. I don't know. Just how powerful and amazing you become when you really want to," Cynthia said.

"So, what you're saying is, the other times I don't really want to, I'm not powerful and amazing?" he asked.

"You know what I mean," she said. "You make me feel safe."

"That's all I want," he said smiling.

She began to shuffle furiously in the backseat. Isaac wanted to stop the car, but he didn't want to waste any time. Every moment he wasted, Cynthia was closer to infection or even worse, death. But at the same time, what if she was having a seizure? She'd lost an incredible amount of blood already. Isaac almost became ill at the sight of her leg. He knew the second he saw it, that she'd never be the same again. He just hoped he'd been vigilant in his efforts to save his wife.

"Are you okay?" he asked nervously.

"Fine," Cynthia said. She groaned quietly. Isaac wasn't an idiot. He knew she was hardly containing herself. The pain was beginning to be too much for her.

"There's no need to be tough with me," Isaac said.

"Nothing about me is tough right now," Cynthia said.

"So, what you were saying about helping people. With the amount of Immobulum we have, we can make some serious changes in our community," Isaac said.

"I would like that," Cynthia said. "It's what we tried to do with Science Supreme. But the Pinnacle decided against that, obviously."

"I know," he said. "We would have enough money to start everything over though. Even our own lives."

She didn't say anything. In fact, they didn't speak to each other for almost thirty minutes.

"Cynthia?"

"I'm thinking. We could start over, but I'm tired of running from the Pinnacle."

"What do you mean?" Isaac asked. "We haven't run from them at all."

"In a way, we have. Our entire lives have been about not causing ripples. We've always tried to be the two minorities who white people could trust. It's gotten us far, no doubt. But Isaac, this money gives us the opportunity to really make a difference. And not an acceptable one in the eyes of the Pinnacle or American government," Cynthia said.

Her words both inspired and terrified him. For one, this is the exact mentality Isaac wish he had daily, but he didn't. He didn't wake up thinking about the plight of his people in America. He was no fool about the realities of systematic racism in his country, but it didn't gnaw at him constantly. He didn't know if it was the recent shootings or just some part of his subconscious. But now those thoughts were alive and well. At the same time though, all Isaac truly wanted from life was to have a family. He had one. A beautiful, vibrant wife, and a confident, joyful daughter. Isaac had thoughts often of what he would do if given the impossible choice between his race and his family. He wanted to believe that his heart fought for the greater good. But deep down, he knew the truth was something he didn't like. He wanted to run. But he knew he needed to fight. Cynthia wasn't making this easy on him.

"What about Alisha though? My mother? Your family?" Isaac asked.

"Your father is one of the most recognized civil rights leaders in this country. Not only is he recognized, he's respected. No scandals, no history to be ashamed of, no fear. You've been a target ever since they realized your father was a good man," Cynthia said.

"You're not wrong, well, kind of wrong about my father," Isaac said laughing a bit. "I am tired of the Pinnacle though. If someone can figure out a way to take them down, it's going to be us."

"We'll keep Alisha safe at all costs," Cynthia said. "And I know you don't have the best relationship with your father, but how did your father keep you safe all these years?"

It was an interesting question. As far as Isaac could remember, there was never a special protocol in place for dealing with nut jobs when he was younger. Isaac's father taught him how to fight at a young age. He also taught Isaac how to use a gun properly and defend himself with a knife by the time he was fourteen. Isaac grew up with a sense of strength. More strength than most fourteen-year-old boys had at that time. There was one time, during high school, that Isaac realized his father would go through heaven and hell to protect him. A student at Isaac's high school was brutally beaten. The principal at the school suspected that the beating was racially motivated. No one could prove it at the time, but everyone in school was on the lookout. Isaac knew who had done the beating. Three white boys who had their own Nazi gang were going around and beating up minorities. They eventually came for Isaac. They broke his nose and tried to break his spirit, but Isaac fought off the three boys. He broke one of their orbital bones' and gave another one a concussion. The boys then tried to sue Isaac for assault. Isaac was pulled out of class one day and was going to be sent home. His father showed up arguing with the principal about how stupid it was for Isaac to get suspended when he was attacked. One of the fathers of the three boys was there as well. A heated exchange took place which ended in the boy's father pulling a gun on Isaac. Isaac remembered how scared he was that day. His father didn't hesitate to jump in front of the man. He startled the man enough that he wrestled the gun away from him. It went off and a bullet struck the Principal in the arm. Isaac's father apprehended the man until the cops arrived. His father was called a hero and it only added to his spotless reputation.

"My father didn't do anything special," he finally said. "He equipped me the best he could. When it came time to protect me, he didn't flinch."

"There's your answer," Cynthia said. "We can do that exact thing with our little Alisha."

"You're right. How's your leg?" Isaac asked.

"Hurts like hell, why?"

"We're at the hospital now," Isaac said. He could hear his wife sigh a sigh of relief. He let one out as well. He noticed the blood has soaked through the bandages he wrapped her in. Gently, Isaac picked her up with the last bit of strength he had. She perked her lips, indicating she wanted a kiss. He laughed.

"You're too much," he said. His arms felt like they were going to fall off. But they would fall off before he dropped Cynthia on the ground. They made it into the hospital. Doctors immediately rushed to Cynthia and took her into the ER. Isaac slumped onto a chair and was fast asleep before Cynthia even made it down the hallway. He knew she was a fighter. He knew she was going to pull through. His queen had much more resolve than he could ever hope for. He liked it that way. Isaac didn't like feeling the weight of the world on his shoulders. That was his father's job.

CHAPTER 6

merica didn't feel any different. Isaac wasn't sure what he thought he was going to feel as he got off the plane, but it wasn't much. His body was still fatigued. Sleep, water, and rest were the only things that were going to help him, and he hadn't had much of either recently. Cynthia had made progress. The bones in her leg were completely shattered. The muscles, tendons, and nerves in the leg were either completely torn or 90% torn. Her recovery time was pegged for at least a full year. She wouldn't be able to walk for at least a couple of months. The doctors gave her a wheelchair for now and a special cast. While she was happy to be alive, Isaac could see the frustration on her face as he had to roll her through the airport. Cynthia was the most independent person he knew. Pride wasn't getting in her way, she just didn't know how to let someone help her. If it were anyone else helping her, she'd have a fit every five seconds. Isaac appreciated the fact she kept her composure during their trip. Now though, they were back home in San Francisco. Home wasn't home though without his daughter. Cynthia's attitude changed too as they approached Isaac's mother's house. They couldn't stop talking about their little girl.

As Isaac pulled into the driveway, something rushed over him. Some sort of energy. Science was his main field. Science made the most sense to Isaac. He understood that science helped explain the unexplainable. He also understood that science couldn't explain everything. He wasn't sure if science would be able to explain the wave of energy that just rushed over him. It felt physical. He closed his eyes for a moment. In his mind, he tried to envision the energy leaving his body. He saw it. A mist or some sort of fog escaping the car, headed into his mother's house. He felt a chill come across his neck. Instantly, Cynthia spoke up.

"Did you feel that breeze?" she asked.

"I did," he said quietly. He opened the car door to see if the wind had picked up at all. Nope, just dry heat. He tried to close his eyes again. Nothing. The energy was gone. Science had its chance. His brain had a chance. But now, the unexplained won another round. He was frustrated. He helped Cynthia into her chair and they went into the house. Isaac entered the house slowly. SpongeBob's theme song was playing from the living room. Isaac was positive he heard Alisha singing along. His mother was sitting at the dining table, facing away from them. She didn't so much as flinch when they walked into the dining room. Isaac needed answers. He approached his mother and realized that Grandma Rose was fine. Her breathing was normal, skin a reasonable color, and she was attentive. Still, Rose continued to sit there, not even acknowledging her son and his crippled wife. Cynthia broke the silence.

"What's wrong with you Rose?" she said.

Isaac jumped slightly. That was the loudest Cynthia had ever gotten with his mother.

"Are you deaf, woman?" Cynthia asked.

Enough of this.

"Cynthia, that's enough," Isaac said in his most stern voice. He wasn't trying to assert dominance over his wife, but she wasn't going to continue to disrespect his mother that way. Cynthia didn't say anything else. She rolled to the other side of Rose, who was still alive, but didn't move.

"Momma," Isaac said quietly. "Momma, it's me, Isaac."

After a while, his mother finally turned to face her son.

Isaac slowly smiled.

"Where's Alisha?" he asked. His voice sounded angry, but he didn't mean it too. He had just scolded his wife for her attitude. They both just wanted their daughter. But his mother couldn't speak. She tried too. Isaac noticed her age for the first time in a while. His mother usually looked full of life. Now though, she looked like a ghost had ripped her soul from her body. Her hair looked fragile and her face shook with the force of a jackhammer. Isaac ran into the living room. All of Alisha's toys were there. Rose's carpet was thick enough too that Isaac could see the imprint of Alisha's feet and butt. She was here. Isaac's mind began to race.

"Where is my daughter?!" he yelled. "Momma I need you to snap out of it and tell me where she is!" Isaac couldn't contain his emotions anymore. Cynthia was becoming hysterical as well. His mother finally spoke.

"She's gone, Isaac," she said.

He ran back into the dining room. Grabbed his mother by the shoulders.

"Where did she go?" he asked.

"I don't know. One second, she's sitting there. You drive up to the driveway, and SpongeBob plays on the TV. She starts to sing, you turn your car off. I was looking at her the entire time."

What the hell is going on? Isaac wanted more than anything to understand right now. That's all he wanted. That energy overtook his body the same time his daughter disappeared.

"Did she evaporate?" Isaac asked.

"Into thin air," Rose said. "Not a scream, not a sound. She was singing the song. Then, she was gone. I saw the whole thing."

Cynthia perked her lips. She didn't want a kiss this time.

"Are you fucking kidding me? Where is my daughter?!" she demanded. Isaac realized that his wife's condition had worsened. The pain medication she was on made her irritable, but now, she was losing it. Her hands were shaking, and she was sweating. Cynthia's leg began to shake violently. To the point that she had to grab it. When she did, tears rolled down her face. He rolled her into the living room and attempted to calm her down.

"Breathe. Breathe," he said calmly. She copied the noises he made. Her leg had finally stopped shaking. Isaac sighed deeply. The last thing he needed was for his wife to have a mental breakdown.

He went back into the dining room.

"You're sure you saw her disappear, Momma?" he asked.

Rose nodded slowly.

"No doubt about it," she said. The shakiness was gone from her voice. She was sure of herself now.

"I don't know what's happening," Isaac whispered to himself. Taking a moment to gather his thoughts, he realized something bigger was at play here. Isaac believed in the concept of different universes, but all the theories on that type of science were exactly that, theories. No one in the history of science had successfully gone to a different universe, collect samples, and return to their world to tell everyone about their findings. It was ludicrous and was an area reserved for novelists. Pure fantasy. But if Isaac was going to come close to finding his daughter, he would have to engage that fantasy with every ounce of willpower he had. Believing his own mother wasn't hard, it's what came after that made him dizzy. Cynthia breathing had gotten worse again and Rose was still just sitting there. Isaac decided to combine both efforts. He sat down next to his mother, then began breathing slowly, trying to calm Cynthia, holding back tears.

My baby girl is gone, he thought. And my queen is hurt. My mother is hurt.

Isaac would kill Jesus himself to restore his family. Just a couple weeks ago, Alisha was in front of him, Cynthia looked better than she did in college, and his mother was more alive than a child. Now everything was in shambles.

He couldn't contain it any longer. The deep breaths were followed by tears. Rose was crying too. Cynthia continued her hysterical breathing. No one in the Eckspo family spoke to each other for nearly two hours. Isaac's brain was still trying to contemplate a way to access another universe or dimension. It had to be done in strides though. Too much thought on Alisha, and his eyes burned something fierce. Cynthia had fallen asleep. Rose was asleep too. Isaac decided it was time to do some research. He got up from the table and headed towards his mother's computer. Of course, he would have rather been in his lab, but he wasn't going to compromise Cynthia's peace. For the first time in a long time, Isaac noticed she looked like she was getting some rest. He would've stayed up for four straight days if it meant his wife could sleep for four hours.

The search started simple. Isaac pulled up a search engine and input "cross dimensional travel." A couple of hours, and six scholarly articles later, he realized he knew as much as these scholars did about multiple dimensions. Time existing outside of time. There was nothing about achieving this type of travel. One professor tried for years. His idea was that of teleportation. Tearing apart the atoms of an object, containing them in an energy field, and reconstructing that object in an area different than the area it was originally in. Except this professor tried to contain that energy in a machine he was positive accessed a different dimension. His tests were flawed, but one test showed readings of a pencil he had sent through the machine. The readings indicated that the pencil was in fact there, but when he opened the machine, there was no pencil. The professor continued the tests, each time getting worse and worse. His project bankrupted him and that was the end of that. By the time Isaac had finished, he looked up and realized it was night time. Cynthia was still asleep. His mother was awake. She had been watching him for a while, but she didn't say anything.

"I'm trying to find her," he said. He was surprised at the sound of his voice. No, it wasn't that. He was surprised at the weakness of his voice, the frailness of it too. Isaac needed to take a break. He knew it, but he also knew a break wasn't going to solve his problem.

"I know," his mother said. She got up from the couch and walked over to her son. She put her hand on his shoulder.

"Maybe you two should go home," she said.

Isaac laughed a little.

"And wake her up. She hasn't slept in days, Momma. I'd be a fool to wake her up now. We'll stay here tonight if that's fine," Isaac said.

His mother kissed him on the forehead.

"You know it's okay with me, son. I could use the company." She walked upstairs slowly.

Isaac brought his focus back on the computer. His eyes were burning, and his head hurt, but he continued to read. Another two hours passed. Eventually, he peeled himself off the chair and made his way towards the couch.

Cross dimensional travel, he thought. What type of crap is this? I just want my daughter back. I just want my---Isaac finally let himself rest. When he woke up, the sun was shining through the window.

Cynthia was up. Rose was up. A sense of failure overcame him. Yes, it was unreasonable to expect a solution in less than 12 hours, but that's who Isaac was. The longer a problem haunted him, the more of a failure he felt like he became. Maybe it wasn't how the world saw him, but that's how he saw himself. He rubbed his eyes quickly and was back on the computer. He didn't say a word to Cynthia.

I'm going to find you, Baby Girl. I promise.

— · · — — — · · — — · · — — · · — — · ·

Two Months Later

Sunlight. Isaac usually loved being outdoors. In two months though, he couldn't remember the last time he had been outside. The only reason today was the day was to get some fresh air. His head was starting to hurt from the inside air. When he stepped outside, he noticed the two men playing the jazz music. It was the last sound he wanted to hear. They waved at him with the same enthusiasm they do every day. Isaac made a face that said, 'Leave me the hell alone,' but soon realized these two men didn't deserve that type of hostility. They were just doing what they loved. His anger, rather his anger about his current situation, didn't require him to be a jerk to everyone he saw. He approached the men.

They didn't stop playing when Isaac came up to them.

Must be finishing this song, he thought.

It was quite a song. Isaac had walked over during the song's climax. The drummer was beating the drums like he had a gun to his head. The saxophone was screeching, but not in an obnoxious way. Their noise was harmonious. Isaac loved that about these two. That no matter what they were doing, coordinated or not, it always sounded good. He took a moment to analyze them. This was the longest he'd ever looked at them. Both were black. Like a misguided fool, Isaac assumed both men were homeless. Why else would two grown men stand outside for hours a day and play music? But upon further inspection, Isaac realized that they were wearing hand-me-down clothes, but they were well-groomed. The drummer had a grey beard, but it was trimmed and so was his hair. The saxophone player had more black hair than grey, and he had dreadlocks.

The men finished their song. Isaac and six other people were watching now. The people applauded. One lady dropped a fifty-dollar bill in their jar. They thanked her and started to play another song. Isaac came over here to apologize for the face he made at them. But he was starting to think they didn't care about the face he made. This song wasn't the chaotic collaboration the last one was. This was barely involved the drummer at all. It was a soulful wail from the saxophone player. Isaac began to tear up a bit. The saxophone player's face was filled with emotion. Isaac's feet began to hurt, so he sat on the step close to the men. The sorrowful song continued, and the drummer finally looked at Isaac. He smiled. Isaac responded with a smile. More people gathered now as the soulful song reached a crescendo. The drummer was more involved now. His glance went away from Isaac. Their song concluded soon after, more tips were collected, and they began to pack up their instruments.

"Why do you two come here?" Isaac asked. He wanted his voice to sound friendlier, but the question had been on his mind ever since he walked over to them.

They didn't answer.

Isaac wanted to respond with anger, but he didn't have the energy. If they wanted to act like that, it was on them. He got up and started to walk back to his home.

"Do you like us coming here?" he heard a voice say.

Isaac turned around. He couldn't tell who said it, so he looked at both of them.

"I think the whole neighborhood likes you two coming here," he said.

"Then we'll keep coming," the saxophone player said. His voice was deep. They finished packing up their machines and headed down the street. Isaac wanted to follow their cryptic asses, but he had more important things to worry about. Once he was back inside, he took a deep breath. Every time he thought about losing Alisha, he had to take a couple of deep breaths before continuing his work. Cynthia hadn't gotten better either. In fact, she had become distant in the past couple of weeks Isaac hated himself for his part in the deterioration in their relationship, but what was he supposed to do? Just sit around and wait for the ghosts who abducted his daughter to gleefully return her? No, Isaac knew that wasn't the case. He knew he was either going to figure out where his daughter was, or she was gone forever. Rose hadn't been much help in his research. He questioned her again after about a week. She was calmer, but her story remained the same. Alisha was sitting in the living room, watching her show, and she just disappeared. Every time Isaac spoke to his mother, he hoped she changed something about her story that made sense. But he trusted her. After a couple more breaths, he walked upstairs to check on Cynthia. Outside her door was the Immobulum.

They hadn't talked about selling it yet. So, for the time being, their accounts were still frozen. Isaac planned on giving the amount he owed to Walkman. 'Owed' was a strong word. Isaac knew he didn't owe them a damn thing. But still, he knew paying them off would keep them out of his hair. He also knew they wouldn't question where the money came from either. So, once they got their money, things could go back to normal. Isaac was a bit surprised that the deposit in Australia wasn't occupied by the United States Army. It was an obstacle he foresaw right when they landed in Australia. He mentioned it to Cynthia. After two months, he figured they didn't suspect him, but he also figured they knew the Immobulum was gone in that area. They probably didn't want to occupy the area to avoid an international mess, but they had to be scouting the area. He was sure of that. Alisha missing was his priority, but this needed to be taken care of before Walkman and the Pinnacle found out.

Isaac heard a noise. It sounded like someone crying. He opened the bedroom door and noticed Cynthia in bed. She was crying, but not a sad cry. Pain had taken over her body. Isaac rushed to her side, but she pushed him away.

"Oh, now you want to help me? When's the last time you've even come to check on me?" Cynthia's voice was filled with disgust.

"Baby, please. You're irrational and your meds are irritating you," Isaac said.

"I'm fine," she said sharply.

Isaac walked to the other side of the room and laid on the opposite side of the bed.

"I'm sorry," he said. "I know I've been neglectful recently, but you understand I'm only doing this for Alisha."

"I can't believe I'm saying this, but forget Alisha for just one second," Cynthia said.

"What? How can you say something like that?"

"I'm your wife, Isaac. Not only am I crippled for life, but I have been stuck inside for months now. No outside air, no work, it's driving me insane. You know the worst part about it all? The fact you've been here with me the whole time. Not only have you not touched me since we've gotten home, but you haven't kissed me either. You think I'm some sort of repulsive monster since the accident."

Isaac couldn't believe his ears. He did the first thing that came to his mind. He grabbed Cynthia by the neck gently, wiped away her tears, and kissed her. She kissed back of course. It was one of their most passionate kisses they have ever had. When they separated, Isaac saw Cynthia's beautiful smile come back. He smiled back at her.

"I'm sorry. And I love you," he said.

"I love you too," she said. "Sorry I've been emotional lately. I just hate feeling helpless."

"I know. But maybe you can help me make sense of my research. You're the smartest person I know and you're patient too. Look, I have a grey hair coming in because of this nonsense."

"Hate to tell you this sweetie, but that's been there for a while. Not your only one either," Cynthia said. Isaac honestly didn't know he had more grey hairs. The joke hurt him, but he could take it if it meant his wife was finally happy. One part of his problem was solved. Now that Cynthia was out of her funk, maybe Alisha had a chance. He decided to get her something nice. The only thing that could make her happier than a kiss from him was ice cream. He ran to the store down the street and returned upstairs with his notes. After Cynthia stopped eating because she gave herself a brain freeze, he started going over his notes. After he talked for what seemed like forever, Cynthia examined them. She read them repeatedly before giving him an answer.

"Looks like there's not much we can do," she said. "Unless we somehow build a machine that can transport us into a different dimension. Which, even if we succeed, we have no way of knowing what dimension our baby girl got sent to."

"That's what I've been stuck on. You see my notes on that energy I felt when she was taken? I've been thinking of a way to build a machine that can detect dimensional energy in the air. Maybe the energy that passed through me is still at my mother's house where Alisha was," Isaac said.

"It's a plausible explanation. Hell, anything is plausible with this mess. You're going to need a lot of power for a machine like that. I'm guessing you're planning on using the Immobulum," Cynthia said.

"I don't need much. There's not even a guarantee I can locate the energy. If I can though, there's a chance I can locate it with a dimension traveling machine, go there, and save Alisha," Isaac said.

"Worth a shot," Cynthia said. "Do you have a prototype built?"

"Not yet," he said. "I wanted you to look it over first and see if you have any suggestions."

"I think you're on the right track. But I don't know if there is a track here. None of this makes any sense at all," Cynthia said.

She started to cry, but Isaac was there quickly to console her. He embraced his wife for a while before picking up his notes and leaving.

"Do your work in here," she said. "I can't take being alone right now."

"It's late anyway. I'll come to bed for a bit, then I'll head downstairs when you're sleeping. When you wake up, I'll make you breakfast and move my work upstairs. Sound good?"

"Perfect," she said.

For the first time in two months, Isaac slept like a baby. He had a dream about finding Alisha. It didn't make him sad like his previous dreams though. This one involved Cynthia. Her laugh, her smile, her hips, everything about her was perfect. When Isaac woke up early the next morning, he realized her perfection hadn't eroded. He got up from the bed, kissed her, and started to walk downstairs.

"Whatever you make, please make bacon with it," she said.

"Sure thing," Isaac said.

She blew him a kiss and closed her eyes.

Downstairs, Isaac had almost finished breakfast. He wasn't the best cook, but he could whip something up. His special today included bacon, at the request of his queen, some scrambled eggs, a toasted bagel with butter on it, and a pineapple smoothie. Simple, but he knew Cynthia would love it. He loved it too. He couldn't describe the feeling going through his body ever since she regained her confidence. Isaac was positive this was a short victory and that he'd have to support his wife more than he ever had before. That was okay though. He was beyond ready to commit to being there for her. If it meant she was her happy, sexy self, he'd do anything. Together, they could find Alisha. If they couldn't, Isaac never wanted to stop, but as long as his wife was by his side, he could endure. The possibility of finding Alisha seemed low at this point. There wasn't a law enforcement agency that could help him with his predicament. After a while, he knew that he and Cynthia would have to move on. Their lives would be destroyed if they continued to throw money at inter dimensional travel. The thoughts of never seeing Alisha again caused Isaac to pause. A couple of breaths later, he picked up the tray of food again and proceeded upstairs. Except, something wasn't right.

He wanted to dismiss it, but he couldn't. The same energy that overtook him when Alisha disappeared. It was back. Isaac began hyperventilating. He noticed his chest was on fire too. At first, he thought it was his heart, but the longer he stood there, the more it burned, he realized it was his muscles. It started with his chest, but soon spread to every part of his body. This wasn't a part of Alisha's disappearance, but he knew the energy was the same. His muscles screamed in pain. Another wave of energy overcame him. Isaac knew what this one meant. There was no time to waste. Frantically, he dropped the tray of food and ran upstairs.

"Cynthia!" he yelled.

"Yeah?" he heard her respond. "Is everything okay?"

He couldn't focus. The pain had found its way to his eyes. They were burning. Isaac didn't want to stop to wipe them, but his vision was completely blurred now.

Please don't take her from me, he thought. Please.

Isaac charged through the room to find Cynthia's body disappearing.

"It's happening to me---" Cynthia began to say. She was gone the next second. Isaac tried to grab on to her, but no avail. He thought that maybe if he grabbed a hold of her, he could get transported to whatever dimension or universe she was taken to. That was not possible though; his wife was gone. Once again, he failed. Isaac couldn't take it. He could still feel the burning sensation going through his muscles. All he wanted was for the pain to stop. He dropped to his knees and screamed. The pain didn't stop.

"What the hell is wrong with me?" he yelled. Isaac looked up and noticed the room was spinning. No, not spinning, his eyes were playing tricks on him. Not only was the room spinning to him, everything was purple. The sheets, the floor, even his skin.

My skin! What is wrong with my body?

The burning sensation continued. Now though, he could see his muscles jumping, his veins pulsating. They were almost popping out of his skin. Isaac tried to get up, so he could find a mirror. The pain was too great though. All he could do was scream. His body was glowing now. A bold, bright purple light came from Isaac. The more he tried to fight the energy, the more his body glowed. Soon, he began to emit energy blasts from his muscles. He noticed the energy blasts looked like lightning. Still, the pain made him want to die. Since Cynthia was gone, he didn't need much convincing to do the deed himself.

There is a gun underneath the bed, he thought. I feel so weak. Maybe this will kill me before I get the chance.

Walking wasn't an option. Isaac fell to the floor and began to crawl. Every muscle he moved caused more energy to free itself from his body. It was noisy too. Isaac couldn't hear himself think.

The more he struggled to crawl towards the edge of his bed, the more he felt his body rip apart.

Finally, he found the gun. It was in a case with a lock. He always kept the key on him. When he grabbed the key though, the burning in his eyes turned into complete blindness. He put his hand up to his eyes. Now, his eyes were emitting the purple energy as well. He couldn't see.

I have no choice but to try, he thought.

Slowly, he found the gun and cocked it. He felt like he was going to explode. When he tried to raise the gun, he could feel some force, like a hand, pushing him down. The struggle felt like it went on for hours.

"This is bullshit!" Isaac yelled. He refused to give in to this energy. He gained control of the gun and pointed it at his head. All that was left was to pull the trigger. Maybe he'd be reunited with Alisha and Cynthia. If not, he was content never seeing them again. He was a failure and didn't deserve to see his two girls again. The force opposing Isaac returned with a vengeance. He felt the pull of one thousand elephants against his arm. He wasn't going to quit. With everything he had left, Isaac screamed at the top of his lungs, pulled the trigger and waited for time to stop. It did. Everything had stopped. The pain, the energy, the noise, everything.

Finally, he thought. Alone with death.

"Not quite, Mr. Eckspo," he heard a voice say. "Not quite."

CHAPTER 7

Isaac felt uneasy. He felt light. Like a feather. He opened his eyes but couldn't see anything. Darkness. He began feeling his body. Everything seemed to be normal. His muscles ached from the pain he had been in. There were so many questions racing through his head. A yellow light appeared in front of him. It wasn't a blinding light, and it wasn't faint either. It lit the space evenly. He saw a figure step from the light, almost as if the light was his car. Isaac had never seen someone like this before. The figure was human, that was a definite, but the way he dressed was ridiculous. He was wearing a long black jacket with a golden dragon going around it. The dragon was difficult to see though. The man had a gold tunic of some kind under the jacket. It looked like a vest. The boots he was wearing had the same golden dragon design. Isaac had a hard time adjusting, because as the man approached him, he looked as if he were floating on air. Isaac wanted to faint.

The man was black. He wasn't as dark as Isaac, but clearly a black man. His hair was stylized. It was slicked to the right side of his head. The rest was shaved. The man was carrying a sword too. It wasn't massive, but Isaac noticed the holster on his back. He then wondered why someone who dressed like this still sported such a lousy looking haircut. This man clearly wasn't from Isaac's world. Isaac wondered why he looked distinctly human yet looked like he was another species entirely.

"It's nice to finally meet you, Isaac," the man said. His voice was youthful. Deep, but youthful. He smiled at Isaac with a genuine smile. Isaac wanted to smile back, but given the circumstances, he couldn't.

"I'm sure this atmosphere is disorienting to you. Apologies. Where would you like to go?" the man asked.

"I've never been to Madrid," Isaac said.

The man waved his hand and within seconds, the pair was standing on top of a massive building.

"This is Prado Museum, Isaac. Present day," the man said. Isaac had to catch his breath.

Did I just travel at lightspeed? Or did I teleport? The science part of his brain began to question everything. He wasn't against what was happening, he just wanted answers.

"No more games," he said slowly, still breathing heavy.

"Fine," the man said. "We should probably leave though. People are starting to stare." Within seconds, they were atop a mountain. Isaac looked out and noticed how beautiful the green of the mountains was.

"Where are we?" Isaac asked.

"Ireland," the man said. "This is one of my favorite places to come and think."

"You from Ireland?"

The man shook his head.

"I'm from New York. Brooklyn, actually."

Isaac's face stiffened. There was no way this man was telling the truth.

"I'm not an alien. I'm from America, but my parents were from Mauritania. They raised me until I was 18. Then, I moved out to purse my dream in law. I helped people who couldn't help themselves."

"A defense attorney? I needed one of you when the Pinnacle shut me down," Isaac said.

"I know. I didn't intervene then, but I could have. This struggle with the Pinnacle has only enhanced my convictions in you," he said.

The wind nearly knocked Isaac off his feet. This man was so unassuming, so kind, he forgot the pain his body was in. The pain his heart was in. This man had answers, and Isaac needed to find out where his two girls went. That's all that mattered.

"Where are my girls?" he asked shakily.

"I don't know," the man said.

Isaac wanted to punch the man. Except he figured this man was God, or some form of God. He needed to stay alive for as long as possible. He figured this man needed him to do some terrible task for him, and taking Cynthia and Alisha was all a part of his sick, twisted game. He'd be no good to them dead.

"I know you want to kill me, but I need you to know, that I am your friend. And your biggest admirer," the man said. He reached behind him and pulled out his sword. It was entirely made of gold. He stuck it in the ground and placed his hands-on top of it. The gloves he was wearing had the same dragon symbol. The wind continued to push against Isaac's back, and it made the man's hair flow gracefully.

"On my sword," he said, "I am a friend."

"Are you God?" Isaac asked.

The man chuckled a bit.

"No, I killed God, though" the man said.

Isaac felt his knees almost give out.

"What the hell do you mean by that? How can you kill God?" Isaac asked.

"It's a long story. Look, Isaac, I'm from the future. About 80 years But I'm also from a different universe. Killing God gave me these powers."

Isaac wanted to hit this man in the face, stab him with the golden sword, and find his way out of Ireland. Something about this man wasn't right, but Isaac felt he was telling the truth about how he got his powers. Isaac's mother watched Alisha disappear out of thin air. Cynthia disappeared out of thin air. Nothing made sense, but Isaac relished in the unknown. He just hated not knowing.

"In my universe, the main difference is the importance in the role of men and women," he paused for a bit. The wind continued to blow. The man picked up his sword and put it back in the holster on his back. "In my universe," he continued, "Women are the dominant gender. Men aren't less important, but women have done a marvelous job running the world. I must admit, it's weird to see women objectified as they are in this world. Not you, though. You treated Cynthia like a queen. You treated Alisha like a princess. Racism and the false narrative of black men still exist where I come from, too. It warms my soul to see a black man so passionate about family."

"Thank you. So, you really don't know where they're at?"

"Sadly, no. I've just recently gained these powers to travel between universes. It's scary. When I first got them, I didn't want to do anything. Isaac, I've lived for over 1000 years. I've done everything a human can possibly do. Every experience we can experience, I've gone through it. These powers only add to the depression that is my life."

"So, you're immortal?" Isaac asked.

"Perks of killing God," the man said with a smile. "I'm sorry. If it's one thing I noticed from my universal travels, it's that a good sense of humor is a unique thing. I, personally, don't have one, but I would've become a bitter man a long time ago if I didn't laugh sometimes."

Man? The question that entered Isaac's mind when he first saw the man, jumped into his mind.

"How old are you? I mean, how old were you when you became immortal?" Isaac asked.

"Twenty-Five," the man said. "Haven't aged a day since."

There was something about this man. The tragedy of life, all life, was written on his face. He had seen empires, be it financial or military, rise and fall. He had loved and lost, and loved again, and lost again. It wasn't possible for someone to have a drive for that long. Isaac couldn't imagine trying to live a meaningful life for over 1000 years.

"Why have you taken me away from my family?" Isaac asked fighting back tears.

"The rulers of the many universes don't care for this one. There are billions of planets, but they all share the same common flaw. Corruption. They don't have any solution for it, but I think you're the answer."

"Billions of planets? So, there is alien life out there?" Isaac asked.

"Some planets just have water and fish. I don't know if you could classify a trout as an alien," the man said. Isaac smiled this time.

"Why am I the answer to all of this?" Isaac asked.

"There are few people in this world as good and pure as you are. I know it sounds ludicrous, but I can sense it. They have a sort of smell, if you will. You have the purest soul of anyone in your universe. Out of all the planets, all the species, all the people, I was drawn to your energy."

"Wow," Isaac said. Truthfully, he didn't know what to say.

"You can say no to this. I can find someone else who is worthy, but why not start at the top of the list? Isaac, as I've said, I've lived over 1000 years. During that time, I wanted to find purpose in life again. When I acquired these powers, it hit me. I decided to eradicate hate, evil, and corruption from the most hate-filled universe I could find. Suffice it to say, the universe I come from is near perfect."

"And this universe is the worst?" Isaac asked.

"Not just this universe, this planet. Earth in this universe is one of the vilest places in all of existence. Your reliance on technology, your hate towards fellow man, and the laughable leadership. This place isn't far from destruction. Be it a nuclear war or financial collapse, all could have been avoided if someone had the courage to change."

"You think I can help Earth change? I'm not sure that's possible." Isaac said.

"I believe it is. America is the epicenter of this ongoing chaos. It starts with you, and I'm not going to lie, I'm happy you're black because this journey is going to be tougher than expected," the man said.

"What does that mean?"

"I want to give you powers. Some of my powers in fact. You won't be able to do everything I'm able to do, but close. I want you to be the hero your world, your universe, needs," the man said.

"A superhero," Isaac said.

"Exactly. Your country will reject you the minute they find out about you. Questions about your motives, origins, and all of that will pop up, but race will be the main factor."

"How you figure?" Isaac asked.

"Don't play dumb," the man seemed irritated. "Racism is the foundation of America. It's destroying the Earth and if people don't unite, things will get out of control. That starts with them seeing a black man in power."

"Do I have a certain task? A certain target? You can't give me powers and not have a plan," Isaac said.

"You know who you need to hit. You know who to expose if this is going to work," the man said.

It didn't take Isaac long to conjure up an answer.

"The Pinnacle."

"You take them down, and heads will turn. You make villains like Walkman suffer, the country will be behind you."

The reality of the situation just hit Isaac. He stepped away from the man to adjust his thoughts. He wasn't sure he could do this. Did he even want to do this? A couple of months ago, his family faced financial problems. Big ones, but that was a normal problem that Isaac felt he could figure out. Now, this man, this stranger, claims to be from a different universe. Claims to have found Isaac because of the pureness of his soul. And now, he wants Isaac to help him in his depressing crusade to save Earth. No, Isaac didn't want this. Not one bit. But then again, without his girls, he wasn't sure what choice he had. He had no working theory on how to find them. Everything he fought for, was gone. This man though, offered Isaac a new take on social justice. Oh, his father would be proud.

Isaac walked around the mountain for a bit. Erasmus just watched him. Isaac then sat on top of a rock and began to breathe deeply and slowly. Erasmus walked over to him.

"On your sword, you swear you didn't take my girls?" Isaac asked.

"Yes," the man said. "I'm still new to this universe. Each universe has its own protectors. Its own gatekeepers. Powers similar or even greater than mine at some level. Maybe perhaps, I've angered someone enough that they took your family away."

"And you aren't in touch with these gatekeepers? Why is there no communication?"

"This is why I believe I'm right. The gatekeepers operate under the premise that they are either agents of God or Satan. Every universe has one. Every universe has religion. These gatekeepers are powerful beings but know nothing of the real workings of reality. They do not know the rulers exist. And they do not know that their God and Satan are a cooperative team. Whoever the gatekeeper of this universe is, his first act was a bold one, but I will find him. You have my word."

Everything was starting to set in. Isaac's new mission involved finding this gatekeeper.

"You won't be able to find him," the man said. "You probably won't be strong enough to face him even if you do. You must train and harness your powers."

"Do I have the powers already?"

"You painfully experienced your main power," the man said. "You reacted violently to it at first. I suppose that's my fault for not coming to you sooner. Your main powers are cosmic electricity. You draw power from the multiple universes, but mainly your own. At full power, you can kill any human with it instantly. But, you still must train your body. I have given you durability as well. Try it now."

Isaac didn't feel different. During their conversation, his muscles had relaxed. The burning sensation was gone. He tried to focus on getting that feeling back in his body but was unsuccessful. Then, an image of Alisha popped up in his head. He remembered watching cartoons with her on Saturdays while he did her hair. If he couldn't find this gatekeeper, his girls would be gone forever. He wouldn't let that happen. The burning in his muscles came back. He could feel his veins pulsating. The ground beneath him started shaking.

"Control it," the man said. "Serenity and anger is the perfect combination. Think about your family. They're gone right now but think of the positive as well. Why do you get out of bed in the morning? Why did you start your company? All of that, not just anger, or the pain will continue."

Isaac calmed his mind. The burning stopped, and now he noticed the purple electricity was circling around his body. His vision wasn't purple this time. The power flowing through his body was intoxicating. He felt like a God.

"Damn, your fast," the man said. "I knew you would be. I've already given you your other powers. You have superhuman strength, flight, and teleportation."

The first two were self-explanatory. That last one caught Isaac's attention.

"How does the teleportation work?" he asked.

"The same way mine does. There's no limit on where you can teleport, but your body must be prepared to take the punishment. If you tried to teleport back to San Francisco right now, you might die of a heart attack. It's the same as the rest of your powers, practice, and you will become stronger. Maybe stronger than me. That's my plan with this anyway."

"You want me to become a ruler of the universe?" Isaac asked.

"No, you're free to do whatever you want. I just want you to use these powers to help America overcome their flaws. After you've achieved that, you can do what your heart desires."

"Wait a minute. This isn't going to happen in a couple of years, maybe not even ten. You gave me immortality, didn't you?"

The man didn't answer.

Purple energy erupted underneath Isaac. He came face to face with the man.

"What's to stop me from killing you right now?" Isaac asked. "You probably have no intention of helping me find my family. I could kill you and harness this power by myself."

"You could," he said calmly. "And I wouldn't strike you back if you tried. I gave you my word that I didn't take them. And I gave you my word that I would help you. That's all I can do."

Isaac was ashamed. He knew he shouldn't have gotten so angry.

"I can't live for a thousand years like you. That might be how long it'll take to help Earth. I don't want to watch the people I love die in front of me while I stay the same age," Isaac said.

"It needed to be done. You can be killed by someone or something of equal or greater power, though. You aren't completely invincible," the man said.

"Feels like it. Did you not come up against many people during your time on Earth?" Isaac asked.

"No," the man said. "I was the King of Earth for over 1000 years. Ran the most effective Empire the world had ever seen. United everyone under one single cause. We uplifted each other. I didn't need to do much. After I killed God, people elected me the King. Some opposed, some were killed. The bloodshed continued for a long time until I was able to turn it around. You aren't as dumb as I was. You'll figure it out much faster than I did. Besides, I could take the power of immortality away from you at your request, by the way. You are not my slave, I have no ulterior motives in doing this. I just want good people to have power throughout the universes. I want good people making the power moves, calling the shots. After you finish your task, however long it may take, and you wish to relinquish your immortality, just ask me."

"Okay," Isaac said. "I will do it. But I need time to come up with a plan. The Pinnacle needs to be taken down, but I don't have the slightest clue on how to start."

"It's going to take time. In the meantime, you must practice your powers. I've given you all your powers. This mountainous region is a perfect place to practice."

"So, you're not going to teleport me home?" Isaac asked.

The man opened a portal. The yellow light appeared. He smiled.

"What kind of teacher would I be if I didn't challenge you a little bit. You can communicate with me telepathically. I'll be around if you need help."

"What's your name?" Isaac asked.

"Erasmus," he said. And he stepped through the portal, and he was gone.

The wind stopped howling the second he left. Isaac was alone in Ireland, in the middle of nowhere.

Well, he thought. Time to see what I can do.

— · · — · · — · · — · · — · · — · · — · ·

Training was exhausting. Isaac had been at it for a couple of weeks now. Overall, he had gotten stronger. He was able to life semi-trucks above his head now. When he first started, he struggled with normal cars. Flight was easy, but if he didn't want to fly, he had enhanced speed. He could run a mile in almost two minutes. His cosmic electricity was coming along nicely too. Isaac returned to Ireland frequently to blow holes in the sides of mountains. Erasmus warned him to not destroy the mountains too much. Isaac wondered if there was some sort of universal law he was breaking. There wasn't. Erasmus just enjoyed the scenery and didn't want to see Isaac's nonsense ruin his favorite place to escape. Erasmus had been a huge help the past couple of weeks. Isaac assumed he would disappear like most cliché trainers do in the movies. Not Erasmus. He was available instantly whenever Isaac needed help. Isaac usually didn't bother him about his powers usually.

Most of the time they talked, it was about the other universe. Erasmus told him of a universe where white people were the main race enslaved throughout history. Isaac asked if the world was any different. It wasn't. The same fight being fought by blacks in Isaac's universe, was being fought in the enslaved white universe. He found that fascinating. Once he found his girls, he'd probably stop this superhero nonsense, but the possibility of visiting another universe intrigued him. Not to save it, but to study it. Erasmus constantly assured him that most other universes weren't that interesting. Isaac didn't believe that though. He tried to get more out of Erasmus about his universe but was unsuccessful.

"Another time," was always the answer. Isaac didn't mind it. He could see the pain on Erasmus' face whenever he brought up his home. Erasmus did tell him about his family. His mother, father, and seven brothers and sisters. Five of them were killed. Senseless violence. It's what drove Erasmus to do law. He was a fascinating man. Isaac was happy to have such an honorable partner during this crazy journey. A full month after getting his powers, Isaac was nowhere close to figuring out how to take down, or even hurt the Pinnacle. He had regained his freedom again. Erasmus created over 50 million dollars out of thin air for Isaac. Erasmus mentioned how unhappy the rulers would be about his abuse of power, but he explained to Isaac they'd understand since it was a part of his superhero "program".

"Are there others?" Isaac asked him one day they were in Ireland.

Erasmus was putting himself to the test today. He was doing excruciating exercises that required him to use his sword. The motions he was doing looked unnatural, but at the same time, majestic. Isaac felt annoyed with himself for bothering Erasmus during his training. Erasmus put his sword away. He didn't look bothered at all. He was breathing heavy.

"You're the first I've given powers to. But my hope is that you inspire others who have superhuman powers to step forward. As far as I know, there aren't any on Earth though with your level of power," Erasmus said.

"Are there any with some type of power?" Isaac asked.

"Yes. There's a girl in your city in fact. Kamayra Jenkins I believe her name is. Her powers are a mystery to me," Erasmus said.

"Kamayra? That waitress with the bruises on her neck?" Isaac was stunned.

"She didn't get those from a boyfriend. From what I know and have personally witnessed, she has enhanced strength, but not superhuman. She can beat the mess out of the world's strongest man, but she can't lift a car. She also has some sort of combustion powers that make sparks fly from her body. They look like fireworks."

"Interesting. Why not recruit her before me? Especially if she already has this powers thing under control," Isaac asked.

"She's on her own path. She works in the summer and attends school at the University of Georgia. Looks like her focus is the underground crime rackets. She's determined, that's for sure. I didn't want to distract her. Plus, as I've said, your soul is the purest I've felt in my life. I had to dedicate my powers and time to the person I felt deserved it the most," Erasmus said.

"Stop it, you're going to make me blush," Isaac hopped up and went almost twenty feet in the air. Teleporting was still something he was struggling with. He decided to practice that a bit more. He teleported to another mountain in the distance, then another, another. Teleporting always felt weird to him. He didn't disappear into nothing and reappear where he wanted to go. No, Isaac's mind was present the entire time it happened. Maybe, that's why he was struggling. Every time he teleported, his body would feel as if it was getting dragged at a speed faster than lightspeed. That's because it was. Erasmus explained to him that it wasn't true teleportation. "You're just moving very fast," he would say. He told Isaac the reason his body felt like it was getting snatched was because Isaac was moving along a network of rays that humans hadn't even discovered yet. Completely untapped energy that only the rulers of the universe could access. Humans had the capability to figure it out, the science was just too advanced.

Erasmus constantly talked about how glad he was that humans hadn't figured out the science to this method of travel. He said that almost everything, war especially, would become extremely intense. Humans in this universe hadn't yet figured out that transgender people are just people. They couldn't handle a discovery like that. Still, Isaac was struggling to let go. Erasmus told him once he let the universe take over, he'd travel even faster and with less headaches. It was going to take time. He teleported back on the mountain Erasmus was on.

"Are there any others?" Isaac asked. "I just want to know, because I do feel like their cooperation is going to be necessary to save the world."

"I agree. There's only one more I know of. Her name isn't known. The only name I've heard is Sofia, but I doubt it's real. No one knows her name, but what she does is known. She controls the Colombian drug trade. She's ending it. This girl acquired her powers from some sort of serum or drug I'm not sure, but she's the complete package. Superhuman strength, durability, all of it. She can't fly, but her powers aren't what makes her dangerous. She's kept her identity hidden because she's known as the world's greatest hacker. And she hasn't used her powers to post nude photos of celebrities on the internet. For right now, her cause is noble."

"She sounds resilient. Something we'll definitely need down the road," Isaac said.

"If you want to get in contact with her, that's your choice," Erasmus said.

"Two women. One black, one Colombian. That's incredible," Isaac said.

"It is," said Erasmus.

They said their goodbyes soon, and Isaac was back in San Francisco moments later. The trip was the easiest one yet. He was in his bedroom. After he showered, he decided to make some food. There was a picture of Alisha and Cynthia on the fridge. He hadn't thought about them for a couple of days. Alisha looked so happy. Cynthia looked so beautiful. He sat down to eat and for the next couple of hours, that's all he thought about. The thoughts weren't filled with sadness though. Only joy. He imagined playing with Alisha and taking her out for ice cream after. She always worked up an appetite after a day at the park. His memories about Cynthia were mainly sexual. His wife was the most beautiful woman he'd ever seen. On most days, he just missed her presence. Her smile, her voice, her personality. But today, he missed her body. Isaac didn't decide to marry Cynthia for her body, but he'd be lying if he said he didn't like it. All he wanted to do was make love to his wife. He knew he couldn't though and the thought left his mind. He decided to turn on the television to see what was happening around the world. The news always bothered him, but he needed some direction. Erasmus had some ideas on how to help him take down the Pinnacle, but they were empty just suggestions. He told Isaac the bulk of the work was on him. At first, the powers, the responsibility, all of it, seemed too good to be true. He could have told Erasmus no. He could have aided him in some other way. There was no need for Isaac to be the face of Erasmus' superhero movement.

He looked at the picture again. He had taken it off the fridge. Isaac then realized that if he didn't accept Erasmus' offer, this would have been all he could think about. Not only would he think about it, but he'd become obsessed, as well as depressed. He needed to keep his mind occupied. Working towards world peace was probably the only thing large enough for him to focus on while Erasmus tracked down the gatekeeper, the one responsible for his family's disappearance. Isaac wasn't going to give the gatekeeper a single chance. There was no reason to take his family. Death was the only thing the gatekeeper deserved. The screen then went black on his television. A breaking news alert popped up on the screen. Isaac got a weird feeling. Unfortunately, he didn't need to guess what was going on.

— · — · · — — · · — · · — · · — — · · — · ·

"Hello, I'm Dan Stane. Channel 6 has been covering the story involving the shooting of an unarmed black teen by the San Francisco Police Department."

I haven't heard about this, he thought. He was sure it was going to be about the situation with the man in the car from several months ago. This looked like a boy.

"The shooting happened only a few months after another black man was shot and killed in his car, with his wife and daughter in the car as well. Lonnie Smith was his name. This teen's name is Tamar Reed. Channel 6 has obtained video of the incident. The video shows Reed running away from two police officers. One officer shoots Reed in the leg, and Reed falls to the ground. They handcuff Reed and while they're doing so, Reed struggles and the other officer fires again, this time into young Tamar's back. Police say that Tamar had been a suspect in a store robbery where he stole some cigarettes from a gas station. We must warn you, that the video contains graphic images and language. Please change the station or leave the room to avoid the video"

The video played, and it was exactly as the newscaster described. The first officer shot Reed in the leg. He appeared to struggle when the other officer shot him in the back. Isaac was appalled. He knew there was no need to kill the boy. He looked younger than 15.

\

"Reed, 14, was skipping school during the time of the shooting. Both officers have not been suspended by the San Francisco Police Department. Joining me now, we have local activist..."

Isaac couldn't listen anymore. Not suspended? They killed a young boy. Images of the boy immediately began to pop up in Isaac's head too. He could see the story people were going to try and tell about Tamar Reed. They'd paint one of a juvenile delinquent who regularly skipped school. Records, everything negative that is, would come to light. Whether he sexually harassed a girl, or didn't brush his teeth before bed, the media, more specifically racists, were going to crucify this boy. Isaac was nervous about the oncoming unrest this would cause as well. He didn't agree with violent protests, but he understood them. He had participated in a couple himself when he was younger. Isaac never physically hurt anyone, but he did smash the window of a local store one time. His father found out about it and gave Isaac hell for it. He never saw eye to eye with his father when it came to racial politics. Isaac's father was one of those activists who did great, meaningful work in the community, but he had a propensity for condescending language. Isaac felt as if his father thought better of himself, simply because he was doing more than others. As a teen, it burned Isaac to the core to hear his father shame certain areas of black culture such as rap and sports. Isaac didn't listen to rap much or play sports, but he understood the necessity of the men participating in those things. He was able to keep his nose clean with his father most of the time because of his love for science, but he knew his father didn't see the full picture. He got up from the couch. Then, there was a loud pop outside. Isaac ran to the window to see what was going on. It had been only twenty minutes since he stopped listening to the news broadcast. The people of San Francisco united fast though. Down the street, Isaac noticed a group of people. They were chanting, marching, and to his sadness, rioting. They were throwing trash cans, lighting things on fire, and destroying property. This was his chance. Except Isaac didn't move. He wanted to bolt out of his house and break up the riot. Maybe he could get the people to listen to him.

But why would they? Because of my strength, or my flight. I can't just go out there in my street clothes. I don't even have an outfit or a costume. The protest only increased in people the longer Isaac stood in his house pondering what to do. He could see the police now. Riot gear on, as expected. The people were blocking an intersection now. Isaac still didn't move.

"Do you have a plan on how to handle this?" Erasmus asked.

Isaac wasn't used to Erasmus jumping into his brain just yet. He almost fell because the voice startled him.

"I'm thinking," Isaac said. "I think I might just go outside to see what's going on."

"Their bullets won't hurt you at, but I'd recommend keeping a low profile. If you want to go full power, that's fine too. I'm just giving you a suggestion," Erasmus said.

"Thanks," Isaac said.

Finally, he had moved. Not only did Isaac move, but he was unlocking the door. Once, he was outside, he noticed a cop approaching him.

Damn, I wasn't outside for more than five seconds.

The cop looked annoyed.

"Sir, you need to get back inside," he said. There was a rudeness in his voice that Isaac wasn't fond of. He decided to stand up to the cop.

"Legally, I'm allowed to stand on my property. This step is my property and I'm not breaking any laws by standing here," Isaac said.

The cop scoffed.

"A fucking legal guy huh? I'll tell you what sir, you looked smarter than that. This is a serious situation and I need you to get back inside your home," the cop said.

"There's been no decree ordering anyone to stay inside their homes. If I wanted to step down, walk into the street, and join the group of people peacefully protesting the disgusting murder of Tamar Reed, there's nothing you could do to stop me," Isaac said.

He'll more than likely pull his gun out now, Isaac thought. Nothing more a white middle-aged man hates more than a black man telling him he's wrong. It's killing him inside because he knows

I'm right too. Thing is, his weapon and badge clear him of all accountability when it comes to my life.

The cop pulled out his gun. Isaac could sense the anger in him.

"Hands behind your head and turn around."

Isaac did as the officer said. In the distance, he could see the protest starting to get out of hand. The officers in riot gear had moved down the street. They launched what appeared to be tear gas into the crowd. People were forced forward into the barrage of cops. They responded by beating the protesters. One protestor was a young woman. Isaac noticed it was a white woman. She was one of the first people that was forced into the pile of cops. They showed her no mercy. When she tried to fight back, they just hit her harder. Isaac couldn't watch. His senses had been heightened ever since Erasmus gave him the powers. He could hear their screams. It was as if they were right next to him and the arrogant cop. He could feel his body beginning to heat up. This wasn't the time or place to explode though. Or was it? Isaac could go save those people. He could do the job the cops were supposed to be doing.

"Your men just provoked them!" Isaac yelled.

"Oh, you mad, nigger?" the cop said.

There it was. Isaac couldn't help but laugh a bit. The last time someone called Isaac that was a few years ago when Science Supreme was at its peak. Every slur from nigger to monkey was shouted. Isaac was determined not to turn the discussion into one like that. The two men were escorted out and it left a weird aura around the audience. He was forced to address it. The word made him mad, but not because of its history or anything like that. Isaac just hated being called out of his name.

"Sir, my name isn't nigger," he said to the police officer. His voice was stern. He meant it to be.

"It is now. I'm giving you a couple more seconds to get back inside," the officer said.

"Are you going to shoot me? Even if I wasn't listening to you, I haven't run or posed a physical threat to you. Why not arrest me?" Isaac said. He heard the gun cock.

The cop was laughing now. Isaac's head started to hurt too. The noise of the protest was becoming too much. Isaac was almost positive that the woman who was forced into the crowd of police was dead. He could hear at least three more people getting beaten viciously by cops. The smoke from the fires was intense. Too intense. Isaac was losing control. He couldn't focus on anything. If the cop shot him, the bullet wouldn't hurt, but he couldn't just up and leave either. The cop would become suspicious.

I have to do something, he thought.

He noticed the cop was by himself. The group he walked down the street with had moved on to terrorize more citizens. Isaac turned his head to look at the cop. Instantly, the cop's expression of annoyance turned into one of rage.

"Turn back around!" he yelled.

Isaac was ignoring him. He saw a building behind his old Science Supreme building, which hadn't been destroyed. All his focus was on that building. Isaac flew at lightspeed. He was on top of the building. The cop fired his weapon the second Isaac turned his head back around. Not one shot, but five.

"Where are you?" the police officer yelled. He began to run back down the street. Alone and scared. Isaac noticed an opportunity. He appeared just far enough behind the officer, so he could chase him down. The officer wasn't in the best shape. Isaac caught him and tackled him down to the ground. The officer didn't resist. Instead, he curled up in the fetal position, crying.

"Please don't kill me," the cop pleaded.

Isaac wanted to laugh. The thought of killing this man never entered his head. But since he could, he thought he'd strike some fear in the man. Mission accomplished already. Except Isaac wasn't done. He decided to use only about one percent of his powers. The cop was still curled up, but Isaac easily moved his arms. Then, he began to punch the cop. Not to kill him, but Isaac didn't want this cop to forget him. Every punch he landed caused damage. On the last blow, Isaac felt the man's nose break. Isaac let him go. The man rolled over on his side in pain. Blood was pouring from his nose. Isaac could hear him trying to breathe through it, but it sounded like boiling water as the blood mixed with his mucus. That satisfied Isaac enough.

"My name's Isaac Eckspo," he said. "Say it."

"I—Isaac E—Eckspo," the cop struggled to say. He spat up more blood. Followed by a couple teeth.

"I'm sorry about that," Isaac said. "But you approached me in a respectful manner at first. Then, when you noticed I was a black man unafraid of the police, you decided to impose your will. That's what bothers me about police. We're supposed to respect you, not fear you. Now, not everyone is like me. They can't stand up to you the way I can. But I need you to promise me that you'll treat everyone with your respect. Just like everyone else in life, you need to earn it."

The cop looked bewildered.

"Surprised I didn't kill you? Yeah, to be honest, I am too. I wanted to. There's still not a soul on our street. If I would've gathered some protestors they might've joined. But I'm not trying to contribute to the cycle. I'm the last black person you call nigger. Understood?" Isaac said.

The cop nodded.

He grabbed the cop by his shirt. He raised his fist. The anger couldn't be controlled now. Isaac's fist began to glow a bright purple. The cosmic electricity followed. Immediately, he put his hand down, noticing his mistake.

"Sorry," Isaac said. The cop didn't move. His breathing was still obnoxiously loud, but he didn't move a muscle.

"You seem like a good cop," Isaac said. "Please just treat everyone with respect. This world sucks. People are vile sometimes, I know. Just think before you talk."

"I will," the cop said. He didn't scurry along like Isaac thought he would. In fact, the cop stood up, and walked over to Isaac.

Has he not learned? The energy began to flow through Isaac. The cop put his hand on Isaac's shoulder though and the energy subsided. He couldn't believe how irrational he was being.

"Thank you," the cop said.

Isaac nodded, and the cop started to walk down the street. There was an almost painful silence surrounding Isaac. His brain was moving too fast, thoughts weren't being accurately processed. Anger, love, hate, fear, envy, everything was circulating in his head and heart like an intricate soup. The protests were still going on. But he wasn't interested in that right now. His head started to hurt. More than it did before, and it wasn't because he was sensing the pain of others. It was his own pain this time that caused him anguish. Isaac began to scream. The louder the scream, the brighter the purple energy field around him. His clothes were tearing apart due to the electricity. He noticed certain people looking out their windows. Not only could he not control his powers, he was doing it in front of people.

"Erasmus!" he yelled. "I can't focus. Take me to Ireland!"

He felt his body moving.

When he reached the top of the mountain, it was time to unleash. The electricity began to flow from his body. Isaac flew up into the air and began smashing into the sides of mountains. With every hit, he wanted to destroy another. The mountains began to rumble. He couldn't see anything. Everything was purple. Everything was loud. He saw the yellow light of Erasmus appear on their favorite mountain, but he couldn't stop. The bedlam continued.

Erasmus flew up into the air.

"You need to get yourself under control," he said.

"I can't" Isaac yelled. "You did this to me. What's happening?"

"I didn't do anything," Erasmus said. "Unfortunately, you're experiencing something every human goes through. Except with us, that rage, if not controlled, can destroy us. We lose focus and can lose ourselves in the process."

Isaac's face and body continued to burn.

"What the hell are you talking about?" Isaac said. Erasmus was directly in front of him now. Isaac saw the punch coming but couldn't stop it. The punch nearly broke his ribs. Isaac swung back, but his punch was caught. Erasmus threw him down to the top of a mountain. He charged Isaac, but Isaac was ready this time. He charged enough energy and blasted Erasmus from the top of the mountain. Isaac got to relax for a moment. Erasmus was flying up the side of the mountain though and he was at the top again. This time, he had his sword out. Isaac dodged the sword attack and he grabbed Erasmus by his black cape. Erasmus fell to the ground and Isaac heard him grunt. The next energy blasts that Isaac let off didn't miss. Erasmus was on the ground. Isaac pulled his hand back, but Erasmus was too quick. He swiped the outsides of Isaac's legs with the sword. The pain was too much. Isaac retreated and fell to the ground. Erasmus wasn't stopping. Isaac realized his mentor was done playing now. Erasmus was swinging the sword like how he was the day they were training. Isaac was doing his best to avoid the slashes, but every swing was calculated to perfection.

After a bevy of hits landed, Isaac was running low on energy. He had one more trick up his sleeve. The next time Erasmus tried to swing his sword, Isaac teleported behind him. He put his hands around Erasmus' neck and began to squeeze.

Something wasn't right though. Erasmus was struggling in Isaac's grip. But Isaac felt something behind him. It wasn't the air of the mountains, which was making his tattered shirt and pants swing in freely. No, something was touching his back. Before he realized what, it was, Isaac was tripped up by the object and lying flat on his back. Erasmus appeared in front of him. The Erasmus who he had subdued was gone.

"Didn't know I could manipulate people's thoughts, did you?" Erasmus said. "It's a power I'm not proud of and I don't use it often. But, this is for your own good."

"Fuck you," Isaac said. Erasmus raised his sword and stuck it directly into the leg of Isaac. Isaac began rolling around on the ground, trying to pull the sword out, but he couldn't. It was stuck in the ground too. Erasmus backed up.

"When the shield goes up, you can explode as much as you want," Erasmus said. From the sword, a yellow force field came out and surrounded Isaac. He could hardly see Erasmus anymore. He let out another scream, followed by more energy. His head was throbbing. He continued screaming. Continued to exert as much energy as he possibly could.

I'm sorry Alisha. I'm sorry my love. I can't do this. One more scream and he let out everything he had left. He felt his veins popping, his muscles tearing themselves apart. The electricity was so fierce. A couple more seconds and the noise of his powers faded into nothing but Irish wind. Isaac Eckspo passed out from exhaustion. He had hoped he was dead. Unfortunately, he wasn't.

— ·· — ·· — ·· — ·· — ·· — ··

When Isaac woke up, his leg was completely healed. The sword was gone too. The shield Erasmus had put up wasn't there either. He was still in Ireland, but everything seemed normal. Isaac looked down at his body. His clothes were ripped to pieces, he was practically nude. All the pain he had felt recently was gone too. Head, muscles, everything felt completely relaxed now.

"Morning sunshine," he heard Erasmus say.

Isaac leapt to his feet. He wasn't sure if Erasmus was going to come after him or not.

"Are you serious?" Erasmus asked.

Guess not, Isaac thought.

"Sit down," Erasmus said. "You need to rest, and we need to talk about what happened."

Isaac did as he was told. Not because he feared Erasmus, but because he was ashamed at how he acted last night.

"Any explanation?" Erasmus asked. "Any at all."

"Not really," Isaac started to say. "Did anything like that happen to you when you got your powers?"

"No. I haven't been that angry in hundreds of years." Erasmus asked.

Isaac didn't say anything.

"Was it the riots?" Erasmus asked.

Isaac shook his head.

"I don't know," Isaac said. "Maybe I'm not ready for this. Last night, I almost killed a cop. Not because he threatened me or even because I hated him, but because I could. I could have killed him and hidden the body somewhere in these mountains. No one would ever find that racist son of a bitch." His own words scared him. Again, he felt the energy flowing through his body. The anger was starting to empower him again.

"You have more hate in you than I thought," Erasmus said.

Isaac put his head between his knees. He wanted to cry, but nothing came out. He made the noise of sobbing. Surely, Erasmus thought he was being a child. But, Erasmus continued to impress Isaac. He came next to him and slowly patted his back. It was soothing.

"Your anger fuels your powers. They make it come alive in ways I couldn't predict. I thought your love for people and your family would do that. But no, this anger you hold in your heart, it runs deeper than I could've imagined. Although I should have seen it coming," Erasmus said.

"What's that supposed to mean?" Isaac said.

"Isaac. Last night was one of the worst moments in American history. Well, in your universe anyway. Over one hundred people were killed last night during those riots. They continued into the morning and have only just calmed down. The people in San Francisco are in shock, and the rest of the country is outraged. That made you mad, yes?"

"Well, yeah, but it doesn't explain--," Isaac said.

"I'm getting to it. Isaac, you remember what I said about your powers being connected to the universe?" Erasmus said.

"Yes," Isaac said.

"I think their pain was yours last night. I go through it sometimes too, but never that much. You're already progressing faster than I thought you would," Erasmus said.

"I don't know," Isaac said. "It just hurt to see people in general go through that pain. No one, black or white, deserves that type of pain."

Erasmus sighed. He looked relieved.

"You're a better man than me at your age," Erasmus said. It was the saddest he had sounded since Isaac met him.

"Thank you," Isaac said. "I was also upset at my lack of action during the riot."

"There wasn't much you could've done," Erasmus said. "I think something like this needed to happen before you made your move."

"Yes, but this doesn't help my case against the Pinnacle. Now, the statements and fake relief will come pouring in from them. They'll be the heroes who controlled the chaos in San Francisco. The way I see it, the main way I'm going to expose them will be from financial corruption and scandal. Something I don't need powers for," Isaac said.

Erasmus was silent. He sat down now on the grassy mountain. He began pulling the grass up from the ground.

"I suppose you're right," Erasmus said.

"The powers will help though. They can't do anything about me stopping crime. And as far as I know, I don't have some scary villain to fight. How's the search coming for the gatekeeper by the way?" Isaac asked.

"No luck. He's good at keeping his energy hidden. He doesn't want to be found and the rulers refuse to give me his name or location. They said he forbids outsiders to know of his whereabouts. But I assure you, he won't be a problem. When I find him, your family will return."

Isaac trusted Erasmus. Of course, he could be lying to him about the existence of this gatekeeper. Isaac was in a position where he was forced to believe anything that came out of Erasmus' mouth. But, he did believe it. Either he was telling the truth or Isaac was dealing with the most dangerous being in the universe. Either way, Isaac knew he didn't have many options.

"These powers can be a symbol. More than anything. I know someone who might be able to assist me in hacking the Pinnacle and finding their secrets. We expose them, the country starts to unravel, but at least they'll know the truth," Isaac said.

"And if they ask for a new system to be put in place?" Erasmus asked.

"You think they would?" Isaac asked.

"Possibly. When I killed God, and achieved immortality, it was almost a unanimous decision that I was the one who was destined to lead us into the future. I was elected King of the world soon after."

"I'm not sure if I would want that," Isaac said. "Don't you think taking down the Pinnacle would be enough?"

"It would. But as I told you earlier, my hope is that you become a protector of the universes as I have. Defeating the Pinnacle would only spawn more problems, which will spawn more problems, which will continue to grow until you reach a utopian society," Erasmus said.

"And it took you almost a thousand years?"

Erasmus nodded his head slowly.

Isaac let out a deep sigh. He wasn't sure if this life was for him. This life was filled with sorrow and constant planning. Isaac grew up wanting to explore the meanings of the world. Science Supreme and his inventions were fun, and they were ways to get the community involved, but he wanted to understand the way the world worked. Now, this god-like being spoke to him daily and claims he came from a different universe. Isaac felt defeated by his life's work. He felt moronic for not seeing any connection when researching different dimensions and universes when his daughter went missing. Human nature was almost harder to figure out. Isaac wasn't sure he had the patience to find the solutions Erasmus wanted him to find. He was confident in himself, but this confidence Erasmus had in him made him nervous. He wanted to live up to his expectations, but if last night's rampage happened too often, would Erasmus leave him and not try to find his family? That pain was something Isaac couldn't live with. Surely, he'd kill himself if that happened.

"How did I heal so fast?" he asked trying to change the subject.

"Your powers," Erasmus said.

"Makes sense," Isaac got up off the ground and dusted his body off. He flew up into the air extremely high and came back down in a few minutes. His strength had never felt better.

"The next time I go out," he said to Erasmus when he was finally back on the mountain, "I need a costume. Can you conjure up one of those?"

"I could, but I think it should come from your imagination and your heart. You need a name too," Erasmus said.

"A name? Boy, we really are going all the way with this, aren't we?" Isaac laughed a bit.

Erasmus joined in the laughter.

"Thank you again," Isaac said. "For helping me last night and believing in me."

Erasmus smiled.

"Thank you for giving me something to believe in," he said. They shook hands and went their separate ways. Isaac was back in his apartment.

A costume shouldn't be too hard. But a name? What the hell is my name?

CHAPTER 8

Two Years Ago

"**O**kay, I hope you all had a good time. Did you have a good time?"

All the kids yelled at the top of their lungs. Isaac couldn't help but smile his biggest, cheesiest smile. He looked over at Cynthia. She gave her thumbs up, showing her approval of his most recent show. Isaac got lost in the moment. The camera was still on him and the kids had stopped cheering. They were waiting for his special send off.

"Sorry about that," he said. "Thinking about science all the time, you can get lost in your thoughts. Okay, if you use the household tools I showed you today, you can be on your way to making your very own rocket. But, maybe wait until your parents are gone first."

There was laughter from the kids and some smiles from the adults in the crowd.

"Seriously kids, always remember to get parent's permission before doing any experiment I show you. Because if you love Science---,"

"You must obey Science," the kids said.

"Now, go out there and be as supreme as you can be kids. Oh, and one more thing. How many of you have seen Star Wars?"

Most of the kids yelled their answer.

"Well, next week, I can't wait to show you my very own, very real, lightsaber I made. Tell your friends and I'll see you all next week! You can tour the lab with your parents if you want, just make sure they are with you at all times.," Isaac said. The cameraman left and so did most of the parents. A few always stayed behind to ask Isaac about his work. Even though his main focus was engineering, which gave him the knowledge to make the inventions he made, all science was important to him. Physics, Biology, Geology, Astronomy, you name it, Isaac studied it. Whether it was a course in school or in his free time, he was always learning. Some professors would come to his shows and compliment him on the ease with which he'd explain such difficult concepts to children. Others would come to critique him. Some would write articles on his shows. He didn't mind what type of person came, as long as they came. Today was routine. The parents who stayed were first timers. They were intrigued, like everyone was, with his hover boots, gravity sphere, and his robot assistant, Carl. When they left, the only people left were Cynthia and Alisha.

Alisha was playing with some of her dolls. She was growing into such a beautiful girl. Isaac was proud of her. She wasn't doing anything noteworthy yet, he was just proud she was living life to the fullest at such a young age. Always running around, asking questions, questions he'd answer gladly, and just having fun. Cynthia had been nothing but supportive during the beginning stages of his show. Sometimes, if he was feeling ill or asked her to, she'd fill in for him. She'd joke that the kids and parents liked her more than him. He never argued because it was true. Her eyes probably did it for people. Isaac could get lost in them. Both of his girls came up to him and gave him a gigantic hug.

"You like the show, Baby Girl?" he asked Alisha.

She nodded cheerfully.

"Another one down," Cynthia said and kissed him on the cheek. "Alisha, you want to get something to eat?"

"I want pizza!" Alisha said.

"We had pizza yesterday. You can have leftovers when we get home," Cynthia said.

Alisha pouted.

"What's wrong baby girl?" Isaac said.

"I want different pizza, Daddy," she said.

Both him and Cynthia laughed.

"Okay, okay," he said. "We can get different pizza tonight. But, tomorrow, promise me we'll eat some vegetables?"

"I promise," Alisha said. Isaac picked her up and kissed her on the cheek.

"That's my girl," Isaac said.

"I don't even want pizza that bad," Alisha said. "Mystic Man does!"

"Mystic who?" Isaac asked.

"Mystic Man," Cynthia said. "Her imaginary friend."

Isaac laughed.

"You got to stop taking her to see those superhero movies. Who's your favorite hero, Baby Girl?" Isaac asked Alisha.

"Mystic Man!!" she yelled.

"Okay, well, he can eat pizza too. But tomorrow, he eats vegetables just like everyone else," Isaac said.

Alisha jumped out of his arms and ran around the lab for a little bit. Isaac warned her to be careful.

"Where did she even learn the word, mystic?" he asked Cynthia.

"Probably from SpongeBob. They talk about everything in that show," Cynthia said and they both laughed. "Hey, your sensor is still on," she said.

"Oh, you're right, I forgot," Isaac said. Isaac recorded every show he did, but he used a motion sensor that acted as a camera. The main reason he did it was to have copies of every show, but also so he could study himself.

"Now, there'll be a copy of us talking about pizza in my files," Isaac said laughing.

Cynthia laughed and went to grab Alisha, so they could go eat. Isaac switched off the sensor and left with his family.

— ·· — ·· — ·· — ·· — ·· —

Present Day

Making the suit wasn't hard for Isaac. It took him a while, but it wasn't difficult. The city of San Francisco was in a tailspin ever since the shooting and the riots. It was all anyone talked about for the next couple of weeks. Isaac paid attention to the news, but he didn't let it depress him. He had ignored some calls from his mother since he'd last spoken to her. No calls from his father. He knew his focus needed to be entirely on building the perfect suit. He needed to make a statement with it, but it also needed to be comfortable. At first, Isaac wanted to make a suit similar to something Iron Man would wear. He saw the movies and loved the sleek design of the later suits. Except, his powers weren't focused on technology, rather magic.

Is that magic? Is that what Erasmus is? Isaac didn't have an answer, but he knew it didn't need to be mechanical armor like that. He thought he should go a route similar to Batman, but he did want the armor to be stronger than anything Batman would wear. The answer was to make something in between the two. A bit of technology to help the suit's durability, and the non-technical parts would help with his comfortability.

Since he could already fly and teleport, there was no need to put any boosters or rockets in the suit. So, he focused on the armor, mainly on the torso and quadricep areas. Isaac was able to build the suit mostly out of Immobulum. The element was easily moldable and was comfortable enough to walk in. Next, he focused on the back. He didn't want it to be as armored as his chest, for flexibility reasons. This, and the joints, is where Isaac let science work for him. He created mini generators in the suit that amplified his muscle movement. They also helped stabilize his joints and muscles in case his powers ever failed him. So, if he fell from a building, depending on the fall, he'd maybe break his legs and not die. The generators gave him an extra pop in his punches he really liked. When he tested out the left hand of the suit at full strength, he nearly destroyed his entire wall of his lab. Next, was the mask. He didn't want to make a helmet, he wanted people to be able to tell he was black. The mask was easy enough to make. He layered that with Immobulum as well and tested it out. Fire, water, hammers, bullets, nothing penetrated it. Isaac decided to increase the frequency of his cosmic electricity by creating two tiny reactors in his suit where his energy came out. Then he thought, why not lace the entire suit with reactors since the energy was capable of coming out of every part of his body. It was a brilliant move. In the next few weeks, he was able to generate force fields around him. They nearly sent him to the ER every time he did them, but they worked. Finally, the suit was complete, and he was ready to take on the world. He invited Erasmus to his home to give it the okay.

"You've been hard at work," Erasmus said.

"While you've been lazily searching for this gatekeeper, I assume?" Isaac said. Erasmus had a look of embarrassment on his face. Anything else would have been a red flag.

"I'm sorry," Isaac said. "You didn't come here to listen to me berate you."

"It's fine," Erasmus said.

Isaac started his demonstration. He flew around the lab, blew some stuff up, and showcased the suits abilities, such as the generators for the joints and the reactors for his energy.

Erasmus was impressed.

"It looks outstanding," he said. "But, do you think that black is the right color?"

"Black on black not doing it for you?" Isaac said laughing. "No, I know the color scheme is off, I just don't know what color I want it to be. I'm not a fan of colors. Black looks the best to me."

"An all-black armored suit would only work for a white man, and you know that," Erasmus said.

"You got Bruce Wayne on speed dial?" Isaac said. He was trying to lighten the mood. He felt bad for his comment earlier. He truly admired Erasmus. He couldn't believe everything he'd been through. Isaac knew he had a good mentor and friend in Erasmus. Or as they called him, The King of the World.

"I'm sorry if this is hitting a nerve, but what was your wife and daughter's favorite color?" Erasmus asked.

Isaac paused for a second.

"You fight for them," Erasmus continued. "Combining their favorite colors on here only makes sense. The public doesn't need to know what it means. But you will."

Isaac heard Erasmus, but he didn't respond. All he could think about was his family. Their smiles. Their laughs. Completely identical. Isaac remembered the time Alisha heard Cynthia laughing so loud that she decided to copy it. From that day, Alisha always laughed in the obnoxious way her mother did. When Isaac was frustrated or came home from Science Supreme upset, they'd do the laugh together just to get him to smile. It always worked. Tears started to come to his eyes. Then, he realized he was still wearing the suit and Erasmus was still sitting in his lab. He shook his head and came back into reality.

"It wasn't my place. But whether the color is teal or pink, I think those two colors are what represent you as a hero," Erasmus said.

Isaac sighed.

"Purple," he said. "Both of my girls love the color purple."

"Black man flying around in a purple armored suit, saving people and exposing corruption. I can see the tweets now. Have you thought of a name?" Erasmus asked.

"There's only one that makes sense" Isaac said. "Mystic Man."

Erasmus's eyes lit up with joy. It was the happiest Isaac had ever seen him.

"I love it," he finally said.

"Really?" Isaac asked.

"The suit, the color, your name. All of it. You can't make this up," Erasmus said. Isaac could see he was starting to cry.

"You were born for this," Erasmus said. "I can't believe this is happening."

Frankly, Isaac couldn't either. All of this was happening so fast. It had been months since he got his powers. Months since the two women in his life were taken from him. Sometimes, he forgot they were gone. He'd wake up, make his breakfast, get dressed, and teleport to Ireland without a care in the world. The green of the mountains, the crispness of the air, Isaac could sometimes go a full day without thinking about his family. Sometimes. When it hit him, it was almost had a paralyzing effect on his body. Maybe it would last hours, most of the times though, it was only a couple of minutes. Erasmus was extremely understanding. The weight Erasmus had been carrying seem to be lifted ever since they met. Still, Erasmus wore that pain on his face. Isaac couldn't contemplate living for a thousand years. Maybe once he got his family back, he would consider keeping his immortality for a bit longer, but he didn't want to out-live Cynthia. That was out of the question. Erasmus didn't have a choice. Now though, Isaac could sense that for the first time in who knows how long, Erasmus had found hope. He left his universe, travelled through time itself, and managed to find Isaac. That type of journey would weigh heavily on anyone, most couldn't take it. Isaac walked towards Erasmus and gave him a hug. Erasmus was sobbing now. Isaac felt his mentor go weak against his body. He wasn't heavy.

"Thank you for all that you've done," Isaac said.

Erasmus laughed a bit.

"No, thank you," he said.

"I think it's time I suit up and test out my new suit. Purple and all," Isaac said.

"People don't know what's coming," Erasmus said with a smile.

For the first time, Isaac heard the young man in Erasmus. Not the thousand-year ruler of Earth with the burden of humanity on his shoulders.

"No, they don't," Isaac said.

Part Two

THE PEOPLE'S HERO

CHAPTER 9

"Welcome back to *The Conservative*, I'm John Crane. Today, we're talking about something the country has been talking about for days. The state of the country, specifically San Francisco. This city has been ground zero for the worst race riot in American history. Constant uproar after the killing of a young black male by a white cop. The riots started soon after and over 200, yes everyone, 200 people have been killed during these riots. Some by police, some by citizens of San Francisco. So, where do we go from here? How does this city recover? Actually, let me rephrase, how does this city not burn to the ground? Riots are still going on, buildings are being burned, and this city is still suffering. Enough from me though, joining me now, in studio, is Conservative senior reporter Marion Woods. How's it going Marion?"

"How's it going? America dissolving right in front of our faces. The media focusing on nothing but PC and race rhetoric. That's how it's going John."

"So, Marion, how does this city move on?"

"We can't move on, John. Not until we can come to terms with how we think about race and police officers. We must admit that there is no connection. There is no racism in police department. Statistics show that black males commit the most crimes. All of these scenarios put our cops, be it white or black, in a compromising position. They are forced to act based on the numbers."

"Marion, what would you say to the people who say, in this situation though, this boy was only fourteen?"

"I say the reports say he was resisting. We'll never fully know everything that happened, but John, I'm trusting policemen before I trust these liberal bloggers on the internet. These riots are a direct cause of the Obama Administration. This false idealism that white men are the terror of the United States, it holds us back from reporting real stories and fighting the real enemies."

"No argument there, Marion. President Trump calls it fake news, right?"

"This narrative that police go out and hunt black citizens is ridiculous. I'll be saying this until I'm dead in the ground, John. When is the black community going to take some responsibility? When? All this talk of respect and yet, I continue to see disrespect from their so-called leaders. This is getting tiring."

"Well, Marion, we have someone on the line who might disagree with you. From Russia, we have Pulitzer prize winning journalist and social exile, Walter Daniels. Let's not waste any time Walter. You aren't fond of us here at *The Conservative*. Do you agree with anything that Senior Reporter Marion Woods is saying?"

"You know I don't, John. Look, Marion is nothing more than mouthpiece at this stage in his career."

"But you're older than me, Walter."

"You stopped reporting a long time ago, Marion. Now, you just suck paychecks from *The Conservative* and spout hateful, ignorant rhetoric. I'm getting off track though. These riots in San Francisco are just the continued examples of America not coming to terms with its history. Until America realizes the atrocities they have committed to black people, relations between police and black citizens will not get better."

"And so, it begins."

"Now, Marion, you had your time, let Walter finish. Now, Walter I hear that a lot. What exactly does realizing the atrocities mean? America has vehemently denied it's past and has worked to getting better. You know that is a fact. It's a fact no one can argue."

"We see things from different perspectives, John. And no disrespect, but mine offers more clarity because you've always been on the outside looking in. See, in America, be it black civil rights, or women's voting rights, these issues were never resolved solely by the American government. Activists, organizations, and other movements help bring issues such as police brutality and segregation to the light. Without these groups, things would have continued, business as usual. The government couldn't ignore the people. They couldn't ignore the progress America was making. Blacks becoming more educated, inventing things such as the traffic light, and gaining wealth. The white men in the government were completely fine, be it at the federal or local level, with keeping black citizens at the bottom. Transition now to the year 2017. Racism isn't popular how it used to be. But those mentalities still exist today. The men who fought tooth and nail to keep America white those 50 and 60 years ago, their children are now running companies, their children are attending college. So, when I say---"

"Organizations? Please. Don't tell me you think that organizations such as Black Lives Matter are really going to change anything. They incite violence against police. They organize nothing but riots."

"I guess you'll never change your view on them but there haven't been any formal attacks on police officers by **BLM**. Ever. The organization doesn't condone or justify the mass killings of police. And the only person you can reference is the Dallas Police Killer. Marion, this is my entire point. There has been officer after officer killing unarmed black men throughout the country. Different states, different precincts, because they all operate on the same principals. That black citizens are more dangerous and more criminal."

"You make this too easy, Mr. Daniels. Cops see black citizens that way because, unfortunately, black citizens commit the most crimes in the country. You can't refute stats."

"You can when they are biased, Marion."

"Are you not being racist by generalizing white people? You wouldn't want us to categorize you in such a way, why do it to us? It's reverse racism, Walter."

Walter sighed and rubbed his eyes. These idiots. I don't know why they even invited me on. Maybe they thought I was going to get upset or something. I've dealt with smarter racists than them my entire life. Crane isn't so outspoken about his racism and bigotry. But he's just as bad as Marion. They aren't interested in listening, just asserting themselves. They want me to shake on their show.

"You brought me on here to discuss the state of San Francisco. Honestly, there's not many solutions to what's happening at this very moment. It's how we respond after the riots, weeks, months, years after that matters. But now, you're transitioning to a different topic when it comes to our American justice system. I know we don't have hours to talk but our justice system is and has always been slanted towards black men, And not in a good way. What you said is true, but it's a half-truth. Black men get reported the most when it comes to crime. Stats show that if a white man and black man commit the same exact crime, the white man is almost guaranteed to get the lighter sentence. Be it something serious like murder, or something simple like weed possession."

"Well, gentlemen, it seems like we're out of time. I'd like to thank Walter Daniels from joining us all the way from Russia. Marion, thank you for joining us as well. Next, we'll talk about the President's recent budget proposition to Congress. Will it make it to the floor, or is deadlock our fourth branch of government? Next, here on *The Conservative*."

The camera turned off in Walter's room. The media workers were gone soon after. He was alone. He wanted to laugh and actually, he did. Loud. Just as the conversation was starting to get going, Crane probably got the call from production to end it. They knew that Marion Woods, famed reporter and conservative pundit, didn't have the patience or knowledge to go toe to toe with him. Walter didn't get upset by empty gestures of respect from white people anymore, but they were as easy to see as the sun on a hot day July. Truthfully, Walter enjoyed even the slightest bit of conversation nowadays. Even if it was someone as close-minded as Marion Woods. A younger Walter may have lost his cool just now, but his lack of human interaction gave Walter much needed clarity when he was dealing with lesser minds. There wasn't much left to do in his day now. He thought about working on his piece about the riots in San Francisco, but he was exhausted now. Walter didn't like to focus too much on one thing. It often turned his mind to mush when trying to write about it. Instead he would try to watch some television.

As he sat on his bed, he smiled at the fact his television had American channels and connection. One of the best things about being a first-class exile. His fridge was always stocked with whatever he wanted, and his apartment was spacious. Literally, whatever Walter wanted to do, he could do. Except leave Russia, of course. Today though, all he wanted was to watch television. Maybe some cartoons, or a funny movie. No politics or bad news. Not to his surprise, he ended up watching CNN. Walter wished he could stop caring about the world around him. He really did. But he knew it was never going to happen. Something big was happening though. There was a breaking news alert and there was constant live footage. The top corner of the screen read San Francisco. Possibly more riots. Then, Walter noticed the headline at the bottom of the screen. He almost collapsed when he read it. A couple of minutes of staring didn't change it. The footage wasn't showing much, just a bunch of cops standing around talking. Finally, Walter read the headline aloud to make sure it made sense.

"*Superman Is Real. And He's Black*," he said slowly.

— ·· — ·· — ·· — ·· — ·· — ·· —

Isaac was standing on top of an old building. For some odd reason, he was nervous. He'd been practicing with his new powers for months. Flying at death defying heights, lifting cars, all of that. But he was still nervous. Maybe because it was the first time he was wearing his suit. It felt great. Strong, but flexible. Every time he let the energy flow through his body, he felt the motors in the suit begin to churn. The mask had needed the most work before he stepped out in public. Isaac didn't want people seeing his eyes all the time. So, he developed and installed purple lenses in his mask that covered the eyes holes. They were somewhat hard to see out of, and he mainly wanted to use them when talking to others, so they only saw his mouth, or scouting the rooftops. The suit was basically one big computer. It didn't have an AI but, Isaac installed some custom operating systems so that he could look up information on the fly. The readings came through the purple lenses. He was proud of his work. He activated the suit and turned on the police scanner. The display in his lenses showed the frequency of the scanner in the right eye, in the top corner. Below it, he saw the names of the officers on duty in his area.

"Any of these officers indicated in the recent riots?" Isaac asked his suit.

Every name flashed.

"All of them huh? Show me the ones who have history of police brutality. Anything from harassment complaints to actual charges being brought forward." The suit showed three police officers who were located a couple of blocks away. Isaac teleported to their location soon after. He wasn't sure what he was going to do on his first night out, but if a riot broke out, he didn't want police abusing their authority, especially if the "riot" was a peaceful protest.

Hours went by. Isaac almost fell asleep a couple of times. He felt like a rookie.

"I'm too old for this," he said allowed. Then he laughed because he remembered his immortality.

A couple more hours passed. It was almost 3am. The night was quiet. For the first time in weeks, San Francisco was quiet. Isaac was watching newscasts to pass the time. Reading police reports to learn more about local police. He was ashamed of himself for not knowing about some of the men working for his local police department. One man had shot an 11-year-old a couple years ago. There was a deep investigation, but he was still employed. Another was suspected of prostitution. But it ended there, with just a suspicion. From what he could tell, there weren't many clean cops in his area. The surrounding area outside of the Pinnacle was even worse. But the transition from television corrupt cops, to boy scout Robocops was quick once you crossed into the Pinnacle. It made Isaac sick. At that moment, an idea came to him. If he could publish these files under and write a piece about the link between cop behavior and where they're placed, he thought it would create some worthy discussion. He also liked the idea of not having to use his powers to do that. Isaac wasn't sure he could control his powers. Not after that incident with the racist officer a couple of weeks ago. He spent the next hour figuring out how to hack the San Francisco police department.

It was around 4 am when Isaac felt the presence of his mentor enter his mind. Erasmus didn't waste time when his spirit became felt. That gave Isaac comfort. His natural human skepticism still doubted Erasmus, something that Isaac wasn't sure he'd ever get over. Erasmus began to speak.

"How's the first night of patrol?" he asked.

"Thankfully, quiet. Been doing a bunch of research. I have some ideas that I want to run by you," Isaac said. He told Erasmus about his findings on the police and the systematic separation. Erasmus didn't interrupt once.

"I was hoping the powers would be a gateway to thinking like this," Erasmus said.

"So, I wasn't supposed to fly through buildings, fighting bad guys?" Isaac said laughing

Erasmus chuckled. He then appeared next to Isaac. For the first time ever, Erasmus was dressed down. No longer in his ceremonial black and gold outfits with the fabulous sword sash and shiny boots. He clothes reminded him of a Jedi. He looked like a monk almost. The colors were still black, but he looked comfortable.

"Going for a new look?" Isaac asked.

"I was so used to dressing for the entire world every day, I forgot what it feels like to be casual."

Their conversation was cut short. The suit was going crazy. Isaac activated the lenses and began processing the information. He then put them away because he could see the situation with clarity. There was a robbery going on.

"I'll leave you to it," Erasmus said. He was gone seconds later.

Isaac took a deep breath. A minute ago, he was almost ready to call it a night. Now, real crime was happening in front of him. He could hear gunshots too. The robbers were in a car that the police couldn't keep up with. From the looks of it, one cop had already been killed. There was no time to waste. Another deep breath and Isaac stood on the ledge of the building. For a moment, time slowed down. He knew his powers weren't going to fail him, but he was still nervous. The longer he hesitated though, the higher the possibility of the robbers getting away. Thinking of Cynthia's beautiful eyes and Alisha's perfect smile, Isaac jumped from the ledge and into the air. The wind brushed up against his face, it was a bit rough and almost distracted his flying, but he was used to it. Now he understood why Erasmus had them train on those mountains in Ireland.

Once he got closer, Isaac decided he needed to teleport into the car. It was the only way he was going to stop the car. Or he could just teleport in front of the car and stop it, but he didn't want the force to hurt the robbers. He wanted them alive, so they could go to jail. He decided to split the difference. He accelerated and teleported on the top of the car. He had teleported a million times, but this time, he felt alive, like a child. The lights of the city blurred together to make one big color he didn't recognize. His breath stopped momentarily, giving him the sensation that he might choke, even though he knew that wasn't the case. When he stopped and landed on the car, he almost slipped because it was going so fast. The police were still shooting at the car. Bullets didn't bother him though. One of the robbers noticed him on the roof of the car. The driver turned down an alley and evaded the police momentarily. The robber in the back seat poked his head out the window.

"Who the hell are you?" he asked. Isaac was disappointed that the robbers were black. They were all young too. He could see the jewels they stole. The cops weren't going to stop until these men were dead.

"Pull over now," Isaac said.

"Fuck you," the robber said.

"Kill his ass," the one in the front seat said. The robber in the back began firing up at Isaac. Isaac put his hand up and blocked the bullets. He could see fear on the robber's face.

"You done?" Isaac said and smiled. The robber threw his gun at Isaac and proceeded to roll up his window. Isaac couldn't help but laugh. The cops had caught up again. It was time to end this. He flew out in front of the car, dug his feet in the ground and made it come to a complete stop. The cops closed in. They weren't shooting, but all of them exited their vehicles with their weapons out. Isaac knew he had to get on top of this. He flew up into the air so that everyone could see him. A huge spotlight was on him. There were multiple helicopters above him. News choppers were his guess.

"The world is watching now," Erasmus said.

One of the cops exited the car. He seemed to be the one in charge. He was a big man, not fat, but muscular. His mustache was one of the thickest Isaac had ever seen. He didn't look terribly old either, just a couple of years older than Isaac. He had a megaphone with him.

"Stand down," he said over the megaphone.

Isaac slowly flew to the ground. Before he was fully on the ground, he turned around and said something to the robbers.

"You run now, they will shoot. They already want to kill you, and some would say their justified in doing so. Don't give them a reason." The only one who acknowledged any understanding of what Isaac just said was the one in the back. He had witnessed Isaac's power first hand. A slow nod was all that he could muster, but Isaac knew it was respectful. He slowly approached the cop in charge. They were a few feet apart. The helicopters still going, the cops behind the boss still had their weapons out. Isaac was a bit offended.

"Tell your men to put their weapons away," Isaac said.

The cop laughed.

"Who the hell do you think you are? You appear out of nowhere and you expect me to take orders from you. You could be an alien for all we know," the cop said.

"That's reasonable. But I'm no alien, sir. I know this area quite well actually, this is my home," Isaac said.

"Oh yeah? What's your name, boy?"

"Don't insult my intelligence. If I wanted you to know my name, I wouldn't be wearing the mask. But your men don't need their weapons right now. I stopped the robbers and they aren't going anywhere," Isaac said.

"How do you know that?" the cop said.

"Because I won't let them," Isaac said.

The cop scoffed. He ordered some of his men to arrest the robbers. They rushed in quickly. One officer began mercilessly beating one of the robbers. The robber was handcuffed and wasn't fighting back. Before another blow was dealt by the officer's nightstick, Isaac had teleported and caught the weapon. The officer was struggling a bit. He then tried to take a swing at Isaac, but Isaac disarmed him and pushed him away from the robbers. He could hear the cocking of guns around him.

"Since the media is here," Isaac began to yell, "Let me make one thing clear." He had programmed a feature in his suit which allowed him to use the same broadcast channel the local news stations and police were using. Mainly for moments like this. He could talk as quietly as he wanted, but they would all hear him.

"This city has been suffering. I love this city. I'm here to help everyone live a better life. The cops, the citizens, everyone. Now, I know the media and the police like to distort the truth. But I'm here live, with them, you can't distort this. After I stopped a robbery in progress, this man's men, I'm sorry sir what's your name?" Isaac yelled at the head cop.

"Mills. Sergeant Mills."

"Mr. Mills and the rest of his officers moved in for the arrest after I stopped the car. One of Mr. Mills officers began to brutally beat one of the robbers after he was handcuffed. I don't know about you, but that to me, is the definition of police brutality. Don't believe me, my suit recorded it and the video is being uploaded now. This is why I'm here. It's small moments like this that lead to protests and riots that we've seen. Everyone needs to be held accountable. Police, citizens, myself included. From now on, I'll be here to protect the people. I'm not an alien or a social recluse who will only appear at night. No, this city needs more than that. It deserves more than that." He ended the transmission and walked over to the Mills who didn't look happy.

"I don't know who you are, or what you are, but you have a lot of nerve proclaiming to be the savior of this city," Mills said.

Isaac could feel the man's anger. He wasn't even sure if Mills cared that he had superpowers. No, Mills cared more about the fact he didn't praise the police for their arrest. And that Isaac was black. He could see it in Mills' eyes.

"The sooner you realize I'm here to help, the better Mills. This city needs changes. And beating up every brown person you see isn't going to solve that," Isaac said. He started to fly off when Mills said something else.

"Maybe if your brown people didn't act like animals, my boys wouldn't have to beat you."

The words stung. Not because they hurt Isaac's feelings, but because he knew no one else heard them. Classic power racism. Only let it show when you know no one can do anything about it. Isaac wanted to drop Mills from his favorite mountain in Ireland. Flashbacks of his meltdown popped into his head.

"Oh, there you are. Maybe you are from around here. You brown people get awful quiet when someone finally stands up to you," Mills said. Isaac got as close as he could to the man. They stared at each other for nearly thirty seconds without talking. The helicopters still whirring, the guns of the officers still cocked.

"I'll make sure you lose your job, Mills. You're a disgrace to the police trying to impact their communities in a positive way. You're talking tough now, but you know there's nowhere left to hide anymore. Not while I'm around," Isaac said. Mills didn't say anything. Just stood there, with the same angry expression on his face. Isaac levitated slowly into the air again, so that everyone could see him, and then he went into lightspeed almost instantly. He was gone. All things considered, Isaac thought his first night had been a success.

— ·· — ·· — ·· — ·· — ·· — ··

Walter Daniels couldn't believe his eyes and ears. He was taking sporadic notes, but there was so much to digest. So much to take in. A superhero in San Francisco. Walter began furiously looking on the internet for tracings of other superheroes. After hours of searching he found reports of some devil girl in Colombia, but nothing concrete. If there were more superheroes out there, they were well hidden. This man though just stood out in the open for the world to see. The news sites had his speech playing over and over again. The passion with which he spoke, reminded Walter of himself when he was a young reporter. Except this man had superpowers, of course. And he seemed like a genuine ally of black people in America. He uploaded the video of the policemen beating the robber. The video also showed him taking down the officer. Walter couldn't really deduct the full extent of this man's power, but he clearly possessed immense amounts of it. Walter loved his costume too. It wasn't dark and menacing. The dark purple fading into a lighter purple was a brilliant idea. The cape had the same effect and it made this man look extravagant. It was all every news site was talking about. Is he an alien? What are his intentions? Was that message a declaration of war? Everything was being talked about as it should. Modern human history as they knew it had taken a massive leap. Walter began reaching out to his contacts in the States. He wanted to see if this man had any other plans, or if speeches were his big thing. Walter thought either would be good. Having a leader like this at the front of the black community could make some real change.

Walter fanned the flames of his excitement for a bit when he thought about all the negatives that would most definitely arise from this. While he saw an opportunity for a superhero to be the face of freedom for people, especially black people, all over the world, he knew that leaders, especially some of the black ones, would look to use this man as a weapon. Military, terrorist groups, politicians, were all planning their move the moment this man appeared on the news. The main positive from this was that this man owned the next move. He could never show up again and he'd become the biggest folk legend in human history. Or he could become the next step in human evolution, both physically and mentally. Walter was confident it was the second option. He only hoped this new hero wouldn't be swayed by corrupt black politicians and activists, looking to play the race card, only to advance their gain and secure incumbency. No, Walter knew that this man could either provide the hope that black and white people needed in America, or he'd be the last piece needed to solidify the gap between the two cultures.

All of this was happening too fast. There were so many possibilities. Walter hadn't been this excited in a long time. He had momentarily completely forgotten about the piece he was working on about the Pinnacle. It was one he had been working on for almost 20 years. It's the piece that got him sent here. For the moment, he had completely forgotten he was in Russia. The thoughts were rushing to his brain and then, he had an idea.

Maybe this man can help me expose the Pinnacle, he thought. He must have a handle on technology, hacking into broadcast frequencies the way he did. If the article comes from him, this might shut down the Pinnacle forever. Walter couldn't contain his happiness. He had hope once again. He had hope.

A couple of weeks passed, and Walter was keeping up with San Francisco's newest hero as if it were his job. He was everywhere. Bank robberies, simple muggings, and even riots, which we were even more slim now that this mystery man showed up. From what Walter could gather, police brutality reports had gone down too. What really impressed Walter about this new hero was that he wasn't restricting himself to one area, and he wasn't shy about speaking out on issues. There was a violent protest in New York City, something related to Wall Street and the mystery man made his presence known. He assisted police officers, assisted civilians and he gave a passionate speech at the end of the protests, about coming together. The next place Walter remembered him popping up was Florida. There was a string of murders in Orlando. People thought they were terror related, but it was drug related. The hero also released files that helped the local police arrest the drug lords. His game wasn't brute force. In the weeks that the mystery man had appeared, he had caused almost less $20,000 dollars in damages. He broke one of the drug lord's jaws in Florida and he paid for the lowlife to have it fixed. This man wasn't leveling buildings, killing innocents, none of that. Walter couldn't believe the hold he seemed to have over his powers. That presented a problem though. It had been almost two months since he came onto the scene. Whenever crime was going on, really in any part of the world, the clamored for the man in purple. They begged for God to come and save them. Most of the time he did. But Walter had a hunch this man was simply that. A man, who somehow acquired extraordinary abilities. Or was it something more? Was it God himself granting powers to a black man so he could help the poor and impoverished? All the prayers that poor people and black people said every night, were they answered in the form of this man?

Walter's suspicions of him being some God-like being who didn't need rest was soon gone. One afternoon, he was watching the man give a press conference. He was fresh from saving over 200 people in a fire in Queens. Now, he was back in San Francisco, he helped the police catch a serial killer. He was talking about neighborhood watches and everyone pitching in to make the community safe. It wasn't his best speech. Walter enjoyed listening to him speak. He spoke with clarity and passion. He used his powers as a platform. If someone misquoted him or didn't understand a point he was trying to make, he would speak informally, but still in a way that was acceptable for news broadcasts. The only times Walter remembered him getting upset was when talking about racial issues. There was one time too, that he seemed especially choked up when he rescued a family from a killer but was too late to rescue the family's youngest daughter. When talking about the daughter, Walter noticed how hard it was for him to speak. Did he have a daughter? A family? Walter told himself at the time he was looking into it too deep. Then, he told himself that he wouldn't be doing his job if he didn't ask questions like that. He didn't dig too deep into it though. The man wore a mask for a reason. And whenever he spoke, two things threw off anyone who would be trying to figure out who he is. There was a clear voice modifier being used when he talked. It didn't make his voice raspy or robotic, but it did distort it enough that you couldn't hear his real voice. The second was the mask itself. The eyeholes had purple lenses over them, so he looked eerie at times, but once again, no one could see his eyes. Sometimes, he'd have them off. From what Walter could tell they were brown, but he never let them show for long. Today though, he did, and the voice modifier wasn't on. Walter could hear his voice with extreme clarity. Funny thing though, the voice with the voice modifier and his voice now didn't sound too different. It was clever. Even though he was exhausted, he was trying to shield his voice, and honestly, Walter couldn't see anyone noticing. It was the eyes that gave it away. He looked as if his eyes were about to fall out of the mask. When the speech ended, he flew away; people applauded, and the day went on. For the next couple of days, he was nowhere to be found. He hadn't tied himself to any particular organization, he made it clear from his first outing that he would show allegiance to no one with agendas, no matter how pure or right he thought they may be. He had said, "The only agenda I stand for is decency." It was kind of cheesy, but he had stuck to it during these past few months. And when he teleported away from a scene or press conference, that was the end of it. People were waiting for him to appear again.

In the days he didn't show up, crime wasn't rampant in San Francisco, or really any part of the world. The news sites talked about the mystery man's absence. Some criticized him for not showing up, but most realized that the amount of work he was doing deserved a couple days off. On his third day off, something big happened. The man could be anywhere, anytime, but he was just one man. Walter woke up from a nap, and it was still dark outside. He went to the bathroom, washed his face, and opened the fridge to see what he had in there. Not much. He put in an order for room service soon after. He was enjoying a cheeseburger and fries. Walter knew he ate this meal too often. He hated the hotel for making it so well. As he sat down on his bed, and turned on the news, his phone vibrated at the same time. It was a number he didn't recognize, but the subject matter made it clear it was one of his sources back in the states. There wasn't much text, but the words he saw hit him like a train.

"Dr. Eckspo has been killed. White Supremacist group."

Walter couldn't believe it. He had lost his fair share of people during his life. But this one stung. His colleague, his mentor, his best friend.

— ·· — ·· — ·· — · — ·· —

Isaac woke up late that day. He couldn't stop watching the television. Erasmus was with him as well.

"This isn't good," Erasmus said.

Isaac didn't say anything.

"You want me to leave?" Erasmus asked.

Isaac shook his head. He wanted to talk but couldn't find the words. Mainly because he could have slept for another 8 hours. His eyes hurt. His back was sore, and he could feel the energy in his body being drained just from sitting on his couch. During their training in Ireland, Erasmus had told him about the dangers of over exerting himself, but Isaac did so anyway. Now, he was paying the full price of it. Bullets and missiles couldn't kill him. But he could certainly kill himself. Still, he was up because his father had just been murdered. His father wasn't invincible. Bullets didn't bounce off his skin. The bullet the terrorist group used went directly through his head. They gave this impassioned speech about white power and how the media empowers white genocide. Isaac listened to it all, he took notes. He couldn't wait to find the men who killed his father. He watched the news cycle through other stories as well, something going on in Colombia, more vigilantism in Atlanta. Isaac knew it was the two girls that Erasmus told him about. Kamayra and the one who no one knows. One day, he'd reach out to them. Maybe try to form a team of some sort. If not that, at least let them know they have support. But, maybe, they didn't want to be contacted. Isaac was the biggest celebrity in the world. Unless these two women lived under a rock, they knew who he was. Why hadn't they reached out yet? Isaac didn't dwell on the fact too long, he was too focused on his father.

A couple of hours past. Isaac fell asleep without knowing. When he woke up, Erasmus was still sitting there, on the couch, watching the news.

"What the—you've been here the entire time?" Isaac asked.

"Yes," Erasmus said plainly.

"You never make any noise. It's weird," Isaac said.

"I've been thinking about your father. Something isn't right about his death. It seems random, or I guess, planned. He's a well-known black activist. The group appears to be, and is known, as white supremacists. But something about this is off. I can sense it," Erasmus said.

Usually, Isaac wasn't in the business of believing statements like that. But, he could feel it too. Yes, his father was dead, but something bigger was at play here. He couldn't sense it in its fullness, but the energy flowing through him now felt like the one he felt when his wife and daughter were taken from him.

"I'm guessing you feel it too," Erasmus said.

"I do. But what does it mean? These powers, they give me great abilities and allow me to basically be God. But, I'm powerless against this energy flowing through me and you right now. Like, it's dark energy or something," Isaac said.

"I don't have a clue what's going on," Erasmus said.

"You think this Gatekeeper did this? The one you can't find?" Isaac asked. He could feel the power surging through him. His skin began to glow, and his fists began to spark rapidly with cosmic electricity.

"You need to calm down," Erasmus said. He stood up slowly. Isaac stood up as well. The energy flowed faster now. His body was heating up.

"How long has it been, Erasmus? You told me that this Gatekeeper could be found. The only reason I agreed to do this is because I need my family back. I need Cynthia and Alisha!" Isaac yelled.

"I get that, Isaac, I do. I swore to you on my sword I would find them. I'm trying. But, that powerlessness you feel, I feel as well. Whoever this Gatekeeper is, whoever gave him his abilities, it is dark magic and mysticism beyond my abilities. The only way we are going to beat whoever this is, is if we do it together," Erasmus said.

Isaac had a headache. He instantly regretted doubting Erasmus again.

"I'm sorry," he said. Isaac sat down on the couch. He sighed and let a few tears roll down his face. Erasmus sat down next to him, but not too close. The news was still playing on the television.

"My father and I never got along," Isaac said in tears. He wasn't sobbing, but the pain in his throat was almost unbearable. "I'm not even sure why," he said. "His entire life was dedicated to helping my people. I guess, I've always had a place in my heart that hated him, because he acted as if helping me was a chore. You know, a father is supposed to play catch with his son. Teach him how to be a man. You know my father cheated on my mother? Multiple times," he was still crying, but laughing as well. Not hysterical laughing though, just a chuckle.

"He wasn't a horrible father by any means, Erasmus. But the media painted our lives as if we were wiping our ass with gold. My mother struggled to keep me and my sister in line all while dealing with his mess. His crusade against the white man," Isaac said.

"You have a sister?" Erasmus asked.

"Had a sister."

"I'm sorry," Erasmus said.

"It's fine. I mean, look at this. They're using his death to declare a war on white people. Erasmus correct me if I'm wrong, but white cops have been shooting blacks forever, right?" Isaac asked.

"You're right."

"Then why the fuck is my father more important to these people than Tamar Reed, Lonnie Smith, Alton Sterling, Tamir Rice, Eric Gardner, Mike Brown, and Philando Castile. And the hundreds of blacks killed this year by police?!" Isaac was screaming now. He didn't mean to.

"Your father was captured and murdered. It was broadcasted live online," Erasmus said calmly.

"So are the bombings in the Middle East. So was that mass killing by that army in Africa. What are they called, The Trees of Hope? No one lifted a finger to save those people," Isaac said.

The news cycle finally picked up another story. This one was about corruption in the White House. Isaac was finally able to breathe normally again.

"I don't want to become him," Isaac said. "I was thinking about this the other day. If I get my family back, I'll become just like him. All the good I've done so far, all the people who look up to me as some sort of symbol. I can't stop now. But, how can I balance this life and my family?"

"You're a good man, Isaac," Erasmus said "You think about the well-being of others more than most. You're riddled with guilt just like I am because of all the inaction you've taken in your life. I can see that. I can feel that. You can't let that guilt destroy you though. If you want to keep this fight alive, I will help you. We can figure a way for you to be with your family. With the money I gave you, maybe you could help the community in other ways. Maybe open Science Supreme again. Powers doesn't have to be the way."

"I thought that too for a while. Especially when you first proposed this to me. But, if Mystic Man exists, people have hope. He's a symbol that isn't going to be replaced with a new library downtown or my inventions. I want it to be that way. Really, I do. And I plan on helping that way as well. But these powers help people in ways money or my father never could. Mystic Man helps them in was no one ever could. He doesn't have an agenda, allegiances, and he doesn't cut deals. Mystic Man is a true representation of someone who can't be corrupted. But, just like my father, I could lose sight of the end game. All because I think I'm the one who is the cause of this. If I ever start to think I alone, am the reason the world is becoming a better place. When in reality, it's about the people I inspire. Those are the ones who make the world a better place. Not me," Isaac couldn't control himself. He was sobbing now. "I won't become my father!" he yelled. "I won't!"

Erasmus put his hand on Isaac's shoulder.

"I never met your father, but I can tell you now that you're the farthest thing from him," Erasmus said.

"Alive for one thousand years but you still understand the effect of an empty sentiment," Isaac said. "Thanks." He laughed a bit and smiled. Erasmus smiled back.

"You need rest. Get some rest, then figure out what you want to do next," Erasmus said.

He's right, Isaac thought. I'm losing my mind.

Isaac got up from the couch. When he looked next to him, Erasmus was gone. The television was still going. Isaac didn't have the energy to turn it off. As he walked upstairs, he passed a picture of his wife and daughter. He smiled because in it, Cynthia was extremely sick that day. He pleaded with her that taking the photo didn't have to happen that day. Cynthia was stubborn though. All she ever wanted to do was take coordinated family photos. This was their first, and she had a fever. Throughout the whole thing she was sneezing and coughing, but when that camera clicked, she held it together. It was hilarious. He gently rubbed the glass of the picture and finally made his way to bed. No more thoughts entered his mind once he laid his head down. For the first time in a long time, Isaac slept like a baby. When he woke up, he decided the best thing to do was to visit his mother.

CHAPTER 10

20 Years Ago

"**B**oy, if you don't hurry up! We got places to be. And tell your father to hurry out of the bathroom," Rose yelled from the car. She knew Isaac couldn't hear her word for word, but he looked at her from the store as if he did. She loved watching him. Whether he was doing some crazy experiment in their garage or he was buying candy in a store. He was special, and she knew it. All his teachers talked about how he was the smartest fifteen-year-old they've ever come across. Girls liked him too, but Isaac wasn't worried about girls right now, and she was thankful for that. Science was his first love and she saw the passion in his eyes. Whether he was talking about it, or practicing it, science made Isaac feel alive. She didn't know where he got that from. She herself was more of a literary person. And his father, her husband, was focused on social justice and politics.

Rose sighed as she thought about her husband. She thought about how the one day, today, that he promised to be home all day, he just took the family around the city on errands. She wanted to get angry with him, and sometimes she did. There were times she couldn't hold her anger, even in front of the kids. The man she fell in love with all those years ago didn't exist anymore. Rose couldn't remember the last time she felt loved. At least, by a man anyways. She knew her kids loved her. The amount of respect they showed her was sometimes mindboggling, but she wasn't complaining. Isaac was her outspoken one. Gabriella though, was the definition of an introvert. Rose had forgotten her only daughter was even in the car. She looked back at her. Of course, as she always did when her mother looked at her, Gabriella smiled. It was angelic. Every time Gabriella smiled, Rose felt the weight of the world, the weight of her marriage, lift.

"What are you doin', girl?" she asked.

"Nothing," she said smiling. She wasn't lying. Gabriella most of the time was quite literally, doing nothing. If psychics existed, they'd probably be amazed at whatever was going on in her mind. Whatever it was, it kept her happy and it kept her satisfied. At thirteen, she was starting to come into her own. Her body was developing, and her beauty was already starting to showcase itself. Rose often thought about how different Gabriella looked. Every member of the Eckspo family was dark-skinned. They were people who couldn't pass for anything other than black. Gabriella though, all the time, was met with questions about her ethnicity. Everything from Hispanic, Native American, Rose even heard Australian once. Gabriella was beautiful. She didn't look like anything to Rose, just her daughter.

"He said he's almost done!" Isaac shouted from the door. He was in the car soon after. With a bag of candy and a pop. He was lucky it was a "family day" or that sugar would have to go.

"Okay, good," Rose said.

"Mommy, can we go to Olive Garden tonight?" Gabriella asked.

What? This was the very first time Gabriella asked to go anywhere. She usually just sat in the car and went along with everything. She didn't throw tantrums over food and never cared where they ate. Rose worried that she was going to start that phase now, at thirteen, when most children go through it much younger. She didn't know what to say.

"Why do you want to go there?" she asked.

"We went on Isaac's birthday and I really liked it. Plus, it's right down the street, I can see it," Gabriella said smiling. Rose laughed.

"I'm sure since it's so close, your father wouldn't mind going there. Doesn't waste gas," Rose said.

"I second that," Isaac said, his mouth filled with candy.

"You eat one more piece of candy and we aren't going anywhere. I'm not washing anything if you throw up when we get home," Rose said.

Gabriella gave Isaac any icy stare. A stare that said, "You're my brother and I love you, but if you ruin Olive Garden for me right now, I'll kill you." Isaac complied and put the candy on the floor in front of him. He returned her icy stare with an apologetic look. They just had a full-blown conversation without even saying a word. Rose didn't know if she wanted to be proud or if she wanted to laugh. So, she decided to do both. She let out a loud laugh.

"You two are too much. I'll talk your father into going. I'm actually craving some All-You-Can-Eat pasta," she said.

All the happiness her kids gave her was soon replaced with disappointment and anger. Fifteen minutes had passed. Her husband was out of the bathroom, and now he was just walking around, buying pointless snacks. The entire day had been wasted. Drawing inspiration from her daughter, she was determined to salvage family day with a dinner at Olive Garden. But, just as her husband was coming out of the store, Rose heard tires screeching behind them. She didn't pay much attention to it, just some teenagers trying to show out. It wasn't until the tire sounds came closer did Rose begin to worry. She undid her seatbelt and started to open her door. The car, along with another, had them closed in. They couldn't move. Her husband sprinted into the car and tried to start it. But once Rose saw who was in the car, she knew they weren't moving.

Four white men in the first car. Three in the second. They didn't get out, but something did peak out of the windows. Guns. Assault rifles, submachine guns, and pistols. The men weren't even wearing masks. They wanted the famous Doctor Eckspo to know who killed him. Except this time, they were all targets. It wasn't the first time either. Well, not the first time her husband had been targeted. It was her first time on the front lines. The bullets started flying.

"Fucking niggers!"

"Stop killing cops, you fucking monkeys!"

"Go back to Africa, nigger!"

She could hear their joyous taunts as they shot the car.

"Kids! Get down!" she yelled. She couldn't risk putting her head up. All she could do was hope they were safe. She could hear everyone near or inside the store screaming. The bullets finally stopped, and the cars sped off down the street. Luckily, and to

Rose's surprise, there was a police car just down the street from them and they began to pursue the car with four men in it. The other car drove away in peace, but Rose hoped that someone called the police during the madness. Her husband popped up from under the steering wheel. He was swearing and yelling at the top of his lungs. A small part of her wished he had gotten hit. She hated herself for it, but she was done fighting the feelings. Her children were turning out great, so he wasn't needed much nowadays. Rose turned around to see if they were okay. Isaac uncovered the top of his head. She let out a sigh of relief. That relief turned into terror as she heard short, raspy breaths coming from the back seat. As rose turned her head, there was Gabriella, back against the bottom of the seat, bullets lodged in her body. The amount of blood in the car was horrendous. Isaac started to scream. It was the first time Rose could recall, that her son showed so much emotion. She rushed out of the car and opened the back door. Gabriella almost fell out immediately. Her short breaths made Rose want to die. The blood was everywhere. Her chest was exposed, organs were showing. Rose didn't know how many times she'd been hit. The only thing she was positive of was that her baby girl was going to die. She was seconds from it.

"Momma..." she tried to say.

Rose, tears obstructing her vision, picked up Gabriella gently. Not only could she feel the life leaving her baby girl, she could feel Gabriella trying to speak.

"I'm here, baby. It's okay. It's okay," Rose wasn't sure if any words came out. There was too much going on. People were screaming, cop sirens were blasting, and her husband had lost his sanity. As she looked up, the hate for her husband only grew.

You son of a bitch. Your daughter is dying as we speak and all you can do is curse and scream? May you rot in hell.

"Momma," Gabriella whispered.

"Stop talking, Baby Girl," Rose said. She held her daughter, not knowing how much longer she would have a daughter.

"I love you, Momma," Gabriella said quietly. She died seconds later, Rose still holding her in her arms.

"I love you too, Baby Girl. You angel, you sweet, sweet, angel," the words barely came out. Rose put Gabriella down on the ground. She almost fainted. The pain in her chest was too much to bear. Her daughter, her only girl, had been gunned down in cold blood. For no reason. No reason at all. The paramedics were on the scene now. People were recording with their phones, reporters filed in with their cameras and crew. Rose didn't leave her daughter's side. Isaac was next to her now. She wasn't sure when he got there, but his emotions were calm now. Tears ran down his face. He wept for his baby sister now. Isaac shut her eyes and wrapped her up in a blanket from the car. When the paramedics said they should move the body, Isaac told them no. When the cops demanded they needed to move, Isaac said lock him up. And when the reporters clamored for answers, he only repeated her name. Gabriella Rose Eckspo. Gabriella Rose Eckspo. Gabriella Rose Eckspo. Because of Isaac, they had a few extra moments to grieve.

Rose's husband didn't kneel at Gabriella's side once. When the paramedics said they should move the body, he asked if they would do the same for a white girl. When the cops demanded they move, he began talking about police brutality. And when the reporters clamored for answers, he said the men who did this were white supremacists. He demanded the city do something about the increasing number of hate crimes in their area. He spoke passionately and clearly about the struggle of black families. How fear and trauma are the two things most associated with black families today because of the government, and agents of the government. He considered these white supremacists the product of a government who didn't condemn racism. They didn't classify acts like this terrorism. Brown people were the only ones who were terrorists in the eyes of America. But today, white men, shouted nigger and killed a little girl. Intended to kill the whole family. People cheered and roared as he spoke about the shooting.

Not once did he kneel beside Gabriella.

— ·· — ·· — ·· — ·· — ·· — ·· — ··

Present Day

The last time Isaac visited his mother, she was on the brink of insanity, having watched Alisha disappear in front of her eyes. He hadn't spoken to her since. He hated himself for that. No matter what his new life demanded of him, he knew his mother needed him more than ever. When he got to her house, he noticed she was in the backyard, doing yardwork.

I don't know why she just doesn't hire someone to do it, he said. Or just call me.

He opened the fence and walked around to the backyard. She smiled as he walked the path to the porch. She was pulling weeds. Isaac helped his mother off her knees and they sat down on the porch. She offered him some lemonade. As usual, it was amazing. Today was a hot day, but he didn't know how hot until the lemonade quenched his thirst. They didn't talk about much for the next couple of hours. Isaac didn't want to upset her, she seemed to be in a good mood for a woman who was spending the day picking weeds. Isaac decided to help. The weeds were annoying and would have been a nuisance without his powers. But with his strength, they got the weeds up in no time. She told him he didn't have to help.

After a couple of hours, the sun was starting to set. It was warm outside, but cool enough that his mother took off her hat. The lemonade tasted better than it did the first time. Finally, she spoke.

"You didn't have to come by," she said.

"I needed to. To make sure you were okay," Isaac said.

"I'm fine," she said.

Isaac laughed.

"Clearly. Those weeds didn't stand a chance today," he said.

She laughed too.

"I'm old, Isaac. Pulling weeds is like going out to a club for me. I get to be outside, smell the air, talk to the neighbors as they pass me. It's an event."

Isaac sipped some more lemonade and laughed again.

"You really do seem to be doing fine. You know, all things considered," Isaac didn't mean to bring her down, but talking about his father, her husband's death was inevitable. Isaac didn't want his mother holding anything in.

"Yeah, I saw it on the news," she said. "At least he died doing what he loved. Or, should I say, doing what he loved got him killed. It's what he would have wanted."

There was an unusual calm in her voice. When Alisha disappeared into thin air, Isaac thought that was it for his mother. Any bit of sanity his mother had was sure to disappear when she watched her only granddaughter disappear in front of her eyes. Isaac was almost certain he was coming to visit the shell of his mother today. Instead, she was coherent, lively, and fun. Still, he worried. Was she manic? Was this some sort of withdrawal? Would the broken woman soon show her face? Isaac was prepared to interact with that woman. He was prepared to see the tears. Listen to the shaky words. No, instead this was the liveliest he had ever seen his mother since he was a child. Then, like a train, it hit him.

"You're happy he's dead, aren't you?" Isaac asked.

"Aren't you?" she said slowly. They didn't say anything for a couple of minutes.

"Come inside, Isaac. I want to show you something," she said.

Isaac listened. They went inside where he noticed how different the house looked. He didn't inspect it the last time he was here. But now that the dust had settled, he noticed something different.

"Dad didn't live here, did he?" Isaac asked.

"Not for the last couple of years," she said. "He cheated on me, Isaac. Some young girl who volunteered for his organization. He's been 'On the road' ever since," she said.

"I didn't know that," he said even though he was lying. Isaac hated himself for not being able to tell his mom what he found out about his father all those years ago. He had buried it deep in his heart. By the time Isaac got into college, the thought didn't even enter his mind.

"Well, that's because I didn't tell you," she said laughing. "But he's betrayed my trust multiple times. All those years, all the times he neglected us, I put up with it. He was probably cheating on me shortly after you were born too. The girls probably respected him more then, so they didn't tell me. This most recent one though came running to me the second she checked out of the hotel room. Your father was still in his underwear when I showed up."

Isaac pictured his father, half-naked and scared out of his mind. It was a comical sight. His father always made sure to never show any sign of weakness. Always made sure to appear to be a man in control. Isaac hated that. There was a time for a man to step up, and be the leader, the provider for the family. Isaac's father took that to the extreme. Everything from the mortgage payments to what the family ate for a pre-dinner snack. He loved control. And frankly, he had mastered it. No reporter misquoted him or twisted his words. Isaac's father was always in control. He could see the mighty Dr. Eckspo with his gut hanging out, trying to get the words out to justify his infidelity. Isaac wished he could have seen it. His father with no control.

"I bet he was scared when you showed up," Isaac said.

"He was. But I didn't yell at him. I wasn't even mad. Over the years he was a terrible father. But I couldn't talk to him about it. Not your father. He would have found a way to twist it into something about his work. He'd ask me if I seriously thought his work should suffer because I was upset. I would answer no, and he would puff his chest out in victory. Son, when I caught that man with his underwear on, man-breasts a hanging, I finally found my victory. He knew it. I knew it. There was nothing left between us," she said.

Her words cut Isaac to the core. All this time, she could have been searching for a man who was worthy of her time. Instead, she wasted her life on a self-righteous activist.

They walked down the hallway. An old family picture was hanging up. Isaac teared up seeing his baby sister, Gabriella. She was so beautiful.

"Do you remember the day your sister died?" she asked.

"Of course."

"Isaac, I did a good job of hiding it through the years. I even kept that mask on after he cheated. Pretending he was a good man," she said. "But, the day my baby girl, your sister, Gabriella died, I think that's the day I stopped loving that man. I know what you're thinking, but my life has overall been joyous. Despite your father disappearing in front of me. Somehow, my two children turned out to be the brightest, most wonderful children a mother could ask for," she turned to Isaac. He couldn't stop the tears from falling now. He couldn't look his mother in the eye.

"Every time you showed me respect, every good grade you got, when you graduated college, got your masters, started your business, and the love you show your wife. Isaac, your life has given me life. I've been critical of you through the years and harsh on Cynthia when I didn't need to be. But seeing you become the caring, loving man that you are today is the only thing that's kept me alive."

He couldn't believe what he was hearing.

"The day your sister died, your father didn't look at her once. He hardly grieved. That day, my love for him officially died. Gabriella deserved so much more. She was too smart and gentle for this world. I will never forget how short her breaths were when I was holding her in her arms. It was almost as if she didn't know she was about to die. Still trying to breathe. And when she did realize her life was over, you want to know the last thing she said to me?"

Isaac nodded slowly. He felt weak, overcome with sadness, but at the same time joy, thinking about Gabriella.

"She said, 'I love you, Momma' right before she died. With her last breath, all that child could think about was love."

Isaac could hardly see. He didn't know why he couldn't control himself. Never, had his mother talked with such emotion. He was expecting to find an elderly woman, struck with melancholy at the loss of her husband. Instead, she celebrated his death, and he, although tears flowed down his face, did as well. But he hated himself for it.

"I'm glad he's gone," Isaac said weeping. His mother opened her arms and he almost fell to the floor.

"Something else is troubling you, Isaac. What is it?" she asked.

Isaac finally regained his composure. He wiped the tears from his face and looked at his mother.

Should I tell her? Am I putting her in danger? She might already know.

"I'm not going to lie to you, Momma. It's about Alisha," Isaac said.

Her eyes got wide. The happiness she felt at her husband dying was wiped away by the thought of losing her granddaughter, who, now that Isaac thought about it, looked just like Gabriella. Now, he understood why she took it so hard. Not only did Alisha look like Gabriella, she acted like her too.

"Did you find her?" she asked.

"You might want to sit down, Momma. It's a very long story."

— ·· — ·· — — ·· — — ·· — ··

Isaac stayed the night at his mother's house that night. He spoke briefly with Erasmus telepathically. Erasmus didn't keep him on a schedule, he was just checking on Isaac. They spoke about what was going on in the world. Erasmus told him to take all the time he needed. He said the people were clamoring for Mystic Man, or as they called him, Mr. Purple, but he needed to make sure he was okay before putting the suit back on. Isaac agreed. And he was grateful that Erasmus understood.

When Isaac got out of bed, his mother was sitting on the couch. She looked calm. Her face was youthful. When Isaac arrived yesterday to help her with yardwork, there was a noticeable stiffness in his mother's face. Although she tried to hide her pain with cheap smiles and jokes, Isaac could tell that his father, her husband's death, bothered her somewhat. Today though, on a beautiful day in San Francisco, she was full of tranquility. Isaac wasn't sure why though. Last night, he told her everything. Everything. He told her about Cynthia disappearing, meeting Erasmus, getting his powers, training, and being the superhero on the news. At first, her reaction was stale. But she smiled about a minute after he was done telling her everything. His mother told him that it made sense that he was the one flying around doing good deeds, because she didn't think anyone else in the world was that good. Isaac downplayed the comment, but she was serious. She reminded him of the impact he made in the weeks since he showed up. Kids had a new idol, governments were nervous, and every company wanted to sponsor the Purple Man. Isaac had to correct her and tell her his name was

Mystic Man. Then, he laughed saying that only he and Erasmus knew about it. To his surprise, she remembered the imaginary character his daughter Alisha created to pass the time. She specifically recalled making lunch for Mystic Man and Alisha one day. That was the end of the laughter though. Tears soon followed from both and Isaac went to bed soon after. He was well-rested now. For the first time in a very long time, his head stopped hurting, his body didn't ache, and the energy flowed through him like the world's strongest river. Everything was looking up and he was glad to see his mother in a happy mood.

"Sleep well?" she asked.

He nodded. She gestured for him to sit next to her on the couch. Once he sat down, she put a hand on his shoulder.

"Thank you for telling me what you told me last night," she said.

"I didn't want to keep it a secret," Isaac said. "You deserve to know if I find Cynthia and Alisha."

"And you aren't any closer to finding this Gatekeeper?" she asked.

"No."

"And you trust this Erasmus? Maybe with your powers, you could find him yourself."

"I've thought about that," Isaac said. "But what if I'm not strong enough to take him on. Erasmus hasn't led me astray yet."

"You hardly know anything about him," she said.

Isaac didn't say anything.

"I already lost my baby girl, Alisha, a member of this family in Cynthia, and a man who was a cheater, but still my husband. I'm not losing you too, Isaac."

He knew losing him would destroy her. It's one of the main reasons he didn't want to take the powers when Erasmus offered. He didn't tell Erasmus that though.

"It sounds like you don't trust Erasmus though," Isaac said.

"You're right. But I don't trust anybody," she said with pride.

Isaac laughed a bit. They ate breakfast soon after and talked more about what he was going to do to help the world.

"Forget the world, people are starving in our own backyard," she said.

"I know, Mama. San Francisco, and the United States in general is my main concern. After that, I'll focus on the world."

"You need to focus on Africa," she said. "I been watching the news and I saw this new group has been killing folks left and right recently. The numbers make me sick. Can't remember what they're called."

"The Trees of Hope," Isaac said. "Me and Erasmus were talking about it the other day. That and something that popped up near Detroit. Apparently, crime is rampant there again. More than usual."

"Don't bother with Detroit," she said. "There will always be problems there. More than you can ever fix."

"Stop it, Mama," Isaac said. "I'll go wherever I'm needed. If that happens to be Detroit, then so be it, they deserve happiness too."

"I wasn't saying they don't."

"Anyways, Africa is probably next, but I want to find something to do here for the time being," he said.

His mother pointed to the television. Isaac was getting tired of television. All he ever watched on it was news now, and that was never good. On it, the news was continuing their coverage of his father. They were milking every angle they could. There was a group of "experts" on the screen right now talking about his legacy. Four in total. The host, just making sure they didn't argue too much, a fat white man who was arguing against everything Isaac's father stood for, an obnoxious black woman who was doing more harm than good, saying "boy bye," every time someone disagreed with her, and a white woman who was the walking definition of a contrarian. After the experts were done talking, they did a piece on the life of Dr. Eckspo. Isaac saw his face multiple times, but they skipped over him quickly. His mother too. Instead, the focus was on Gabriella. His blood boiled because her murder didn't garner this much attention when it happened. The piece last for almost thirty minutes. They had videos of Gabriella at dancing recitals. Pictures that only the family had.

"He must have given those to them," his mother said. "The old man was prepping his farewell tour."

Isaac didn't say anything.

"Someone contacted me about setting up a funeral," she said a couple of minutes later. The panelists were back on television, arguing like children.

"Are you going to be involved?" he asked.

"I wasn't going to," she said. "But I think you should be."

"I planned on going," he said.

She shook her head.

"No, not as Isaac, as Mystic Man. This could be the next step for you. You could speak at the funeral. About the state of America, race, politics. Isaac, if you want to bring a puppy on stage and pet it for an hour people would be interested. You have a great chance to make some changes," she said.

He thought about it for a second, but he didn't need to think for long. She was right in every way. Isaac had no idea what he was going to say though. He wasn't going to get up there and honor his father in the comedic way the news was, but he wasn't going to discredit all the work his father did either. Because some of it, saved lives, changed policy, and gave people hope. And that's what Mystic Man was all about. Hope.

"It's a really good idea," he said.

His mother pretended to flip her hair with confidence. Well, the confidence was there, but the hair wasn't. Still, Isaac admired how graceful her gray hair looked. Not many women could pull the look off. He wasn't sure if she had a choice, but she still made it look good. He got up from the chair, kissed her on the forehead and walked towards the door. Then, he laughed.

"Would it be okay if I leave my car here?" he asked.

"Why?"

"Now that you know about my powers, I kind of just want to teleport home. Traffic is no fun on this part of town," he said.

"That's fine, just don't be poppin' up in here whenever you want. I may be naked," she said.

"I promise to always use the front door," Isaac said laughing. He waved goodbye to his mother and seconds later, he was in his lab, staring at the Mystic Man suit on the wall.

CHAPTER 11

It had been a few days since Isaac visited his mother. He didn't do much except research. There were talks of riots happening during the funeral. A local KKK had planned on marching, and the San Francisco chapter of Black Lives Matter planned to attend as well. Isaac didn't want anyone to get hurt. He announced his presence at the funeral yesterday. His mother got involved and told the group hosting the funeral that Mystic Man would be the only speaker. Well, she didn't say Mystic Man, Isaac didn't think it was the right time, or of the upmost importance that people knew his superhero name. Although he was getting tired Mr. Purple and all its variations.

The wind was strong at the top of the building he was standing on. His cape was making violent noise as it flapped in the wind. If he wasn't so far away, people would have heard the cape and his entrance would have been ruined.

Why the hell am I making an entrance, anyway?

It was his mother's idea. Isaac thought sitting in the crowd would humanize him to the rest of the crowd. She wanted him to maintain his god-like presence in front of vulnerable people. She told him the last thing they needed was to feel powerful in front of him.

"She's right, you know," said a voice. It was Erasmus. He appeared on top of the building next to Isaac, wearing his usual ruler-of-Earth getup. Isaac always laughed when he first saw Erasmus. The man was nice, respectful, and the closest thing to God, but his royal clothes made him look like he was straight from a video game.

"Always listening to my thoughts?" Isaac asked. He knew Erasmus didn't, he would have sensed him, he just didn't have anything better to say.

Erasmus must have known that because he didn't answer. He just walked towards the edge of the building and stared at the ceremony.

"It's a beautiful funeral," he said. "Where I'm from, they're a lot more extravagant, but I enjoy this. Extravagant isn't always better."

"You count beauty as the KKK members sitting in the back with their racist signs?" Isaac asked.

"I wasn't really looking at them, but no, I don't," Erasmus said. "When are you going down there?"

"My mother is going to introduce me here soon. I'm listening for my cue," he said.

"Do you have a speech prepared?" Erasmus asked.

Isaac shook his head.

"Coming straight from the heart, huh? For most, that's dangerous and asinine, but for you, I think it's perfect. What are you going to talk about?"

"A little bit of everything I guess. I want to turn everyone's attention to the Pinnacle, well mainly, the neighborhoods outside of the Pinnacle. No one is doing anything about them. Maybe if I can raise awareness some of these billionaires will take some much-needed action," Isaac said.

"Bold move. Turning your attention from the corruption in the police department?" Erasmus asked.

"No, it's all connected," Isaac said.

"Most of those billionaires have stake in the Pinnacle though. Any words you say to this crowd today may be lost among the masses."

"I have a feeling I don't have any friends in the Pinnacle anyway."

"That's probably true."

"And besides," Isaac said, "There are plenty of men and women with money who don't have stake in the Pinnacle. Athletes are the main one. If I could reach out to them, maybe we can do something."

"You looking to corral the black ones?" Erasmus asked.

"Doesn't matter to me. The neighborhoods affected the most by the Pinnacle are black ones, but anyone can help. Silly to leave out others because they aren't black. But, yes, I would like the black ones to be the main ones who contribute," Isaac said.

Erasmus chuckled.

"What?"

"Even when you're talking about race, you don't stumble over your words," Erasmus said.

"You're proud of me?" Isaac said in a sarcastic tone. Erasmus didn't answer though, he just pointed to the funeral.

"You're up," he said.

Isaac almost didn't want to go now. Erasmus was right about one thing. Isaac's message could get lost here amongst the anger. There were the blatant racists who still saw black people as monkeys, and there were the people who idolized his father. To them, he was up there with Malcolm X and Dr. King. If Isaac didn't spend his time praising his father, he'd be called a sellout and the court of public opinion wouldn't allow him to get his message across. Now, when he was mere seconds from teleporting to the stage next to a coffin that his father was laying in, he wished he had prepared a speech.

— ·· — ·· — ·· — ·· — ·· — ·· — ··

When he landed on the stage, everyone fell silent. He decided not to teleport because he wanted people to see him coming. As he stood there, no one made a sound, everyone just stared at him. It was a beautiful day outside and the birds could be heard at least a half mile down the road. It was that silent. Until one man, in the white supremacist section, broke the serenity.

"Fucking nigger!" he yelled. Instantly, the crowd erupted, the men closest to him got out of their seat ready to fight. Security was there though. They separated the men. The once calm scene had turned into chaos. Everyone was shouting something at Isaac now. Not really at him, but they were voicing frustrations. Some people were complaining about his presence. "We don't need you," was a common phrase he heard in the mayhem. "You think you're better than us?" That was another common question. Of course, it wasn't a question that anyone wanted answered, they just wanted to vent their frustrations with everything that was going on. That was fine to Isaac. He was more than happy to be the crutch for people to lean on.

The uproar finally calmed down and people became silent again. Isaac scanned the crowd. He didn't see much, just a bunch of people who either cared about his father too much or hated him. There was a bevy of people on their phones though. No doubt on social media, tweeting and streaming his speech as he gave it. Some might just quote with no context, others might try to interpret his words on the spot. Either way, he knew he was about to be meticulously picked apart by people who would lick a goat if it meant they'd double their following overnight.

He looked out at his mother. His lenses were up, so no one could see where he was looking. She was beautiful, wearing her best clothes, and he knew it wasn't for the funeral. Having the support of his mother meant everything to him. He took one last look at her, took a deep breath, and began speaking.

"I see a lot of different people out here today," he said and as he said it, he saw everyone look up. Everyone. Racist men holding their white genocide signs, teens who gave him thumb cramps by just watching them text, and the uninterested blacks in the back who look like all they wanted to do was play basketball. Isaac had their attention.

"Different isn't a bad thing. I know it's a cliché saying about America, but there so many different people here. Look around you. Look to your left, look to your right, and look a few rows beyond your group. You might not like what you see, but the fact is that *this* is our reality. I wasn't expecting this many people to show up for the funeral of Doctor Eckspo. I didn't think I'd show up. But, the main reason I decided to come today was to appreciate a man who fought for what he believed in. And that is something I cannot ignore."

No one said anything. No one moved.

"Sometimes, we go overboard with what we believe. Sometimes, it's hard to know what to believe. But when you find that one thing in life that's worth believing, you want to hold on to that with your life. And that's understandable. Life isn't fun sometimes. Society telling you who you should be, how you should dress, what music you should like, how you should talk. When you find something that you, as an individual believes in, it's almost a euphoric feeling because no one can take it from you. That's the type of man Dr. Eckspo was. For years, he fought for the rights and liberties of black people in America."

The white men in the back began to boo. The rest of the crowd became restless. Isaac wasn't going to tolerate the disrespect this time. He held his hand up. Everyone eventually fell silent.

"Now, when I first stepped on this stage, I was greeted by the word, 'nigger'. I don't believe in saying that word in my everyday life. I also don't believe in the hostility you hold for black people, including me. I'm not an alien. I grew up here in the United States. I understand the struggle of black people and it's something I truly believe in. Your beliefs, your convictions won't allow you to stay silent when a black man is speaking about racism. That's a problem. When you called me out of my name, I managed to disregard my personal, core beliefs and let you have your moment to 'Let me have it.' But, do you see the problem with you not being able to disregard your beliefs like an adult? The conversation advances nowhere. It's stuck in a sinkhole so deep, that humans become animals. We start to act on instinct. I know you may be proud of your actions but let me tell you as a human being first, it's appalling."

Everyone else applauded. Isaac wasn't finished though.

"Dr. Eckspo fell into this trap as well. We all do. I'm not here to pick sides. I fight on the side of peace and justice. Unfortunately, black people and minorities need more support than others in America, but as I said, I can set aside my personal beliefs to do what's necessary. Sir who called me a nigger, I probably would never have a drink with you, nor you with me, but trust me when I say I'd save you from certain death if I could. I'm not sure Dr. Eckspo would. He was convinced that white men were the mortal enemy of black people. He never organized any violent protests or even condoned them when they happened, but, he was a victim of his beliefs, even if they are more noble than my friend who called me a nigger."

He said that last part in a joking tone and people responded well to it.

"A noble cause does not make someone noble themselves. Our beliefs, specifically the racially and socially motivated ones, can blind us. I don't care if you're a gay rights activist, a vegan, a feminist, or a civil rights activist, there have been times we find ourselves in a position we didn't want to be in. We find ourselves saying things we might not say. But, we don't care. We don't care because it's instinct and it feels good to let your beliefs known to the world. Dr. Eckspo helped thousands of children struggling in the streets of almost every big city in America. He helped get funding to schools that have been criminally neglected by local politicians and money men. He also fought for the rights of every black citizen in America to be able to feel safe while walking down the streets of America, which still needs work, given our gathering today."

There were a lot of nods from the crowd.

"Still, Dr. Eckspo discredited the work of any person who wasn't black that attempted to help black people. He stereotyped every person who ever challenged him on his ideas and his beliefs. He criticized other black men for marrying out of their race. Didn't want anything to do with them. He discredited the work of doctors, lawyers, directors, artists, and more, all because they were not black. His values and beliefs made him a great activist, but he was shielded by his own anger. I guess that's what I'm here to say today. First, decide if your cause is a noble one. Are your beliefs rooted in nobility? Or are they rooted in insecurity? I promise you, more often than not, you're going to find the answer is the latter. If they are rooted in insecurity, please just go about living your life. Do what you want, enjoy what you want and don't fall for anything. Find out what you truly believe in. And stand by it."

"But if the bloggers and journalists out there only take one sound bite from my words today, make it this. There is a fine line between your beliefs and becoming someone like my friend in the back there. Or, maybe not as disappointing and ridiculous, you become like Dr. Eckspo. Don't let your beliefs dictate how you respond as a human being. This country, and this world needs people who are willing to stand up in the face of tyranny, but also accept the responsibility that comes with the role. I don't care if you're a man in Dr. Eckspo's position or watching and learning about racism through the internet. The second you make the decision to join the cause, whatever that cause may be, you have a responsibility to make sure you don't let those newfound beliefs consume you."

Isaac could see that mostly everyone was absorbing and understanding the words he was saying. There was a man near the front though who seemed unbothered, emotionally, during the entire speech. There were others too. One of them stood up to speak.

"You dare compare the great Dr. Eckspo to that racist? You got no shame? Ridiculous!" it was a young woman. She was full of youth and life. Anger too. Isaac could practically feel the anger coming off this woman.

"If that's all you took from the words I just said, you aren't as smart as you think you are," Isaac said. Some people decided to boo.

"I'm sorry to be so harsh, but in order to come together as a people, we need to understand that everything in life isn't simple. Sometimes, there are layers that need to be undressed. Dr. Eckspo understood the system of racism better than most. He understood the struggles of black people. But do any of you remember his response during the anthem protests? It was a simple protest, and the players involved were model activists whenever they spoke on this issue. Dr. Eckspo said in an interview that the players were just trying to get more followers on their social media. He condemned them for their lack of awareness and protest early in their careers. Simply put, Dr. Eckspo believed the protest was a publicity stunt."

The woman's face softened. Isaac looked at his mother slightly. She could hardly contain her smile.

"Was the million dollars donated, a stunt? How about the countless events that were organized to spread a message of peace and equality? Or maybe the food and supplies sent to Somalia? Dr. Eckspo only allowed certain black men and women in his inner circle of activists. His beliefs muddled his view on a clear black and white issue. There was no grey area in the anthem situation. But selfishness and personal agendas made not only Dr. Eckspo, but a number of other black figures speak out against the athletes. No man is perfect. Every man, famous or not, should be spoken of truthfully when they die. Every way they've impacted the world should be spoken. Not just the positive and not just the negative. When a man of Dr. Eckspo's importance dies, we must learn. He died for a reason that is deeper than hate. It's because we refuse to relinquish our beliefs, and it's killing us. Mentally and obviously physically. I promise you all here today, while I'm alive, I will only continue to evolve my beliefs and become a better person. I owe that to Dr. Eckspo. I owe it to this gorgeous planet. And I owe it to myself. I owe it to you."

He stepped back, signaling he was done speaking. The was a small ovation and within seconds it turned into a roar. Everyone was clapping, including the apathetic teens and racists. Isaac couldn't believe it. His mother was clapping the hardest. All he wanted to do with this speech was make her proud. The ceremony concluded soon after that. Isaac, by himself, carried the casket to its burial place. To the citizens of San Francisco, some random black man with superpowers was putting Dr. Eckspo to rest. If only they knew it was in fact his son. Isaac wasn't a literary person, but he figured this was probably the definition of irony. If it wasn't he didn't care. It was something amazing and something sad at the same time. As he laid the casket in the ground, people started to leave. Isaac decided to stay and meet as many people as he could. There were a bevy of celebrities at the funeral. Singers, actors, athletes, politicians, and some of the world's most famous activists. Dr. Eckspo's reach was certainly worldwide. But, Isaac knew he was the real reason most of these people came. Every time someone shook his hand, they examined him thoroughly, trying to figure out his identity. One lady requested a hug and tried to "accidentally" knock his mask off. It made Isaac laugh more than anything.

The sun was starting to set when he shook his last hand. There wasn't much left to do now, but he wanted to stay at the burial for a bit longer, of course, that meant news media not far behind him, but he didn't mind that. Mystic Man wasn't meant to be a personality.

Isaac had no plans on showing off for the cameras, doing crazy stunts, or saying something controversial. If they wanted to take pictures of him standing next to a grave, that was fine. Isaac's patience was greater than their need to get a good story. After about an hour or so, everyone was gone. Isaac saw this as a perfect opportunity to try his newest power.

Over the past few months since acquiring powers, Isaac had become fond of meditating. He wasn't sure why but meditating always put him in a great mood. Through meditation, he discovered a new power that Erasmus hadn't told him about. Isaac had seen Erasmus do this once. It was when Isaac almost killed himself that night with the police officer. It was a sustainable force field. Sitting down next to his father's grave, and staring at the sunset over San Francisco, Isaac closed his eyes began channeling energy. The energy started small at first. In his stomach was where he felt it. Soon though, it manifested outside of his body. A bright, purple force field was around him. Isaac's eyes remained closed and he felt extremely calm for the first time in a while.

The thoughts circling around his brain varied. The majority were happy. Sometimes, a negative thought would make its way to the front of his senses, but he was able to block it out. Isaac felt light when he meditated. He felt like a purple feather flying over the city. Every time the air changed course, so did his mind. Every smell, every sound, every movement could be felt. And not just in San Francisco. Africa was on his mind recently. The purple feather had been there multiple times. Witnessing the horrors of terrorists who claimed to be warriors of God. Hearing the screams of women as they watched their husbands, their faithful, loving husbands, being butchered like animals. Severed limbs outnumbered people. But he also felt the love of the people. Other spirits, other men enabled by those spirits. Love was plentiful in Africa. It was plentiful around the world. Isaac felt the love in places such as Russia, Australia, and Mexico. The feather continued its journey across the world until Isaac reached a higher level. It had only happened once, and it was on accident. Colors he had never seen before, worlds without a single human, but filled with life. New governments and new cultures. Isaac was witnessing the birth of civilization and a civil war at the same time. Both light years away. Both helping the universe balance. Helping the universe become complete. It was beautiful.

Isaac wanted to cry. The fusion of his soul and the universe gave him a happiness he hadn't felt since Alisha was born. It ended soon though. Isaac couldn't maintain that state too long. He let the energy release and opened his eyes again. A poetic sunset greeted him. He closed his eyes again. Not to meditate, but to just take in the air of the city. Even with the dirt, and smells of the city, Isaac could smell flowers being cut miles away. He could smell pies being made and put on window sills. The smoke of a grill massaged his nose as well. The family was having a barbeque. Everyone was happy.

More smoke.

Isaac opened his eyes. This wasn't joyous. There were hardly any lives near this smoke. The ones he did sense though were--- dead. Isaac jumped to his feet. Scanning the city for a sign, he finally noticed, in the distance, a building smoking. It would have been easy to miss. No one had called it in, there were no firefighters on the scene. Isaac closed his eyes again. He focused and when he opened his eyes he was in front of the building. It was a research lab. It was a lab that he had worked at before starting Science Supreme.

An elderly couple was watching from their window. The fire was spreading now. It lit up the sky and people were starting to take notice.

"Someone call the fire department!" he yelled. He saw people begin to pull out their phones.

Something was blocking him from setting a teleportation spot in the building. He didn't want to teleport directly into the fire. Not because it would hurt him, he just didn't want to startle any civilians that were inside. So, he decided to break open the front door. The fire was uncontrollable now. He tore off the door and fire roared out of the entrance.

"Everyone stay back!" he exclaimed.

Isaac used his cape to cover his face. It was difficult to see anything.

Let's see if anyone is here, he thought. Isaac began flying through the different floors, searching for anyone. He found a total of five people. It was past normal work hours, so he didn't expect to find many people. The ones he did find though were no doubt staying after hours to work on their projects. Isaac teleported them outside. When he rescued the 5th person, the fire department was on the scene. One of the firemen approached him.

"Anyone else trapped?" he asked.

"I don't think so," Isaac said. "I'm going to check the building one more time though, just to make sure."

The fireman nodded, and Isaac was back in the building. Something instantly drew his attention. There was life on a floor above him. He teleported and began searching. This floor wasn't like the rest though. It was a floor filled with containment chambers. The workers here probably used it to house dangerous experiments, whether it was a chemical or an animal. The fire couldn't penetrate the chambers that were sealed. Isaac continued to search but he couldn't find anyone. Then, a faint noise could be heard from one of the chambers. The fire was thick around this area. Isaac noticed that certain areas of his suit were starting to chip away under the pressure. Which was weird because he thought he had accounted for all types of heat. He used a force field to blow the fire in a different direction. The person was inside the chamber. He still couldn't see because of the smoke and fire, but he could see the figure of a person on the ground. They weren't moving much, but Isaac knew they were alive. He decided to break the door open, move as fast as he could and teleport the person outside. There wasn't much time. One punch should have done the trick. But it didn't. the door didn't budge. Isaac hit it again and nothing. Not even a tremble. He blasted it with energy and the result was the same.

What the hell is going on?

He thought hard about what was going on. Something was interfering with the door. That was the only the explanation. Isaac looked closer at the door. It was surrounded by a thin black smoke. The other doors weren't.

"I suppose it's time I reveal myself," a voice said.

The fire roared and the black smoke grew thicker.

"Who's there?" Isaac demanded. "Show yourself, coward."

The smoke inside the chamber dissipated. He could see the body clearly now. It wasn't a worker, it wasn't even an adult. It was Alisha.

"Baby Girl!" he cried out. She looked through the glass door and noticed her father immediately. She ran to the door and tried to open it. With everything in his body, Isaac began to pound the door and blasting it with energy. Nothing. He kept pounding though, screaming in agony. He could see that Alisha was mouthing the word "Daddy" in despair. Isaac cried out with every punch.

"Let my daughter go! You're the gatekeeper, aren't you?" Isaac asked.

"Your mentor had a very hard time finding me. Well, he couldn't find me. I just decided there's no time like the present to make an entrance."

A canister was next to Alisha. Isaac couldn't tell exactly what it was, but he knew it was explosive. The thickness of the black smoke turned thin again. Isaac still couldn't break the door. The smoke took a form all on its own. It took the shape of a man. It didn't have any discernable features, but Isaac could see it creepily standing over his daughter, who was terrified. Alisha fell to the ground and began to scream.

"Leave her alone!" Isaac screamed. The figure laughed. It stalked its way over to the canister. There was a long pause. Isaac couldn't watch.

"Baby Girl, look at me," he said. Isaac took his mask off and began to make funny faces and gestures so Alisha would look at him. She did. Still scared, she stood up and walked over to the door. He continued making funny faces and Alisha even laughed once. The figure sparked the canister. An explosion filled the room. Time slowed during the explosion. Isaac wasn't sure if he was manifesting a new power. He thought about doing Alisha's hair on Saturday mornings. Taking her to the park and to school. The smile was still on her face when the explosion reached her. Alisha Eckspo was then turned into nothing but ash. Sobbing, Isaac fell face first on the hot floor. The figure continued to laugh. The black smoke surrounding the door was gone now. Isaac was struggling but knew this was his moment. His mask still off, he punched the door as hard as he could. It went through the wall and into another room down the hallway. Isaac charged into the room. The figure was full now. When Isaac attempted to punch it, he couldn't. It was literally smoke. He tried to gather energy, but it was too late. There was a choking sensation in his throat. The smoke was sucking the life out of him. Isaac hadn't felt real pain in a long time. He began to seize uncontrollably, trying to fight the choking, but it was futile. The figure began to speak.

"I never knew it would be this easy to kill you," it said.

Isaac felt the life quickly escaping him. All the power he possessed was being stifled by this black figure. Just as he was about to conjure up the last bit of his strength, he looked at the area where Alisha just was. There was nothing left of Alisha Angela Eckspo now. Her beautiful smile was the last thing Isaac saw and in her final moments, he was happy it was the last image in his mind. Isaac fell to the ground. The figure took shape again. This time though it was in the shape of a human. Solid and normal looking. He carried a staff. At the top of the staff, was a ball of black energy. It was enclosed with what looked like glass. The man lowered the staff and whispered into Isaac's ear.

"Goodbye."

———————————————————————

Erasmus wasn't sure where he was at. He wasn't sure what had happened. All he knew though, was this was a place he didn't want to be. Beasts were about, creatures Erasmus had never seen before. There was no color in this place either, but it didn't appear to be completely black. If emptiness had a color, this void was that. Erasmus could move about freely, dodging beats whenever he decided to be brave enough to challenge the void, but there was no way out of this place. He tried hard to remember what he was doing before being in this place. The only thing that came to his mind was Isaac. Then, it all came back to him.

Dammit, Erasmus. Dammit! You're so stupid. He had hoped he wasn't too late. Pieces of his memory started to repair itself.

Erasmus began to remember being hit from behind by the Gatekeeper who was responsible for taking Isaac's family. Erasmus hadn't been able to find him and now, he had placed Erasmus in a beast-filled dimension with emptiness as its atmosphere. If Erasmus got back in time, he wouldn't be upset with Isaac for never wanting to speak with him again. First though, he had to focus.

This wasn't Erasmus' first time in a different dimension like this. In fact, he had studied beastly dimensions when he first acquired his powers all those years ago. When he achieved his universe jumping powers, one of the first places Erasmus went was to what was known as the Middle.

Erasmus attempted to escape. He was unsuccessful with his first few attempts. Then, he found Isaac, but was unable to teleport to him. Isaac was helping people in a fire. A fire that wasn't an accident. The presence of the Gatekeeper made Erasmus' skin crawl as he began to try and conjure a portal. No luck. Isaac had no clue that the Gatekeeper was behind this. Whoever this man was, he was skilled. Erasmus feared that he may not be a match for this person. Still, he continued to gather his energy so that he could help his friend. Isaac now was laying at the base of a door where Erasmus felt another soul enter the room. It was Isaac's daughter.

This Gatekeeper's a monster. Using Isaac's child as bait. Come on, Erasmus. Focus!

He could feel the rage in Isaac. At the same time, he could feel the life being sucked out of Mystic Man. This Gatekeeper was using Isaac's rage against him, baiting him into a fight he knew Isaac wasn't prepared for.

It's my fault. I should have found him sooner. I should have learned where he got his powers from. I should have done something. Should have told Isaac the truth. Dammit, Erasmus. Focus!

Isaac was near death. His daughter's spirit was long gone now. No doubt that meant death. Erasmus could feel his skin beginning to rip as he tried to break free from this void. Slowly but with every passing second, Isaac was dying. Then, a yellow hole appeared in front of Erasmus. He knew he had to be quick.

It's about time, he thought.

Erasmus charged through the hole and drew his golden sword. The Gatekeeper was standing over Isaac, his staffed raised. Erasmus landed a swift kick that sent the Gatekeeper flying and through a hole in the wall. Erasmus tried to wake Isaac up, but it was no use. The Gatekeeper teleported back and swung his staff with so much force, Erasmus almost fell. But he didn't, and a sword vs. staff fight started in the burning building. Erasmus handled himself well. The Gatekeeper wasn't bad with his staff though. Every swipe of Erasmus' sword was met with a swift block. Back and forth they went until the Gatekeeper attempted to send some sort of black energy towards Erasmus. It was a smoke screen. For a moment, Erasmus was blind. When Erasmus broke the smoke screen, he was alone, but not for long. The Gatekeeper flew in behind Erasmus and tried to ram him into a wall. Erasmus teleported outside and landed in the street, his enemy not far behind.

The people of San Francisco began screaming instantly. Erasmus got up slowly and looked around. He knew the news would be all over this. Two super-people fighting in the streets of San Fran and neither one is Mystic Man.

Erasmus wanted to take the fight elsewhere, but he wasn't sure this Gatekeeper would follow. There weren't too many options. The Gatekeeper lowered his staff and blasted an enormous ball of energy. Erasmus returned the favor and blasted his own golden energy from his hand. They cancelled each other out the first time, but the Gatekeeper was raining down dark energy now. He was in the air, black energy surrounding him. This was Erasmus' first good look at him. He wasn't an old man, in fact, Erasmus was surprised at how young he looked. His powers altered his human appearance though. Whatever color his hair used to be, it was now a thick black with energy leaking off the edges. The man's eyes were solid black as well. It was an eerie contrast with his pale white skin. The clothes he was wearing seemed typical of a Gatekeeper from hell. A long black robe with markings all over it. It looked to Erasmus to be some sort of satanic language, but he wasn't sure. Underneath the robes, Erasmus could see some sort of armor as well. His moment of observation was over though as the black energy started hitting the street and ripping it to pieces. All the civilians hadn't cleared the area. Erasmus began forming force fields around the individuals stuck in the middle of their battle. Then, he began to twirl his sword like a helicopter. From that, he began to emit energy. It was so concentrated and so bright, that the Gatekeeper was forced to shield his eyes. Exactly what Erasmus wanted.

"Run!" Erasmus said to the civilians. They followed orders as the burning building began to crumble.

The Gatekeeper flew down to the ground with velocity. When he hit, he stuck his staff in the ground, causing massive cracks in the street. From it, white electricity rose from the cracks. The cars on the street started to levitate as well.

Magic, Erasmus thought. He's casting some sort of spell.

The Gatekeeper yelled something that Erasmus hadn't heard before. As it expected, it was a spell and its effect began immediately. Old, nasty hands the size of the burning building started to rise through the cracks. They grabbed Erasmus and had a firm grip. The Gatekeeper was up next. Erasmus couldn't move but he coated himself in energy. When the Gatekeeper attempted to use his staff to finish Erasmus off, the blast deflected. Erasmus began swiping at the hands from hell so that he could get free. The Gatekeeper charged in and landed the hardest punch Erasmus had ever felt in his life. It was directly in the side and Erasmus could feel his ribs crunch. He went flying down the street and landed on top of a car. When the Gatekeeper met him on top of the car, it was more sword combat.

This time, Erasmus was ready for the moves he had seen before. He could tell this man had raw power, not skill. They traded blows a couple of times before the Gatekeeper attempted to land a death blow to the head. Erasmus ducked and sliced his enemy's leg. The Gatekeeper let out a scream and tried to blast Erasmus off the car, but Erasmus was already in the air. The chase was on. They began to race through the city, energy blasts coming in with ferocity from the Gatekeeper, and Erasmus dodging every one of them. When they got close, sword and staff met. This went on for a while. Erasmus was exhausted. He teleported to a nearby field away from the city. To his delight, when Erasmus landed, he noticed the Gatekeeper was tired too. Both were holding their weapons, waiting for the other to strike. Erasmus decided to make the first move. The

Gatekeeper was ready though, he knocked Erasmus' sword out of his hands. Erasmus was quick to react though. He knocked the staff away. Erasmus enjoyed hand-to-hand combat more than anything. He didn't give the Gatekeeper time to blast anymore dark energy at him or hit him with any more spells. Erasmus was almost touching the Gatekeepers nose, landing punch after punch to his ribs. The Gatekeeper caught one punch and moved Erasmus' arm to the side. He responded with a knee to Erasmus' ribs. The knee was followed by two quick punches that knocked Erasmus back a few feet. He teleported instantly though right next to the Gatekeeper, landing his own punch that sent the Gatekeeper into a tree. They continued to exchange punches for what felt like forever to Erasmus.

Erasmus was amazed at this man's durability. Sure, he should have been durable beyond measure given his powers, but Erasmus didn't know how much he had left. They stood in front of each other, panting.

"What's your name?" Erasmus said exhausted.

The Gatekeeper was definitely a hideous man now, but Erasmus saw some quality features underneath the dark magic. He smiled a bit when Erasmus asked the question. Erasmus didn't really care to know his name, he just needed a break.

"I'm guessing you're tired, like me," he said. "Fine, my name is Theramir."

"Theramir. What business do you have with Isaac Eckspo?" Erasmus demanded.

"You want me to unveil my master plan right here, right now, huh? This is where I'm supposed to brag about my accomplishment of killing his daughter with his wife still primed? I'm not an idiot, Erasmus. My motives don't need to be explained to you right now," Theramir said.

"Fair enough," Erasmus said, "You fight well, but you seem inexperienced, so I'm guessing that you're nothing more than a hitman. After I beat you, maybe you'll reveal who has a vendetta against Isaac," Erasmus said.

Theramir laughed. Erasmus had seen evil before. He knew evil. But for some reason, he didn't sense that in this man, no, this boy. Theramir didn't seem to be older than 25. Something wasn't right about him. Yes, he had just killed the young daughter of Isaac Eckspo, and Erasmus wouldn't utter a word if Isaac ripped Theramir's spleen out, but Erasmus felt something much bigger at play.

There wasn't time to think about that though. Right now, he had a formidable opponent in front of him. Theramir walked over to where his staff was, picked it up and allowed Erasmus to do the same for his sword. Both men firmly gripped their weapons. Just as Erasmus was about to step forward and spring an attack, a gust of wind came through. Erasmus felt the energy at once and knew what was coming next. Theramir didn't though. It was Isaac.

He swooped so fast that Erasmus barely saw him. Theramir's head almost popped off his shoulders from the force. They rolled down to a nearby dock, the collision destroying it completely. Theramir was on the ground when Isaac took him by his robe and threw him down a street. Isaac teleported before Theramir could land, and he delivered a punch so brutal it destroyed the windows of all the nearby buildings. Theramir landed on top of the hill where Erasmus was. Isaac was on top of him a second later landing punches. He managed to scurry away for a moment though.

"Don't touch him," Isaac said to Erasmus.

Erasmus backed away.

"Yes, I've been waiting for this fight," Theramir said.

"This won't be a fight," Isaac said.

Theramir chuckled.

"Bring it on, purple man," he said.

"Mystic Man," Isaac said and with that he charged forward with bright purple energy around him.

— ·· — ·· — ·· — ·· — ·· — ·· — ··

Isaac could hardly see. The purple field around him was extremely bright. He didn't need to see much though. The bastard that murdered his baby girl, Alisha, was easy to see. One of the ugliest men, or rather things, that Isaac had ever seen. When Isaac went in for a punch, it landed flush, sending Theramir flying into the city. Erasmus was still on the ground, Isaac could tell he was exhausted.

"I can handle this," Isaac said to him.

"I hope so," Erasmus said. "His name's Theramir. I've never fought someone so powerful before."

There wasn't much time for talking, Theramir had hatched his next attack. The sky became filled with black smoke. It circled the city, then settled calmly around the city. Isaac could hear the people in the city screaming. He could also sense them running into each other and into objects.

"He's covered the city in some sort of smog. It's blinded everyone who's inside the cloud," Isaac said.

"That cloud is him," Erasmus said. "The dark arts are his specialty. Both of you are extremely powerful, but both of you are inexperienced. Get him out of the city, no one needs to die during this fight," Erasmus said.

Isaac nodded. He flew into the smoke.

At first, he was just as blind as everyone else. Stumbling through the city, hitting cars and occasionally people. When he got close to someone, they could tell who he was. As Mystic Man, of course, not Isaac. Everyone reacted differently. Most pleaded for him to make the cloud go away. A couple of drunk citizens threatened to fight him. One girl even offered her "services" during what they were calling the black out. No sign of Theramir though. The smoke became thinner and thinner the more Isaac searched. It was condensing into one area that was down the street. Isaac teleported there.

A shadowy figure was standing next to a building. It beckoned for Isaac to come closer. Isaac learned his lesson from last time. He decided to emit as much energy as he could so the smoke would evaporate. By doing this, he wanted to be able to tell if the figure standing in front of him was Theramir, or just another stand-in that almost killed him in the lab. The structure of the figure looked real enough. Isaac channeled his energy and flew directly into the figure. Except, when he grabbed what he thought was Theramir, the figure disappeared. Isaac tried to stop but he couldn't. He had done everything right. The light revealed the tissues and bones within the figure. Isaac went head first into the base of the building the figure was next to. The force of the blow sent a ripple through the city. Isaac teleported himself back outside the building, but the damage was done.

He dusted himself off and noticed the black smoke around the city was gone. Theramir was floating though. He was about ten feet off the ground, smiling.

"Your powers are incredible," he said. "But, I've mastered magic. It's wonderful what the mind can conjure up, isn't it?"

Isaac wanted to snap his neck. But, his trickery had worked, and Isaac didn't have time to banter with Theramir. The building Isaac had rammed was an apartment building. Isaac could sense life in the building. Hundreds maybe thousands. The building was coming down fast. Just as Isaac was about to teleport into the building, Theramir blasted him with dark energy. It almost knocked Isaac unconscious.

"Are you insane?" Isaac asked. "All of those people are going to die!"

The building was halfway down. Isaac could still save them.

"You think I care about them?" Theramir said. "You're my only target. Anyone else who gets in the way doesn't matter."

Target? Erasmus did say he was inexperienced, Isaac thought.

"Who are you working for? Who ordered you to kill my daughter?!" Isaac demanded.

Theramir clicked his tongue.

"Come on now," he said, "You don't want the whole world knowing who you are, do you? Besides, if the world finds out who Mystic Man is, they'll probably kill you anyway, especially if you let those people die."

The building was starting to crumble. There wasn't much time left.

"I'll leave you to it," Theramir said. "After this, stop what you're doing. Give up your powers and this all ends. You might even see your wife again."

Cynthia, Isaac thought.

The building was almost in pieces. Theramir disappeared and Isaac began teleporting as fast as he could. He started at the highest floors first. It must have been at his twentieth person that the building fell into nothing. In that moment, Isaac could feel the life in the building die. Over four hundred souls lost. He was on the thirteenth floor when the building crumbled. A little girl was in a corner with her teddy bear and a woman who appeared to be her mother. When Isaac attempted to grab their hands, they fell through a hole in the floor. Isaac did his best to catch them, but they fell at such a high velocity, he lost sight of their bodies in the debris. The weight of the building surprised him too. It crushed Isaac and sent unconscious.

He had wished his mind had faded away completely, but the agony of death haunted his mind. Not just death in the building. He could feel death throughout the city. A fight between Erasmus and Theramir came into his mind. Cars toppled, windows destroyed, and bodies broken from debris. Souls in other parts of the world were in pain as well. Isaac couldn't believe the irony. Not too long ago, he was sitting atop a hill experiencing the endless amount of love the universe had to offer. Now though, the pain in Africa returned to him. Pain on a nearby planet as a child was killed for something they didn't do. His energy was exhausted. He had no idea where he was, but he had no desire to get up anytime soon. Isaac let the failure overcome him. He laid in the rubble of the building, underneath a pile of bodies, and slipped further into unconsciousness.

— · · — · · — · · — · · — · · — · · — · ·

When Isaac woke up, he was worried that his mask wasn't on. He was relieved when he felt the mask and the thickness of his suit. That was the first part. Isaac knew the next part was going to be the worst moment of his time as Mystic Man. He wasn't sure how many people had seen Theramir. It didn't matter. He could sense the swarm of people outside the debris. Hiding wouldn't solve anything, and Isaac didn't just want to teleport to his home or his spot in Ireland. Owning up to his mistakes was something Isaac wanted to be known for as a hero. This was his first mistake in the eyes of the public. Running away would only turn the public against him.

The debris wasn't difficult to get off. Isaac's main concern was hurting any first responders who were trying to get people out. Slowly, he started to pull rocks off his body. As soon as he saw a light, Isaac teleported to the outside. He didn't get a good look at how many people were there, but he knew it was a couple hundred at least. They didn't look pleased with him. They began shouting the moment he appeared from the debris.

"You let those people die!" a woman screamed.

"This is all your fault"

"We don't need you in our neighborhood."

"He was trying to save those people."

"He's the reason the blackout started!!"

"Leave San Fran, purple man!"

The hate was strong. People started to surround Isaac. He attempted to speak, but the yelling was too loud. Police and EMT's tried to break up the crowd, but their efforts were futile. One man swung at Isaac and missed. Others felt empowered. Hands and feet were flying at Isaac and he didn't know what to do. The only thing he was sure of was that he couldn't use even a morsel of power on these people. As they punched and kicked, he felt every blow. And they saw it was hurting him.

"Isaac, what are you doing? I sense that your powers are gone. Get out of there, now," a voice said. It was Erasmus.

"I can't" Isaac responded telepathically. "If I leave, I look responsible for this."

"If you stay, they'll kill you," Erasmus said.

"I'll be okay."

Isaac dropped down to the ground in an effort to escape the crowd. One lady tried to grab his mask but a shock from the mask stopped her. She responded by kicking Isaac in the ribs. The rest of the crowd joined in.

"Damn you," Isaac said. "I was trying to help! If you just let me explai---" the crowd wasn't listening though.

"He's trying to get away!"

"This motherfucker's going nowhere."

"He isn't so tough!"

"You ungrateful idiots!" Isaac yelled. Enough was enough. Isaac closed his eyes as he continued to get kicked in the ribs. The power returned to him and the next kick that hit his body felt like a blade of grass. The people noticed too. Isaac didn't stand up though. He had no interest in making a speech or making some grand exit. He let the crowd continue to be furious and continue to punch and kick him. They were chanting now, although he couldn't hear what exactly. Isaac began to imagine somewhere better than this place. San Francisco had become his home over the past few years. The people were friendly, there was a bunch to do and overall, it was just a nice place. This though, this was something hideous. Isaac had seen the ugly face of humanity plenty of times before in his life. The Pinnacle, one of the most corrupt cities in the world, was mere hours from his home. What Isaac witnessed here though, was something different. The anger in their faces was palpable. He already blamed himself for the deaths of those people, he hoped the citizens would understand. How did no one see Theramir? It wasn't his battle to fight right now. When Isaac opened his eyes, he was on top of a mountain. The mountain appeared to be in the middle of a desert of some kind. It was peaceful, and best of all, quiet. It was here that Isaac finally let the emotion of the last few minutes out. Now that he had control of his powers, he wasn't too worried about doing any damage to his body. He started with a couple of healthy screams. How dare those people punch and kick him? After everything he had done? Then, he flew to the bottom of the mountain and attempted to pick it up in pure anger. Isaac didn't expect to move it at all, but it did slightly. Isaac flew back up to the top of the mountain and let out some of the strongest energy blasts fly from his body. He screamed and screamed until tears started to come to his eyes. He removed his mask and threw it on the ground. Isaac dropped to his knees and started to pound the mountain. All he wanted to do was save those people. All he ever wanted to do was see his daughter and wife again. One of those would never happen again. Alisha didn't deserve that death. Isaac continued to sob and pound the mountain. He screamed out in the dry heat of the desert.

"What's wrong with us?!"

CHAPTER 12

E rasmus first learned about meditation when he got his powers. Every man and woman who claimed to be enlightened stepped forward to try and help the new King when Erasmus took leadership. Many were fools, some were just book smart, but all of them were arrogant. The person who helped Erasmus open his mind to a world beyond his own was a man by the name of Alistair. Alistair was only about ten years older than Erasmus. The two men formed an instant bond when Alistair decided not to show up for his meeting with Erasmus. At the time, Erasmus didn't take it well. The first thing he wanted to do was teach Alistair a lesson in respect. So, he went to the man's city, all the way out in the Netherlands, and decided to speak with him. It was there that Erasmus realized he knew absolutely nothing about the power he had just acquired. The two men talked for hours. Alistair said he didn't want to meet because he truly didn't know what to say to Erasmus.

"I'm regarded in this region for being a profound scholar," he said, "but I'd be lying if I said I thought I could help you in any way."

Instantly, Erasmus knew this man possessed more knowledge than the thousands who proclaimed to have knowledge.

"What is it you study, Alistair?" Erasmus asked.

"A little bit of everything. But my main love is metaphysics.," Alistair said.

"A man of Platonic Dualism, are you?" Erasmus asked. "Or do you subscribe to the ideas of Heraclitus? Everything is fire!"

Alistair chuckled.

"More like Platonic separatism," Alistair said.

Of course, Erasmus wanted to know what he meant. Alistair began to explain the way in which he thinks the universe is organized. Well, not just one universe, but multiple. He wasn't the first man or woman to conjure up such a thought, but his key to exploring such a reality was in what he called, 'dimensional walkers.' Something he clearly believed Erasmus had become since the war.

"My theory is that the universe is somewhat like a day job for the beings we call Gods. Each assigned to their own universe where they are in complete control of how the universe functions. When it comes into being, the rules that govern it, how much control they want, etc. It isn't a game per se, but an experiment. Each universe abiding by different rules based on what that God wants." The ideas made Erasmus think harder than he ever had before. Alistair didn't have an explanation for the devil, other than that he probably doesn't cause evil things to happen, rather, he deals with evil things that happen. Mainly people. Alistair's view was that the devil was in sync with the God of each universe, and that the majority of these realties, created the stories of evil and deceit in order to give the God something to oppose.

"Fascinating," Erasmus said. "So, you think I can walk among the universes?"

"Not only that, I think you're the sole owner and facilitator of this one," Alistair said. Erasmus nearly fell when he heard those words. He couldn't fathom his brain creating people from nothing, making a hurricane to teach people a lesson, or causing a fire to arise from nothing. The only thing he noticed about his powers were the fact that they made him a modern-day Superman. Strength, immunity to disease, immortality, durability, and everything in between. Not once, did he think about his role in the universe, or as Alistair theorized, the multiple universes. Without Alistair, there was no exploring the cosmos for beings greater and smarter than himself. Without Alistiar helping him reach a state of peace and inner clarity, there would be no transfer of powers. There would be no Mystic Man.

In fact, there was no Mystic Man now. Erasmus opened his eyes. For a moment he had forgotten he was floating in deep space above Earth. For a long time, it almost used to kill him whenever he came this far above Earth's atmosphere. But now, it felt like a second home. For a place that was supposed to be silent and devoid of sound, Erasmus always heard the cries of humanity.

"I miss you, old friend," Erasmus said thinking about Alistair.

The world was screaming. Erasmus, floating almost right above North America, closed his eyes and focused on the souls of America. He concentrated, and sure enough, the words of hate could be heard, even in space. Words of disgust about Isaac and what happened in San Francisco. Thousands, if not millions blamed him for the deaths of those people. The ones who claim to have saw Theramir, are being labeled insane. News reports talked about Isaac. Every hour, on the hour. The topic of race was brought up. Many ask the question, "Can America handle a superhero, especially one that is black?" People wrote papers trying to answer the question. People argued for almost a month about it. Riots happened here and there, but nothing serious. A white scientist is jailed for experimenting on children to achieve superpowers. A white woman is killed at a white supremacist rally. The media continues to ask where their purple hero is. Erasmus' soul hurts hearing these conversations. Nothing gets solved. No one is listening to each other, people need Isaac, but he's nowhere to be found. Out of nowhere, that's when it hit Erasmus.

Theramir knows who he is, he thought. Of course, both he and Isaac knew this, but Erasmus had never given it much thought after that. But, Erasmus began to wonder how he knew who Isaac was. Doubt began to creep into Erasmus' mind. Something in the back of his mind was telling him that this man was from his past somehow, but Erasmus didn't recognize him. Even without his smoke black hair, and stone colored eyes, Erasmus wasn't sure he knew anyone who looked like Theramir, at least, he didn't make enemies with someone like Theramir. Erasmus then realized how foolish he was to assume that in his thousand plus years of existence, someone like Theramir didn't exist. It was possible on every level. Just when he was about to close his eyes again, Erasmus heard a faint noise. A voice. No, it was a question.

— ·· — ·· — ·· — ·· — ·· — ·· — ··

"So, this is why you like it up here so much?" the voice said.

"Isaac," Erasmus said quietly.

In front of him, Isaac appeared. A beard was starting to come in, and he wasn't wearing the best clothes, but overall, Isaac looked well rested and peaceful. He floated in space next to Erasmus.

"Took you no time to master deep space, did it?" Erasmus asked.

"About a week or so," Isaac said.

Erasmus laughed.

"Better than me in so many ways," Erasmus said.

Isaac laughed back and the two just sat there for almost an hour. Isaac closed his eyes and began to meditate. When he opened his eyes again, Erasmus asked him a question.

"Where did you let your mind just go?"

"There's this universe I've been intrigued by lately. Very peaceful but on the brink of war. Reminds me of Earth, but this world actually deserves saving," Isaac said.

Erasmus raised his eyebrows.

"I don't mean it like that," Isaac said. "Still plan on doing what I can here, but now, with everything that's happened, I have a new plan of attack."

"Let's hear it," Erasmus said.

"I lost my daughter. Have searched for my wife for the last month or so as well. Nothing in my life makes sense or is going well right now. I can hear the screams and the anger just as well as you can. And it hurts. Some are calling me racist since most of the people who died were white. Others are saying I'm a sellout for not being around when it really matters. Obviously, none of that is true, but I needed to look at myself hard for a while. Only so much my brain can take. I decided to rededicate myself to science. Tinkering here and there, reading scientific journals. I even made some improvements to the suit." Isaac stopped mid-sentence and began to float away from North America. He ended up right above South America.

"I was too focused on San Francisco, too focused on the Pinnacle," Isaac said. "This world, it's massive. So many different people, so many different ethical codes and ways of thinking. So many people in pain. Oppressed by governments and powers they have no hope of fighting or beating. The Pinnacle is sucking American dry right now. Soon, they'll be dealt with, but America's made it clear that they don't want me."

Erasmus chuckled a bit.

Isaac raised his eyebrow.

"I never expected you to stay in San Francisco," he said. "Your powers are growing every day. I'm starting to think even I don't fully understand them. The Pinnacle is an important step to ending corruption and attaining peace. But, I agree that it's best to move on from America right now."

"I did let them down though," Isaac said.

"Don't speak like that. Theramir has more power than either of us thought. He tricked you, and nearly took me to the brink. Things like this are going to happen, Isaac," Erasmus said.

"They shouldn't happen though. I'm a scientist. I understand this reality better than most. And now, a man from a different universe gives me unexplainable, god-like power, and I have to come to terms with the fact that I still have limits?! It's just frustrating sometimes. I thought I would be able to find Cynthia and Alisha the second you gave me these powers. I've found everything but them since then," Isaac said.

Erasmus didn't say anything. Isaac didn't either. They just continued to float in space, now above Africa.

"Do you hear it?" Isaac asked Erasmus.

"I do," Erasmus answered.

Constant civil war and chaos. No one to fight it. No institution strong enough. Yet, those people endure, in hope of a better day.

Hold on. Wait. What is he doing?

When Erasmus looked back up at Isaac, he was wearing his Mystic Man costume. He could see some of the improvements that Isaac was talking about. The suit looked more aerodynamic, but at the same time, it looked bulkier in the upper leg and bicep areas. The mask looked a bit tighter too, and the purple was more luminous than before.

"Changed the color too?" Erasmus asked. He didn't know why the brighter shade of purples on Isaac's suit stuck out to him right now, but they did. The cape too, had the same brightness, but it had a fading effect of some kind. The top of the cape, was the bright purple which was also on the chest, legs, and feet of the suit. The middle of the cape faded into the darker purple and the bottom of the cape, along with the rest of the suit, was the darker purple that the suit was before. In some ways, Isaac looked ten times more heroic than he did before with this new suit.

"Like it? I wanted to revamp my image. I'm not going to fail again, Erasmus," Isaac said and just like that he was gone. Erasmus knew that Isaac didn't need his help, but he stayed on standby in case Theramir showed his ugly face again. Instead, Erasmus allowed his mind to follow Isaac down to Africa where he landed in Nigeria. He was near a small village. Isaac landed and immediately went into action. A lady was tied to a post. A man, wearing militia gear, was about to set her on fire. There was a huge crowd around watching with about fifty men dressed in the same militia gear as the man. They were wearing black clothing with golden trimmed boots on buttons on their shirts. The man who appeared to be the leader of these men, had a pin on his shirt that resembled a tree. Isaac flew in with great velocity. He knocked the man down to the ground. Everyone in the crowd instantly screamed, and some of the other men began shooting in the air to get everyone's attention. Isaac took care of them too. He swiftly took out every soldier. Erasmus couldn't tell if Isaac was killing the men or not, but his question was answered when he saw Isaac snap the neck of one.

He's filled with rage, Erasmus thought. But he seems to be in total control of his emotions and powers. Erasmus pondered just how strong Isaac had become in this past month. How much training had he done? Or was it even training at all? Isaac seemed driven now. Not like Erasmus had ever seen before. It made sense of course. When Erasmus had found Isaac, it was during a turbulent time in Isaac's life. Erasmus could sense the hesitation every time Isaac charged his cosmic energy, and when he threw punches. He didn't hold back against Theramir, but that was uncontrolled rage. This rage, the one Isaac was displaying in this small village in Nigeria, was calculated. Isaac finished with the men, but the battle wasn't over. Just outside the village, was an outpost. By the outpost, the militia had tanks, rocket launchers, and machine guns. None of which mattered to Isaac, but the militia thought they did. Soldier after solider began to pour out of the outpost. Firing their automatic weapons, pistols, some were even attempting to throw knives. Erasmus could hear Isaac laughing a bit.

Isaac flew head first into the bullets. He then flew high enough so that they were blinded by the sun and couldn't see him. When they could see him, Isaac was hurling a gigantic ball of purple energy at the outpost. The soldiers scrambled. The ones who didn't were instantly killed. Some men started to flee, but Isaac had no intentions of leaving any survivors today. He flew down on the battle field and began taking men out. Erasmus did notice that Isaac wasn't killing these men. Some of them, but not all. Erasmus could only guess that he wanted some alive so him attacking didn't come off as completely inhumane. Or maybe he wanted to give the Nigerian government a chance to prosecute some of the men and take some credit in the terrorist group's downfall.

The tanks and soldiers with rocket launchers began to fire at Isaac now. One hit Isaac dead in the chest, but he didn't even flinch. Erasmus could sense the pure fear in the soldier who fired the rocket. Isaac did in fact, kill him, and the others firing rockets. For the tanks, there were two in total, Isaac went and picked one up. He flew it higher than any tank had gone before. Then, he descended, but still a couple hundred feet in the air. With all his might, he threw the tank down at the other tank on the ground. The impact instantly smashed both. Isaac then conjured up energy in the form of cosmic electricity and he unleashed his power on the tanks. One explosion later, and nothing was left of the tanks, the outpost, or the terrorist group that was stationed outside this village.

Amazing, Erasmus thought. Absolutely amazing.

— ·· — ·· — ·· — ·· — ·· — ·· — ··

Death was something that Isaac didn't enjoy taking part in most of the time. But he could sense the pure evil in these men's hearts. It almost felt like the evil within them was singing to him. There was no choice but to kill these men and free these people. Isaac had no intention on just flying away and waving to the people. This was an enormous act of war he just waged on this terrorist group. He had been researching them from months, even while in San Francisco. The Trees of Hope. They had successfully driven out powerful groups such as Boko Haram, and now, Nigeria, and its multitude of resources were theirs for the taking. The men Isaac had just killed, represented a small portion of the terrorist group. Isaac knew they would look to take revenge at some point, but hopefully, with the display he just showed, he had given these people some time. When he flew back over to the village, the people were still standing around the woman tied to the post. Everyone looked to be in complete shock.

About a minute passed before Isaac landed on the ground. The people instantly backed away, horror in their eyes. Isaac was confused.

"They think you're going to kill them," a voice said. It was an elderly man who appeared to be in great shape for his age. His English was a bit shaky, but Isaac understood him well enough. The man stepped forward, unafraid and with a smile on his face.

"I'm not going to hurt anyone," Isaac said softly.

"By the looks of those men out there, I'd say that proposition has gone out the window," the old man said laughing.

Isaac forced a smile. The man was close to him now. They shook hands.

"You have to forgive my people," the old man said. "That group has terrorized us for months now. The lady you saved, she was a reporter. Got a hold of one of their phones. Began reporting, recording, planned to send their atrocities to everyone in the world. They did not like that."

Isaac walked over to the lady. She stunk of gasoline.

"Let me help you," Isaac said slowly. She nodded her acceptance and held her body stiff, so Isaac could tear the rope. Once he did, he could see the tears on her face. She hesitated a moment, then threw herself at Isaac, arms around him, squeezing him tight. Isaac was surprised at first, but he embraced lady. The rest of the people around Isaac began cheering.

"Thank you," she said.

"It's what I'm here for," Isaac said. He helped her up to her feet.

"My name is Jonas," the elderly man said.

"Mystic Man," Isaac said. It was the first time he had told someone the name.

"The purple man from the United States has a name, now," the lady said. She was clearly still weak, but Isaac could tell she was filled with spirit.

The rest of the people gathered around Isaac and began asking him questions, most of them speaking a language he didn't understand. Their happiness and energy were infectious though. Isaac couldn't help but smile. The elderly man told everyone to move back.

"It's really okay," Isaac said. "I'm not going anywhere for a little while. I want to get to know everyone here."

Jonas smiled, and so did the lady.

"Come with me, Mystic Man. We owe you a feast. We'll see what we can come up with," Jonas said.

"Sounds perfect," Isaac said. He was still focused on helping the lady. He put her arm around her, and followed Jonas down the road, the rest of the people cheering in the background.

— ·· — ·· — ·· — ·· — ·· — ·· — ··

"So, your powers came from a God?" Jonas asked.

"No, not really. But a man who killed God. He's from a different universe," Isaac said.

"Fascinating," the lady reporter, whose name was Imani, said.

"I'd prefer if you didn't tell anyone that, though," Isaac said smiling.

"Of course!" Imani said with joy. "I would never. It's Jonas I'm worried about." She made a face at Jonas, who had moved into the kitchen area of the house. Isaac didn't know what these nice people had in mind for him to eat, but it sure smelled good. When Jonas returned, he carried a plate of steamed vegetables. The meat was already cooked, Isaac didn't ask what it was, he just enjoyed their hospitality. He looked around at the house he was in, it looked much better on the inside than the out. Decorative rugs made the floors come to life, and there were paintings on the walls. Some were of cities, some were of babies, Isaac liked them all though. A simple house, like most in this village, but he was comfortable here.

"I saw all of your articles and books when I came in," Isaac said talking to Imani. "What made you get into reporting?"

"Those men," she started to say. "Killed my mother and my father. Jonas here, watches after everyone in the village. Took me in when I was young and taught me how to speak English."

"I lived in the United States for ten years," Jonas struggled to say, his face filled with vegetables and meat.

Imani smiled, but continued her story.

"When they killed my parents, I remember going into the city. Lagos is not far from here. There's a library there. I looked to see if there was any information on my parents. There was, but the websites called my parents enemies of the state. Said they were a part of Boko Haram."

"I'm sorry," Isaac said.

"My parents were killed because they refused payment to those savages. They needed money to help me get medicine. They gave their lives for me."

"How old are you, Imani?" he asked.

"Just turned eighteen," she said, fighting back tears.

"Well, I would love to read some of your articles. Have you published any of them?" Isaac asked.

"No, not yet. The savages stopped me from leaving town when they suspected I had a phone. When they found out, they wanted to kill me," Imani said. She scarfed down a couple more vegetables than got up from her chair. She returned with a small stack of paper and some pictures. Isaac became nauseated at the sight of the pictures. Most were gruesome murders committed by the Trees of Hope. Isaac began reading through her articles. Jonas and Imani just watched him, in silence. Or maybe in reverence, Isaac couldn't tell which. After about an hour, he was done. He looked up at Imani and smiled.

"These are exceptional," he said. "Your voice really shines through in every piece. These men knew you were a threat from the moment you started to learn."

"They'll be back, you know," Jonas said.

"I know, and I plan on being here when they do. I'm going to help you fight this group. And I think it starts with you, Imani," Isaac said.

"Me?" she asked.

"Me," Isaac said pointing to himself, "I'm just the first step. I can't go around and destroy every terrorist outpost in Africa. The change needs to come from people like yourself. I'm just happy to help start the fire. You have to sustain it," Isaac said.

"He's right," Jonas said. "You know, she isn't the only talented young person in this village. Some of the elders have given up, they've seen too much. But the fire still burns bright in some of the youth. They can help as well."

"Perfect, we'll start tomorrow," Isaac said.

Over the next couple of days, Isaac walked around the village talking to everyone. Sometimes, about the plans to stifle the terrorist organization, but most of the time to try new food. The people of Nigeria were delightful, and Isaac enjoyed hearing their stories and their struggles. He felt a sense of calm knowing how much his presence alone impacted their lives. The youth that Jonas spoke too jumped at the opportunity to help Imani. Imani had a reputation for being the smartest person in the village. Her candor could never be silenced. Losing her in a fire would have devastated the entire village beyond repair. Isaac thought maybe that was the reason he heard their screams the loudest, deep in space.

The plan was simple. Head to Lagos and start a campaign to end the terrorist group's influence in the southern region of Nigeria. Isaac had teleported his computer and had already successfully uploaded Imani's articles to the internet. Almost instantly, people picked them up and began sharing them. Brave, courageous, gruesome, unholy, and many more words were used to describe the young girl's articles. Isaac wanted to make sure that people in Lagos read them too, in case the terrorist group had any influence in the city itself. Mystic Man planned on showing the articles and pictures to the governor himself, in hopes of getting government support in the dismantling of this group. Imani told Isaac that almost no one in Lagos believes the terrorist group is serious enough to do anything about.

Isaac teleported himself, and about fifteen youths to the heart of Lagos. There, the kids made extra copies of every one of Imani's articles. They also wrote a few of their own in the public libraries downtown. Isaac expected to be trampled by reporters and press the second he landed, and he was. It was the first time he made a public appearance in over a month. Of course, everyone asked him where he had been. Instead, he told the cameras about the terrorist group and the articles that Imani wrote. He assured them that every one of those articles were legitimate and that he had seen the group with his own eyes. One reporter asked him "Why here, why Lagos? "

"This is the start," Isaac said. "I can't be everywhere. And I know that some places, like America, don't want me. But I'm going to try my best and help those in need wherever I can, no matter your country. Today isn't about me, it's about these brilliant kids who have decided that their voices need to be heard. I'm just the megaphone they're speaking through." The reporters continued to ask questions, but Isaac just walked away, down the street with the kids. They were headed to the governor's office. Along the way, people in cars honked, more children came to walk with him, and the reporters continued to scream their questions.

This is insane, Isaac thought. But wonderful too.

The governor knew about the situation. He claimed to have known about the terrorist group as well, he just didn't want to scare the public or the world. The kids were waiting outside, while Isaac and Imani met with the governor in his office.

"That's not a good excuse," Isaac said to the governor.

"I know it wasn't, but I couldn't do much else," the governor said.

"Now," Imani said, "The people in my village, and villages across this country need your help. You have to send the government after these savages."

"I simply do not have the manpower, my child. And corruption is ripe in this city," he answered.

Isaac paced around the office. It reminded him of the time he was in Walkman's office in the Pinnacle. Then, Isaac was just another negro in the eyes of Walkman. Another pawn in the never-ending game of capitalism. A game that men like Walkman had been winning at for centuries. As he touched the pristine shelf in the governor's office, Isaac noticed the glare from his Mystic Man suit. Now, he was more than just some negro demanding justice. He was the closest thing humanity had seen to a God. And he intended to use that image to help those he couldn't help as Isaac.

"Maybe," he started to say, "If you didn't waste time on things like this nice shelf, or that elegant chair, you'd be able to see why things are going the way they are in your city."

The governor looked ashamed.

"There's still time to do right," Isaac said. "I'm all the manpower you need for now. I'll take out this group's biggest outpost. But after that, it's up to you to handle any corruption or economic turmoil you encounter. The people know. They won't let this stand," Isaac said.

The governor nodded slowly.

"Last thing. I have no idea how the budget is allocated here. But, I want to assist in financing new living quarters for citizens. Imani and the people in her village get first-priority. I know it's not going to happen overnight. But the people deserve something and it's the best I can think of that I can help with. I want it to be the best living quarters in all of Lagos," Isaac said.

"It will be done," the governor said. "I look forward to working with you."

They left the office, and instantly, the other kids backed away from the door. Isaac laughed, and they joined in. Then Imani came up to him and gave him a hug. She was squeezing him tighter than she did when Isaac saved her. The rest of the kids hugged him too.

Isaac wanted to cry, and he didn't let anything hold him back. He let the tears flow down his face as the kids hugged him tighter.

"You're the best," Imani said.

Isaac didn't say anything. He just continued to cry and think about his daughter, his wife, and how he missed their hugs. Imani was doing her best Alisha impression, and Isaac wasn't complaining.

For the next two weeks, Isaac made Nigeria his home. He had taken out most of the terrorist organization. In fact, for the first time in years, analysts were reporting that Nigeria was nearly terrorist-free. The work didn't stop there though for Isaac. He was committed to the promise of improved living quarters for Imani and her people. That involved countless meetings with politicians over zoning issues, budget allocation, and much more. He used most of the money that Erasmus had given him to start the first stages of the project. When he wasn't playing hero, he hung around Jonas and Imani at Jonas' home. Wearing the Mystic Man suit 24/7 was cumbersome, so Isaac disclosed his real identity to his new friends. He trusted them not to tell anyone, and they swore up and down they wouldn't say a word. Isaac found a peace he hadn't known in a long time while in Nigeria. Whether he was in his suit, playing with the children in the village, or dressed as Isaac, playing board games with Imani, it all just felt right. His happiness was stifled one day, when Erasmus called for him. At first, Isaac told him he'd get back to him later, but Erasmus seemed upset.

"It has to be now," Erasmus said telepathically.

Isaac got up out of bed, it was early morning, but a good portion of the village was already up. Imani was outside, doing another girl's hair. When she saw Isaac, she waved. He waved back and gestured to her that he had to leave. A worried look came over her face. Isaac mouthed the words, 'I'll be right back.' With his suit on, he flew up into the sky and when he was high enough, he teleported into deep space, where Erasmus was. But, he wasn't above Earth. No, he wasn't in deep space either. Well, he was, but Isaac couldn't believe where he found Erasmus.

When he finished teleporting, Isaac began clawing at his neck. He couldn't breathe. Erasmus was just floating there, with a smug look on his face. Isaac wanted to punch him. But, along with trying to breathe what felt like fire, there was immense pressure constricting Isaac's body. He couldn't move.

"Calm down," Erasmus finally said. "Breathe, your body is in shock, but this isn't anything you can't handle."

Isaac tried to regain his composure. He still couldn't breathe too well, but instead he closed his eyes and attempted to center himself. He decided to take a deep inhale of whatever gas he was in. Either it would burn his lungs to ash, or it would help his meditation. Luckily for Isaac, it was the latter. The gas flowed through him and exited his body. It was still painful, but he was breathing again. With breathing, came movement. Isaac began to look around. He wasn't an astronomer, but he recognized where he was at.

He brought me to Titan, Isaac thought. A moon orbiting Saturn.

Questions began to circle in Isaac's brain. Was Erasmus testing him? And if so, why? And why test him in such a dangerous way? The roar of water cleared his mind. The blue on Titan was pure, unlike anything Isaac had ever seen before. There were mountains next to him and Erasmus. And on them, it looked to be lava, but the lava was blue. Isaac knew that was a type of water. He also knew that he just learned how to breathe pure nitrogen and methane, along with some other compounds. The rain on Titan burned a bit at first, it wasn't water, but ethane and methane mixed together. Once he got used to it though, the rain began to tickle him. Erasmus seemed to be meditating, so Isaac decided to travel to the world that Titan orbited, Saturn. Saturn's extremely dense atmosphere was much greater than Titan's. Isaac was almost killed when he entered the planet's core. But, after a few minutes, he was able to overcome the planet and stand in the center of the second biggest planet in the solar system. It was impulsive, and Isaac wasn't positive his powers wouldn't fail him in that situation, but now, it was clear to him that maybe Erasmus meant this to be somewhat of a training session.

"Are you done?" Erasmus said.

Isaac teleported back to Titan, where the liquid gas continued to fall, and the mountains continued to erupt blue lava. Erasmus was still floating in the same spot.

"Why are we here?" Isaac asked.

Erasmus looked confused.

"Look at this place. It's beautiful, is it not?" Erasmus asked.

Isaac wasn't in a mood to be messed with right now, but he had to concede that Titan was gorgeous.

"You're growing in power faster than I thought you would," Erasmus said. "And truthfully, I don't know why. I gave you a portion of my power, you should be able to do only the things I can do."

"I sense jealousy in your voice," Isaac said. "And besides, I only can do everything you do. I haven't done anything special."

Erasmus chuckled.

"You just did. You just stood in the center of Saturn in less than five minutes. It only took you about sixty seconds to master Titan. Isaac, it took me months on end to master those things. You're growing at a rate I couldn't have predicted," Erasmus said.

"You say that like it's a bad thing," Isaac said. "What's bothering you?"

Titan wasn't interested in Erasmus' response. The mountain they were close to exploded with great force. The wind picked up tremendously, and Isaac could feel the rain becoming heavier and heavier.

"Let's leave," Isaac said. "Been a while since Ireland. Race you there," as soon as Isaac finished his sentence, both men were atop the mountain in Ireland where they first spoke. Where Erasmus had to contain Isaac after his run-in with the police. Where Isaac trained for months to hone his powers. Now, for some reason, it wasn't as beautiful. Maybe it was the obvious somber mood that Erasmus was in. Maybe it was because he missed Imani and Jonas. He couldn't tell, but something was different.

"I won," Erasmus said dryly, referencing Isaac's race comment.

Isaac laughed and the two looked at each other for a moment.

"Isaac, I don't know what I'm doing," Erasmus said. His voice was starting to break.

"What do you mean?" Isaac asked.

"You're doing a great job in Africa. A tremendous job, and you're doing more than anyone has for Nigeria in years. You gave those people hope, courage, and best of all, they love you. When the people of Nigeria think of Mystic Man, they don't think of a man running around in purple armor, blowing up terrorists. No, they think of someone who advocates for children literacy rates to increase and goes through the trouble to improve libraries. They think of your genius proposal to improve the living quarters. What I'm trying to say is, people think of a friend. Mystic Man is a God, but in so many ways, he's more human than they are," Erasmus asked.

"Thanks," Isaac said chuckling. He made sure not to laugh too hard, because he knew Erasmus was serious. To show Erasmus that he understood how serious he was being, Isaac removed his cowl and stood in front of Erasmus, as Isaac Eckspo.

"You don't need me Isaac," Erasmus said. "You never did. I could have done what you're trying to do for my own world, but I failed miserably. And in my shame, I ran to a completely different universe."

"Well," Isaac said. "I'm still waiting for you to tell me about that shame. But, without you giving me a new purpose, I don't know that I would have had the energy to keep on living. Suicide was a real option for me. Science is my passion. Inventing and teaching children about science was the best hobby I could have asked for. But my girls, my family? Erasmus, I could feel my spirit break when I lost them. And it snapped again when my baby girl was taken from me. But, this? These powers? They've reestablished my belief in humanity again. In my humanity, if you can believe that. I don't meet the brilliant Imani, and wise Jonas without these powers," Isaac said. He walked over to Erasmus and put his hand on Erasmus' shoulder.

"I'm guessing that in your thousand plus years of life, you haven't had many people there for you, if any," Isaac said. "Well those days are over, my friend. You taught me how to believe in something again. And I need you every step of the way in this journey."

Erasmus smiled, but it soon faded.

"What is it?" Isaac asked.

"Theramir," Erasmus said dryly.

"Yeah, what about him?" Isaac asked.

"I said that when we first met, that the rulers of the universe didn't care much about this planet. There isn't life in this solar system, and the life that's in this galaxy, humans won't be able to reach any time soon. I had been working off the assumption that Theramir was the hell gatekeeper. That his powers derived from Satan, himself."

Isaac knew where this was going.

"There is no Satan," Isaac said.

"Even worse, there is no God. Theramir's powers came from someone else. Someone not from this universe," Erasmus said.

"Someone you know?" Isaac asked.

"No. No one I know has such power. I was the only one. What's even more confusing is how he knows who you are. Powers from someone not from here, and no connection to you or me," Erasmus said.

Isaac stood there in silence for a moment. All the progress in the world didn't mean a thing if he couldn't kill Theramir. There was no other option. There wasn't a fancy cosmic prison that Isaac could send him too. Isaac guessed that there probably was actually a cosmic prison. Nothing was off the table nowadays. But, that offer for Theramir expired when he killed Alisha. Nothing was going to feel better than wrapping his hands around that psychopath's neck. Except that the last time they fought, Theramir was clearly the better fighter.

"So, Theramir has just been bumped up to the top of the list?" Isaac asked.

"You know, just as well as I do, that nothing matters as long as he's out there, and knows who you are. He hasn't released that yet, and I don't know why," Erasmus said.

"That might not be what he's after. After all, I am the only superhero with this type of publicity. The other ones you told me about are myths in their cities," Isaac said.

"They're far from myths, but I get what you're trying to say" Erasmus said.

"The girl in Atlanta, she only has enhanced strength, right?" Isaac asked.

"Right, and I thought her combustion powers came from the last Gatekeeper but, now we know that there's no such thing here," Erasmus said.

"Interesting," Isaac said. "I won't bother her, though. She more than likely won't be able to handle Theramir. The one in Colombia though. You think I could recruit her?" Isaac said.

"There's little to no information on her, but from the little I've observed and read, she's ruthless. There's no limits on her power or intelligence. If she physically couldn't fight Theramir, I have a feeling she'd be a tactical asset," Erasmus said.

Isaac took a deep breath. The air atop the Irish mountain almost made him choke, instantly, he missed Titan and the nitrogen tickling his nose. The blue lava, the rain, and the thunderous storms. Isaac wanted to go back there, so that's exactly what he did. He put his hand on Erasmus shoulder and teleported hem back to the moon orbiting Saturn. When they arrived, Isaac took off in the air, trying to challenge his speed and endurance. Why he was overcome with such emotion and joy, he wasn't sure, but Titan was the only place he wanted to be. His cape made loud flapping noises in the air, and when he looked down at his arm, he noticed how his new suit shined as the rain fell on it. When he finished, he found Erasmus near the same mountains they were at before. He had his legs crossed and eyes closed. Isaac decided to join him.

While meditating, Isaac began to think about his family. Not just his girls though, this time he thought about his father, his mother, and his baby sister, Gabriella. The memories weren't filled with too much pain or happiness, they were just memories. One was about the time Gabriella learned how to ride a bike, another was the time Isaac could hear his parents arguing downstairs. He focused and let his mind wander to Earth. There, he found his mother. But she wasn't at home. No, she was at the cemetery. She was visiting Isaac's father. Atop the same hill that Isaac meditated on before his battle with Theramir, Rose Eckspo held flowers in her hand. Slowly, she set them down and began to speak.

"Lord," she said. "Don't take my Isaac away from me."

He shuddered at her words. There was pain in them, but more importantly, fear. Isaac could feel the fear in his mother. That fear amplified as she walked over to two new headstones near her husband. Isaac couldn't make them out at first, but when he did, he almost cried out in agony. Rose, his mother, had gotten burial plots for Cynthia and Alisha. She had some flowers left in her hand. She placed an equal amount where their names were. Isaac could barely breathe but concentrated enough that he could read the writing.

"Here lies Cynthia Eckspo. Wife, mother, and brilliant mind. May heaven appreciate her soul. May she continue her quest for knowledge. May she continue her quest for love."

He read Alisha's next.

"Here lies Alisha Eckspo. Gentle angel. Story unfinished, but the chapters written sing a song of true bliss and wonder."

Isaac couldn't control himself now.

"Thank you, Momma," he whispered. At the same time, Rose stepped back instantly. Isaac had let his consciousness slip into his mother's mind. She knew what was going on though. She put a hand on her shoulder and smiled.

"Anytime, baby," she said.

Isaac removed himself from her mind and continued to think about his family, this time, nothing but his girls. Every memory was positive. Out of everything Isaac missed about them, he thought about doing Alisha's hair. He missed watching SpongeBob and watching Alisha's reactions to some of the crazy things her favorite cartoon character did. The quote underneath Cynthia's name made Isaac miss her brain the most. Her intellect was unquestioned, and some of the work she did with children and disease prevention earned her an enormous amount of respect in the science community. As much as he enjoyed the physical part of their love, Isaac much more enjoyed the fact that his wife was smarter than he was.

When he opened his eyes, he noticed he was smiling a wide smile. Erasmus had his eyes open as well.

"I needed that," Isaac said.

"That's good to hear," Erasmus said. There was a stiffness in his voice, but Isaac knew he wasn't trying to be disrespectful. Isaac knew Erasmus wanted to say, 'You're going to need it.'

The rain had calmed down, but the winds of Titan continued to howl. Isaac checked the readings on his suit. Everything seemed to be okay, he reinforced the suit with a couple of layers of energy, and it glistened, showing its appreciation for the power boost. He made sure his cowl was on tight, the last thing he wanted was his identity to be revealed during a fight with Theramir. Next, Isaac put the purple lenses down in front of his eyes. He balled up his hand into a fist and felt the cosmic energy inside him. As he squeezed his fingers together, he began to appreciate the work he did on the suit. The gloves were connected to the suit, but they were a bit heavy and had twice the generating power of the entire suit. So, when Isaac charged his energy in his hands, it was twice as strong. One last look at Erasmus, and he knew he was ready.

"Are you going to tell Imani and Jonas what's going on?" Erasmus asked.

"Did that while I was meditating. They're upset, but if I live through this, it isn't the last time they'll see me. I'm not abandoning them," Isaac said. "But, Theramir, needs to be stopped. And I might need some help. I guess it's good I've always wanted to go to Colombia." Erasmus smiled and nodded. When Isaac looked up again, he was in the air, high above a city. It didn't take him long to realize that he was in the Colombian city of Cartagena.

CHAPTER 13

Walter Daniels didn't mind the sight of blood, he had seen too much blood during his life, but he always hated seeing his own. This was the longest he has ever tasted his own blood too. The iron taste had long migrated, and a new, sulfuric taste had taken its place. Still, he spat in hopes of getting rid of the taste. No luck. Another punch came across his face. Even though each punch felt as if he was going to die, he could tell this person, no this beast, was holding back. Walter looked at his captor, and his captor smiled a cynical smile.

"Walter, Walter, Walter," a deep, ruffled voice said. The shadow of the room he was in hid most of his captor's face, but he knew whatever was beating him to death, it wasn't human.

"Have you learned nothing from your days as a political terrorist?" the voice asked.

"What?" Walter asked weakly. He had no idea what this demon was talking about. Then, suddenly, he understood. When he understood he closed his eyes and laughed a bit.

"Don't pretend to not know what I'm talking about!" the voice said. Another punch came across his face. This one, broke his nose, and the pain was almost too much for Walter. He screamed out, and his captor laughed louder than before.

"Your will to go on, by some, is seen as heroic, Walter. Myself, I see it as an annoyance. A bug that doesn't know its place," the voice said as it raised its fist, for another punch. But, someone, or something else stopped it.

"There's no reason to kill him, at least not yet," the second voice said. It sounded just as demented, but younger.

"Do not tell me what to do," the older voice said. "If I wanted to kill him, I'd do it already."

Walter had an idea of who the older demon was, but he wasn't one hundred percent positive. The younger one stepped into the light. He clearly didn't care about being seen. For a demon, or whatever he was, Walter noticed some good features about the young man. But, those features were soon forgotten when Walter almost vomited at the sight of his solid black eyes. No white, no pupils, just black. They almost looked like stone. His hair looked like it was on fire as well, but the fire burned black. He was wearing a long black and silver robe too, with some markings on it. Walter didn't recognize any of the symbols. He carried a staff with him as well. Atop it, the same black flame that was his hair, sat on the staff. It wasn't moving much, but when it did, Walter felt uneasy. The young man stood next to Walter, eyeballing him. Then, he looked back at the other demon standing in the shadows.

"What do you want with me?" Walter asked trying to get some answers out of them. But neither answered, and they didn't hit him either.

"If I'm not back tonight for room check," Walter started to say, but the young man cut him off.

"There's no need to worry," he said. "We had a productive conversation with the Russian government. And by productive, I mean we threatened to send him to a different dimension if we couldn't have you. You'd be surprised at how fast they gave you up after that. And just for good measure, we sent one of them to a different dimension anyways. Just until we get what we need from you."

These idiots love to talk, Walter thought. Then again, most evil men do.

"So? Are you going to tell me why I'm being held in this room against my will? Why you're beating me senseless?" Walter asked.

"Do you know an Isaac Eckspo?" the older demon asked. His voice cracked at the end, Walter could tell he was mad.

"He's the son of my good friend Dr. Eckspo, who was murdered not too long ago, but I don't know him," Walter said. "I haven't seen Isaac since he was a baby."

Since he was a baby, Walter thought. Oh my God.

"Isaac is Mystic Man, isn't he?" Walter asked.

"You didn't know?" the older voice asked.

"No, not at all. I had a whole list of people, but he wasn't on it. It makes sense now, why he wasn't at the funeral. I just thought he didn't much care for his father. I don't really blame him," Walter said.

"Your eye for detail is unmatched, Walter," the older voice said.

Walter chuckled.

The older demon attempted to strike Walter, but again, was stopped by the young man.

"My name is--- Theramir," he said. "We've been watching you and your reports on your computer. You seem to be the only person with an idea on where Isaac is."

"Me? All I've done is type of papers about him as a symbol and what he means to the world," Walter said.

"Precisely, and in your most recent paper, which you haven't published yet, you talk about all the other places, Isaac would go next. And given your knowledge on the state of the world, we wanted to know if you knew where he was going next," Theramir said.

"Wait a minute, Mystic Man, not Isaac, was in Africa for nearly a month. Why not attack him then?" Walter asked.

"He's growing," the older voice said quietly. For the first time, Walter heard fear in this creature's voice.

"During his time in Africa, he was anticipating us. His power levels were at an all-time high and his will to protect those people would have outmatched us. We need to surprise him, and we thought you'd be the man to help us," Theramir said.

"Evidently not," Walter said. Theramir hit him this time, and Walter fell to the ground in immense pain. While on the floor, the cold concrete made him shiver. He thought it weird, that with everything going on, his life likely to end here, he focused on how unbearably cold the floor was. He closed his eyes and waited for these two creatures to finish him off.

"This was a complete waste of time," Theramir said.

"Maybe not," the older voice said. "This man, would have been his strongest ally, other than the warrior you fought. Now, we know Isaac is alone. There's one person left on this planet he cares about. We take her away, he'll truly be alone."

"His mother," Theramir said softly.

A loud swooshing noise came, and Walter guessed the older demon was gone. Theramir remained. He walked next to Walter and picked him up. Walter could hardly breathe. Theramir pointed his staff at Walter's chest. Walter could feel the life being sucked out of him, and he wasn't sure if Theramir was doing anything. The ball of black energy began to pulsate. It was mere inches away from Walter's chest. He wanted to faint and escape whatever pain was coming, but that was cowardly. In all his years as an investigative journalist, Walter had faced death many times. This was the third time he'd been captured. Trying to avoid death now, when he welcomed it so many times before, would have made his entire career a fraud. It would have made every time someone commented on his courage false. No, Walter knew that opening his eyes, and facing his sentence was the way to go. Even if he was unsure about what exactly was going to happen.

The next second seemed to go by for hours. Theramir began to utter some sort of spell, but right before he finished, Walter remembered being instantly teleported from that dark room, back in his bedroom in Russia. Walter figured it only took a millisecond to get from one place to the other, but the whole ordeal felt forever. When he looked up, it was none other than Mystic Man in front of him. Walter couldn't believe it. His purple suit looked more impressive in person. It looked like armor in a way but looked as if it allowed for great swiftness. Mystic Man smiled when Walter looked at him. Then, Walter snapped back into reality.

"Isaac," he said. "Don't worry how I know who you are. The one called Theramir is on his way right now, to kill your mother!"

Mystic Man frowned and stood there for a second. He then nodded in agreement.

"Thanks," he said. And he was gone.

Walter laid on his floor, exhausted and struggling to breathe. He knew he needed medical attention but laying on the floor, in his blood-soaked clothes, was all he was going to get at the moment.

— ·· — ·· — ·· — ·· — ·· — ·· — ·· — ·· ·

3 Hours Earlier

Finding who he was looking for in Colombia wasn't hard for Isaac. Just like Erasmus, he could sense certain energies. Whether it was her powers, or the pureness of her soul, Isaac couldn't tell, but he knew exactly where this secretive hero was. Since he knew that, he decided to walk around the beautiful city of Cartagena. Africa's heat was sometimes unbearable, but this felt like Florida. He was close to a beach. The second he started to walk on the sand, people began circling around him. Some children, some adults, and the media soon after. Most were nice, but Isaac could sense the hostility in others, more so then he did his first time walking the city in Africa. One reporter asked him what he was doing in Colombia. Off the top of his head, Isaac didn't have some savvy political response, so he answered truthfully.

"I just want to experience this beautiful city for the first time," he said in Spanish. He was fluent. The reporter thanked him, even though she looked disappointed in his answer. In time, people went on to do their own things. Isaac had gotten used to being in one spot for a long time. He wasn't sure how much time had passed since he first stepped on the beach. An hour? Two? He didn't care. When he finally decided to get up, he pulled up some news readings from his suit. The display on his wrist appeared as a hologram and showed both print and video. Isaac was particularly interested in things about him. Had the world begun to accept him again? To his surprise, the answer was yes, except in America. America was still ripe with racial divide since the recent police shootings in his hometown of San Francisco. Most of the articles he found on him regarding the city talked of abandonment. Across the ideological spectrum as well. Democrats and Republicans both believed that Mystic Man promised to focus on America and broke that promise at the first sign of trouble. The articles supporting him were well-written and made great points, but they were drowned out by the noise. Of course, this made him sad, but even more, he couldn't help but notice that not a single person was talking about his first fight with Theramir. People wrote article after article on Erasmus' fight with him prior, but no mentions of Isaac's encounter.

I suppose it's my fault, he thought. I portrayed myself to be mightier than them in every single way. And while my powers grant me gifts they could only dream of, I still have the naivety of a man. That'll never go away.

Images of his encounter with the police officer began to enter his mind, but he calmed himself down and continued to read news reports.

World news was next. Tons of areas needed his help. Theramir needed to be defeated as soon as possible, so Isaac could help these people. Syrian death tolls in their civil war continued to spike, coups in South America, and Africa continued to be a home for corruption and war. Nigeria was in the news, but for something positive. Imani was writing a book about her time under the boot of terrorism and how the world could learn from her experience. Isaac smiled. There wasn't a doubt in his mind it would be a best seller.

His joy was cut short though, when a weird feeling overcame him. That energy he detected before. It was growing weaker. Why though? Isaac knew what powers he had, but when trying to figure out how they worked, the scientific method didn't always help him out. Most of the time, he just chalked it up to magic or some high form of science. Maybe they were the same thing. But he could feel her energy dwindling down to nothing, as if she was dying. If he didn't teleport to where the energy was, he'd never have a chance to talk with her about Theramir. Isaac focused and within seconds, he was standing in a dark room illuminated by monitors.

He counted at least ten, but there were definitely more. The room wasn't much. To him, it looked like some sort of lab. There was a table on the right of the monitors. The table had an assortment of gadgets as well as knives, and guns. Isaac couldn't even see a door, so he was wondering how whoever was in here, got in here. That's when he saw her, and that's when she heard him. Isaac attempted to step forward, out of the shadow he was standing in, but the girl, with her back to Isaac, spoke first.

"I know you're there," she said in Spanish. Her voice was soft, but Isaac could sense the seriousness, no, the toughness in it.

"Please," Isaac said, "I just need to talk to you."

The girl was sitting in a chair. He couldn't see any part of her except the top of her hair, which appeared to be pink and orange. Her fingers were furiously typing something, the monitor displays were changing every few seconds, it was very disorienting to Isaac.

"You're very proficient with technology," Isaac said. "I don't mean to brag, but I'm sort of a scientist, myself." He attempted to laugh, but the unnerving calmness of the girl made that feel like a huge mistake.

She didn't move an inch.

"I will kill you, if you do not leave," she finally said. Whatever she was doing on her monitors appeared to be done. Now, she was watching what appeared to be a sitcom. Isaac didn't recognize it.

"I don't pretend to know everything about people," Isaac started to say, "but you seem like you need a friend. Believe me when I tell you, I don't want to hurt you, or bring any type of harm to you. I think I might need your help."

There was a long pause. The sitcom continued. Isaac didn't have many options, so he decided to watch. The father in the sitcom was the main character, and his kids were all obnoxious, but intelligent. Isaac continued to watch, and so did the girl. The episode was about one of the children, the only daughter, getting a date for her school dance. The father ended up going with her, embarrassing her, but they ended up having a good time. It was a fairly generic show, but Isaac heard a couple of chuckles from the girl. When the credits started to roll, she paused it.

"You come into my place. Unannounced. Expect me to help you?" she asked.

"I'm sorry. But I didn't know how else to find you. I know who you are and what you can do. But at the same time, I don't know you at all, and I don't know anything about what you do," Isaac said. "My name's Mystic Man."

"I know who you are," she said dryly.

"What's your name?" Isaac asked.

The girl turned around in her chair, and for the first time, Isaac saw the face of this mysterious heroine. She was a pretty girl, Isaac guessed she couldn't be older than 20. Her skin was brown, but she wasn't dark like he was. Her hair was an assortment of colors. The top and back were mainly orange, with the sides being pink. There was purple sprinkled throughout too. She was wearing a white shirt underneath her brown jacket. There was also a bandana hanging out of her jeans. Isaac guessed that was maybe used to cover her face. The same rage and determination Isaac had just heard in the girl's voice, didn't appear to be on her face. She looked embarrassed. Isaac guessed it had something to do with her self-esteem. He felt horrible for intruding on this girl during her most private moment. It's as if he had come in while she was naked.

Her face was full. Her features were all well-defined and her lips looked soft. But it quivered as she looked at Isaac, trying to maintain that tough presence. Her eyes were a soft brown, and that's where Isaac noticed the most discomfort. She could hardly look at him, even though she appeared to be trying with all her night to look into his soul, but it wasn't working.

"Here," Isaac finally said. "I'll turn around, and you approach me however you want to."

He turned around, hoping she understood. She did and when she spoke again, that confidence was back.

"My name is Victoria," she said. Isaac turned around and her face was covered with a mask. He could see only those soft brown eyes. Everything else was covered by a mask that appeared to be a mix of metal and maybe plastic, but Isaac wasn't sure. It muffled her voice a bit, but not much.

"Mystic Man is the fancy name they call me. Well, actually, I gave it to myself but that doesn't matter." Isaac said smiling. "My real name is Isaac."

Victoria's eyes twitched a bit. Isaac had guessed she smiled back.

"Did the people of Colombia give you a fancy name?" Isaac asked.

Victoria nodded.

"The Shade of San Juan," she said. "We're by the San Juan river right now."

"I see," Isaac said. "Well, Victoria, I know that you're special. I really don't have time to explain how I know that, but I do need your help and from the looks of this room, I know how you can help me."

"How?"

"Your intelligence knows no bounds, I see. Computers are your thing, I'm guessing?" Isaac asked.

Victoria nodded.

"Among other things," she said.

"Of course," Isaac said chuckling.

Victoria just stood there.

"There's a powerful man on our planet. He calls himself Theramir. I think your mind could give me insight as to how I can beat him," Isaac asked.

"I don't want to be a part of your fight," Victoria said.

"Why not?" Isaac asked.

Victoria walked over to her monitors. She tapped a few buttons, and the screen changed. It was security footage and it appeared to be live. The camera was focused on what appeared to be some men in some sort of bunker. They were guarding a door, two of them, holding automatic rifles, while the other sat in a chair, twirling a knife.

"In there," Victoria started to say, "In there, little girls are being tortured. Forced to have sex against their will. This operation runs through my entire continent, not just Colombia. As I'm sure you know, not everything can be solved with fists. This, Isaac, is my fight. I cannot help you fight this Theramir."

"I understand that now. I think it was foolish of me to come here and assume you'd put your life at risk for someone you don't know. And what I'm asking doesn't require you to leave this room at all. No, I just want to talk to you, get to know you. I want to get to know the mind of a real tactician. How they operate, and how to think like my enemy. Do you think that's something you could help me with?" Isaac asked.

Victoria removed her mask. Isaac was happy to see her face again. He wasn't sure if she was ashamed of it or not, but she was pretty, and he was happy she felt somewhat comfortable around him.

She nodded her approval.

"I don't fully understand, though," she said.

Isaac laughed a bit.

"Trust me, neither do I. But I'm sure you're used to surviving and adapting," he said.

She smiled, and Isaac noticed that corner of her mouth was cut. He guessed that's why she wore the mask. He extended his hand and she grabbed it firmly, they shook hands for a second and continued to smile at each other. Isaac then walked over to her monitors. He noticed the men on the camera. Victoria looked up at the monitor as well. Isaac could feel the pain in her soul as she watched the men, who were literally just sitting there, doing nothing.

"I don't know anything about this," Isaac said pointing to the monitor, "but I'm eager to learn from you one day."

Victoria's face was expressionless.

"I know, I know," Isaac said. "This isn't my fight. But, I'm not a pawn for America to use. Or Africa. I go where I'm needed most, and it looks like Colombia needs help."

"I am helping," Victoria said dryly.

"I didn't mean to imply that you weren't. All I'm saying is that we're in this together. You may think you are the only one who cares for the girls inside that room, but you're wrong," Isaac said. "I'm not here to tell you how to solve this problem, hell, I'm not here to tell you how to feel about these men. But, we have these abilities. I know for a fact we aren't the only ones in the world either. And there are even some on other worlds. Other universes. It's our job to stick together and help each other. If we don't, men like that will always win, no matter how powerful we are," Isaac said.

"You sound like a cheap commercial," Victoria said smiling a bit.

"I suppose I do, but I think I'm right," Isaac said. Victoria didn't say anything.

"Other worlds?" Victoria asked. "Universes?"

"Millions of them," Isaac said. "I could take you to see some one day."

There was a flash in the room, a bright light, but only Isaac saw it. Instantly, he knew he had seconds to act.

"Victoria," he said. "Or should I say, Shade. It was nice meeting you and I look forward to conversations in the future, but I have to go."

"Why?" she asked.

"Theramir," Isaac said. There was an emptiness in his stomach. Of all the times to show himself, and with such arrogance, he chooses now. The dark energy was palpable. Isaac could almost taste it, and it tasted like garbage. He closed his eyes and let the dark energy's trace lead him to wherever Theramir was. Instantly, he was in front of Theramir, some other creature he had never seen before, and an elderly black man who looked on the brink of death. He picked up the man, and instantly, saw an image of where the man wanted to go. It all happened within two seconds. Isaac was a bit nauseous from the speed of it all. He hoped the man wasn't killed due to shock. The man was on the floor but sprung up instantly as if his face wasn't bleeding, his body not broken by Theramir. This man seemed familiar to Isaac. For some reason, he felt as if he had seen this man before, but what the man said next eliminated that thought from his mind quickly.

Part Three

A MAN DIVIDED

CHAPTER 14

A s he teleported onto a street, Isaac felt uneasy. It was too silent. Isaac's powers had grown to levels he could never imagine. His senses weren't affected too much at first though. They were heightened, sure, but now, Isaac could hear everything. The sound as he landed on the street? Heartbeats. Isaac couldn't tell how many people were outside, but it was the entire neighborhood, at least. He decided to turn his voice modifier off, along with raising his lenses.

I know where this is going, he thought.

Slowly, he walked down the street. The dark energy of Theramir that had called him here hurt his head. Didn't take long for Isaac to see the damage that had been done. About fifty feet in front of him, was his mother's house. There was an enormous hole in the side of the house. Inside, Isaac could see the new demon he did not know, standing next to Theramir. Theramir was what he was focused on though. The young murderer was holding his mother by the neck. She didn't look scared, really, but there was blood dripping down her face. Isaac knew that any rash action could end his mother's life, but the thought of those monsters hurting his mother was almost too much. Slowly, he continued walking.

The people were staring at him. On some of their faces, Isaac knew that some of them had put it together. He knew most of his mother's neighbors. And they knew him. Isaac didn't see a need for his mask anymore. After he hit a button on the side of his head, the mask clicked, and he raised it from his face. When he threw it on the street, Isaac heard some gasps, some chatter, but nothing hateful. The neighbors he did know just gave him a slight nod. It felt weird. During his short time as Mystic Man, Isaac felt as if the people who got behind him, did because of the mystery of the hero. Not knowing if Mystic Man had a day job or spent his days rearranging galaxies. There was no way to know. But Isaac wasn't stupid. He knew that this was Theramir's end game. So, he decided to take at least this one thing from the monster.

One neighbor came up to him, as he continued to walk towards his mother's house. Isaac hadn't noticed until just now, but the sky was almost completely grey. He didn't know if that was the dark energy in the air, or if the forecast called for rain, either way, Isaac couldn't help but feel that this was some sort of weird symbolism.

"Didn't want to miss the show?" Isaac asked. He didn't have a humorous bone in his body right now. But what he had just said sounded better than 'I don't know how I'm going to beat these two, so you and everyone here might die.' Yeah, what he said sounded better than that. It worked too. The neighbor slightly smiled, but it faded as he looked at Rose's house.

"No," he said shortly. "That 'thing' told us to stay and watch. He wanted us to watch, before we died. His words," the man said.

"No one's dying here today," Isaac said. "I promise you that."

"I believe you," the neighbor said.

Do I believe in myself though? Isaac's brain went stagnant as he finally approached his mother's house. There was debris on the ground. As he stepped closer to the demon and Theramir, he stepped on something. It was a picture of his little sister, Gabriella. The glass cracking under his foot startled him. Theramir and the demon continued to watch, Isaac's mother continued to hang on for dear life. Isaac looked down at the photo. His sister, his wife, his daughter, the people lost in the apartment with his first fight with Theramir, the people he couldn't save in Nigeria, the people he couldn't hear in Colombia. How couldn't he hear those little girls crying for help? How? Isaac continued to look at the picture. After about a minute, he looked up at the demon. He looked at Theramir. He looked at his mother. She smiled slightly.

"My son," she said quietly. So quiet he wasn't sure if Theramir or the demon heard, if they did, it didn't bother them. They just continued to stare at him with intensity.

"I hear you all, now" Isaac said closing his eyes. "I hear you all."

"Father?" Isaac heard Theramir say.

"Shut up!" the demon said.

Isaac opened his eyes.

I suppose it's time, he thought.

"I'm glad you've taken the time you needed to prepare, Isaac," the demon said.

Isaac didn't care much about what this new demon had to say. There wasn't a doubt in his mind, this creature was just a grunt hired by Theramir.

"Theramir," Isaac started to say. "This is it. You're going to die today."

"You fool!" the demon said. Isaac could feel his energy spike. For the first time since walking up, Isaac looked at this new demon. Isaac wasn't sure what to characterize this new demon as. His body resembled a gorilla, but only in form. His face, looked almost bearded with dark energy. He looked like Theramir when Isaac watched Theramir kill his daughter. Just an ominous, dark figure. But now, as Isaac looked at him, something felt familiar. The black figure began to shift every time Isaac focused.

"Come on, son. You know," the demon said.

Isaac winced in pain. Suddenly, the energy changed. It was an evil energy that he had felt before. It overpowered him. It forced him onto his knees. The pain was almost too much.

"All the power in the world," the demon said. "All that power. All that will, and yet, you are just as pathetic as the day you stepped in my office."

"Walkman?" Isaac struggled to say. It all made sense now, except it really didn't. Isaac still couldn't stand, whatever energy Walkman possessed was draining him.

"I'd like to introduce you to my son, Jacob," Walkman said. Now, he was in his human form. Isaac looked up and saw the old man who he knew as one of the leaders within the Pinnacle.

"I'm sorry, he likes to be called Theramir these days," Walkman said laughing. His laugh was boisterous, loud, and annoying. Isaac looked at the neighbors outside. Some were beyond terrified, but the rest were just watching intently. The pain had stopped now. Isaac stood up and faced Walkman. He hated himself for not knowing the reality of the situation the entire time. Not only did Walkman possess the same type of dark powers that his son did, he was able to conceal that energy for the past few months while Isaac had his. Isaac also noticed that Erasmus wasn't around either. There wasn't a better time for his mentor to show up than now. But, Isaac couldn't sense Erasmus' presence whatsoever. Was it all a setup? Why? Why would these God-like beings set their sights on him, and no one else in the galaxy? No one in all the multiverse?

"I see your brain is running wild," Walkman said. "Trust me, this has been an ordeal for me, too. Imagine my surprise when my son tells me that he's been gifted these amazing, amazing powers. You can imagine what I said when he first came to me some months ago telling me what happened. I thought he was crazy."

There was something off about Walkman. The usual calm, and dominant man was gone. This was an erratic person in his place. Isaac could see the power was consuming him. Almost all his hair had fallen out, and his teeth were a disgusting yellow. Scars covered his hands and face as well. Instead of skin showing underneath them, the black energy peaked through. Even in his normal form, Walkman looked more demon than human.

"But, I'm a man of calculated risks," Walkman continued. "You've been a pain in my side for a long time, Isaac. A very long time."

"Walkman," Isaac finally said. He put his hands up, showing he meant no harm, at least not yet.

"I can see whatever this energy is, it's starting to rip you apart. Getting back at me for whatever you think I did to you isn't worth your life," Isaac said.

"That's where you're wrong," Walkman said. "I refuse. Refuse! To let you all of people. Become some type of hero for the world."

Walkman extended his hand towards Theramir. Theramir, or Jacob, gasped for a moment. There was a stream of dark energy flowing from son to father. Walkman closed his eyes as a smile came across his face as he absorbed his son's energy. When he opened his eyes, they were completely black. On the ground was a normal boy. Brown hair, young features, and scared out of his mind.

The pure evil that Isaac once felt in this boy was completely gone now. He was wondering if it was ever there in the first place. If Walkman could take the powers from his son with ease, then could he control him? The way Walkman spoke reminded him of Theramir's speech pattern. And the only word that Theramir spoke when Isaac arrived was father.

Rose Eckspo was still hanging in the air though. Walkman conjured a hand the size of himself. The hand was now holding onto Isaac's mother. She still looked as calm as she did when Isaac arrived. This was Isaac's chance. He teleported to his mother. That wasn't hard, but what came next was. He tried to teleport to a local hospital, but Walkman's energy gave him no room to escape. It followed his mind wherever he went. Isaac had one choice. While holding his mother, he made a force field around them and teleported wherever his mind went. When Isaac opened his eyes, they were in Colombia, on the beach where he sat before talking with Victoria, The Shade of San Juan.

"You okay, Momma?" Isaac asked.

"I think so," she said. "Where are we?"

"Colombia, I think. It was the only way I could get us out without them following us," Isaac said.

People were starting to gather around them.

"I shouldn't leave you here. I can take you somewhere else if you want," Isaac said.

"No, I'll be fine. I've always wanted to visit Colombia," she said.

"Really?"

"No, I don't even know where this country is," she answered laughing.

Isaac smiled.

"That man from the Pinnacle. I told you he was no good."

"I didn't think you meant 'evil demon' no good though, Momma."

"Basically. Stay safe," she said. "I can't lose you too."

"I will." Isaac teleported back to his mother's house. Walkman was gone, but Jacob was there. He was awake, and when he saw Isaac he cried out in fear.

"Woah, calm down," Isaac said.

"Don't kill me, don't kill me. It wasn't me. I didn't kill that little girl! My dad made me do it!"

Isaac paused for a second. This kid, who couldn't be older than 18, was out of his mind. He looked like Walkman, but instead just more human. Bloodshot eyes, yellow teeth, blotchy skin, and dirty hair.

"When's the last time you weren't Theramir?" Isaac asked.

The boy was still breathing heavy.

"I—I don't remember," Jacob said. "Last thing I remember is coming home from a friend's house one day, and that's it. I was some monster with powers. No one explained anything to me, not even my dad."

"I'm guessing he hasn't been much of a father recently?"

Jacob nodded.

"He talked about you, you know," Jacob started to say. "I've always known my dad was a racist creep. But you. You really got under his skin."

Isaac looked around his mother's destroyed house. There were still some neighbors in the distance watching. Wasn't a doubt in Isaac's mind that the entire world knew his identity.

"I think that's apparent," Isaac said to Jacob. He extended his hand and helped Jacob off the ground.

"I believe you," Isaac said. "No one deserves to be treated like this by their father. So, you have no idea how you got these powers, or if your father had them first?"

"If he had them before me," Jacob said. "He probably would have killed you."

"Fair point. You don't look too well. Let's get you to a hospital so you can get some treatment. Then maybe you can help me track down your---" A loud boom and it was Walkman teleporting. Except he didn't talk this time. He tackled Isaac and they went flying through his mother's house. Walkman had no intention on stopping. They went through another house. And another. Isaac finally gathered himself enough to teleport them away from people, but Walkman teleported them right back. This time, they were in the heart of San Francisco. Isaac went tumbling to the ground and landed in the middle of the street. The landing caused a huge pothole and a traffic pileup. People began to get out of their cars to see what was going on. Isaac hadn't been hit that hard in a long time. He struggled to stand on his feet. When he stood up, there was Walkman, floating in the air, for everyone to see.

"This is your hero. This is your Mystic Man. Isaac Eckspo," he said. The people around Isaac didn't seem to care what Walkman was saying, they seemed scared. Isaac could sense everyone's fear.

"Failed scientist, son of a terrorist, and a criminal in his own right. This man fooled you with his phony speeches and good deeds. He concealed his identity from you all because he is selfish. What do you have to say for yourself?"

Isaac was still reeling from what just happened a couple of seconds ago. He wasn't sure how this was going to end, or even if he could beat Walkman. But the one thing he did know was that no one was dying here today. All the growth in power meant nothing if he couldn't save people when it mattered most. Protecting these people was the only thing he cared about, and to do that, he started by laughing. It wasn't an obnoxious laugh, more like a chuckle.

"You sound like an idiot up there," Isaac said. "I'm not better than anyone. I don't pretend to be. Some of you from this great city might hate me for letting those people die a couple of months back. Their spirits are forever with me. But a deceiver? A liar? I'm none of those things," he was in the air now. "This man however, is one of the heads of the Pinnacle. You might not be able to recognize him because but that's Johnathan Walkman. Me and Mr. Walkman go way back. You might have read about the Pinnacle shutting down my company not too long ago. Isn't that funny? I can't explain these powers to you all, and I damn sure can't explain how Walkman got similar powers. But, what's hilarious to me is that all of this is happening because of this man's fragile ego. Outwitted and outpowered by a black man. He's a child. Nothing but a sixty-something child. Attempting to expose me as some sort of power play," Isaac started clapping his hands. He could feel Walkman's energy at an all-time high. Exactly what he wanted.

"I have to hand it to you sir," Isaac said. "And I want you all recording this to hear every word." Tears were forming in his eyes now. People positioned themselves closer to Isaac and Walkman.

"I really have to hand it to this man. His ego is so fragile. So weak that he decided to use his powers to take my wife and my daughter. Killed my baby girl in front of my eyes. And I have no idea where my beautiful Cynthia is. You have to respect a man who can hold so much hate in his heart without bursting," Isaac said.

Walkman had heard enough. He flew at Isaac screaming. His eyes closed, the dark energy swirling around him. Right before a punch landed, Isaac focused and teleported him and Walkman to his original training spot in Ireland. He didn't let Walkman finish the punch either. Isaac grabbed Walkman's wrist and slammed him into the ground as hard as he could. Isaac heard a loud thud. Noticing Walkman was on the ground, Isaac decided to try what Erasmus did to him that one night. He knew he didn't have long, or Walkman would teleport them back to San Francisco. So, Isaac put his hands up and focused his energy the best he could. Within seconds, a purple force field covering the entire mountaintop was around them. Walkman was up now and attempted to take a swipe at Isaac, but Isaac was up in the air before the hit landed. Walkman looked around at the force field.

"Interesting," he said. "But it won't take me long to get out of here."

"You want me? Here I am," Isaac said. He wasn't interested in talking with this man anymore. Nothing else needed to be said. Walkman silently agreed and the two of them flew at each other with extreme force. Their fists pounded against each other, and the vibration sent them flying backwards, but the force field was still intact. They flew at each other again. This time though, Walkman teleported behind Isaac, and grabbed his cape from behind. Walkman slammed Isaac into the ground. Walkman then attempted to elbow Isaac, but Isaac swept Walkman's feet from under him. They engaged in hand-to-hand combat.

"I was a boxing champ in my youth," Walkman started to say. "These powers enhance that by 1000."

Isaac dodged another punch. Walkman attempted to throw a right hook, but this time Isaac caught his hand. Walkman threw his left hand, and Isaac caught that as well. A surge of energy left Isaac's body and zapped Walkman like electricity. He let out a brief scream.

Isaac amped the energy up and Walkman continued to scream. Isaac could see the purple electricity beginning to go in every direction from his body. Still holding Walkman's hands, he looked down at his suit. The mini-generators he installed in the suit were whirring with excitement trying to contain the cosmic power flowing in him. Then, Isaac let the energy release from his body. It exited his body from every direction. The bulk of the energy however, hit Walkman, who went flying backward. Isaac could sense the pain the hit had caused Walkman. Isaac deactivated the force field as Walkman went flying in the air. Isaac decided not to teleport, he didn't want Walkman to trap him with some kind of dark energy mid-teleportation. Instead, he flew as fast as he could and landed a punch on Walkman. When he caught up to Walkman, another punch. Another one. One more. Walkman landed in the side of a mountain. Isaac flew with all his strength into the mountain. He and Walkman went completely through the mountain, causing it to explode. Isaac felt Walkman's life beginning to fade.

Maybe Walkman was starting to play tricks on him. Because instantly, Isaac found himself in a city. It didn't take him long to realize it was New York City. He was floating in Times Square. Walkman then appeared and flew into Isaac with tremendous force. They both landed inside a building filled with workers. Walkman was still on the floor, so Isaac grabbed him, and they teleported again, this time to Antarctica. Nothing but snow, wind, and ice surrounding them for hundreds of miles. The wind was loud, but nothing Isaac wasn't used to. He was reminded of his time on Titan with Erasmus.

"You're skilled," Walkman said. He was breathing heavy.

Isaac teleported behind Walkman and landed a punch to his ribs. Walkman screamed for a moment, then turned around and attempted to blast Isaac with a stream of dark energy. Isaac ducked it though. He grabbed Walkman and threw him across the sheet of ice. As Isaac was about to go after him though, he noticed he couldn't move. There were circles of dark energy surrounding his feet. He was trapped on the ice. Walkman teleported back in a few seconds. This time, he unleashed a flurry of punches that dropped Isaac to his knees. Then, another stream of dark energy came from Walkman's hands. He shaped this one though. It resembled a lion. Fully grown, with an outstanding mane, and teeth that appeared to be the size of Isaac. There was nothing he could do but accept the attack from the dark beast. As it scratched and clawed, Isaac was attempting to get free from his dark energy shackles.

How is he keeping me in these? If Isaac didn't answer that question soon, this dark beast was going to kill him. Which was a weird thought given how used to immortality Isaac had become.

During the chaos of the attack, Isaac noticed that Walkman was staying back, and he was chanting something. Isaac figured that whatever Walkman was chanting, it was the reason these circles around his feet weren't budging, no matter how much energy he attempted to conjure. It was some sort of spell. But Walkman appeared to be extremely focused on it. So, Isaac decided to start blasting cosmic electricity from his body in every direction. This ended up doing two things. As soon as the cosmic energy hit the lion, the lion backed off. And second, a stray beam of energy hit Walkman and sent him flying into the arctic snow. Isaac could feel the circles become loose immediately. He was able to break free and one swift punch later Walkman's beast was dead. Isaac then flew to where Walkman was. Walkman attempted get up, but Isaac landed a clean punch. When the punch landed, Walkman attempted to teleport. Isaac was right behind him. Their cycle started with Spain. Another punch from Isaac and they were in Seattle. Another punch landed them in Africa. For a moment, Isaac was reminded of Imani, Jonas, and the great people of Nigeria. Reminded that if he didn't stop this man, world domination wasn't on his mind today, but how long until it was? What happens when others decided to rise against the Pinnacle? Isaac wasn't going to let that happen. He landed another punch. Walkman grunted as they teleported to Titan. Just like Isaac did his first time, Walkman struggled to breathe when they first landed.

Is this it? Do I just let him die here?

Isaac couldn't believe that he was conflicted about killing a man who killed his daughter, but he was. Nothing explained it, but he wasn't sure he could kill Walkman in this moment if he didn't adjust to the atmosphere on Titan. Unfortunately, he did, and Isaac was trapped in his own thoughts for too long. Walkman rose up from the ground and landed an uppercut loaded with dark energy. It was the most pain Isaac had felt since getting his powers. Not only did the hit hurt his body, it almost decimated his suit. Each generator began to sputter, and parts of the suit cracked as well. The punch had gotten through the layer of energy Isaac coated over the suit and Walkman followed that uppercut with a stomp. He teleported right above Isaac and stomped him as if he were a bug in his luxurious office. Isaac was right above one of Titan's many mountains. He landed on it, and blue lava came pouring from it. Walkman teleported next to Isaac, but Isaac blasted him with an energy blast that knocked him off the mountain. Isaac was quick though. He caught Walkman, ready to deliver the final blow.

As he was about grab Walkman by the throat, Walkman teleported. Isaac attempted to follow his energy, but it was weaker for some reason.

When Isaac reoriented himself, he noticed he was standing on a beach. Once he caught his breath, he guessed he was in Thailand or some other part of Southeast Asia, but no Walkman. He could sense his energy, but it seemed to be far away. But somehow it felt close too.

Isaac didn't want to get too cocky, however. But he knew that Walkman was playing a game with him right now. He figured that Walkman was hiding in the forest that was a few feet from the beach. Isaac guessed that Walkman didn't have the energy to teleport again, given the weak energy signal, so he decided to wait his enemy out.

He decided to teleport back to his mother's street, but only for a brief second. It was to retrieve his mask. When he got back to the beach, Isaac put the mask back on, and put the lenses down. The sun was going down, and the beach felt calm. Isaac decided to sit on the wet sand and meditate.

Where are you, Walkman?

His question was answered quickly as Walkman, in his gross human form, limped from the forest. Isaac didn't stand up, he just simply turned around. Still sitting on the beach. The tide was starting to come in, and the cold water was calming him.

Walkman looked like he wanted to say something, but he just stood there. His eyes flickering between normal human eyes, and the black emptiness he had when in his demon form.

"Help me," Walkman said. He fell to his knees, his body shaking. When he looked up at Isaac, Walkman was gripping the sand with incredible force. He seemed to be in immense pain.

He's dying, Isaac thought. Rather, something is draining his energy, no his life force.

"Please," Walkman pleaded. "Please."

Isaac wanted to burst out in laughter. Not because this man was about to die, Isaac wasn't sure if anything could be done to save him at this point. And he wasn't even sure why Walkman was dying. Surely the punches and blasts Isaac had landed hurt, but Walkman was deteriorating in front of him. No, the laughter would come from the irony. This man, this human, who before he had these amazing powers, wanted Isaac dead. Maybe not dead, but he wanted to inflict pain on Isaac in the worst way possible. Why? Isaac told the world his theory not too long ago, and he was sure that they'd configure their own, but watching Walkman right now, Isaac realized there was something bigger at play. Figuratively and literally.

It was still a mystery as to how Jacob gained these powers in the first place. Walkman took advantage of his own son, who was hardly an adult. So literally, something else was going on here, and Isaac was determined to figure out what. But figuratively, this was a weak man. A man who had more power than one person should. Hardly any checks, and absolutely no balances. Walkman was the main man within the one percenter community known as the Pinnacle. He ran his office with brutality, never letting anyone out of his clutches. With that fear, he ruled. Fear is a powerful thing. But so is anger. Isaac could sense the anger in Walkman even before he had

218

these mystical, cosmic powers. He had sensed it in himself that night he came across that cop. So much so that his fear and anger manifested itself. Maybe that's why Walkman was so powerful for so long.

Maybe it's why my powers have grown, Isaac said. Fear and anger don't drive me like they did when I first met Erasmus.

Thoughts of Alisha and Cynthia came into his mind. The last thing he wanted to do was cry with his helmet on and his lenses activated, but his heart didn't care.

All this power, he thought. And I can't sense Cynthia. I couldn't save my daughter.

"Isaac," Walkman said slowly. Isaac decided to get up this time. Walkman's body was starting to evaporate. Most of his left leg was gone, along with some parts in his face. It was evaporating in the air as black dust.

"Where's my wife?" Isaac asked.

Walkman didn't say anything.

"I'm going to ask you again," Isaac said, "Where is Cynthia?"

Walkman's eyes lowered. He looked upset. He looked embarrassed.

"He," Walkman began to say. "He told me I didn't need to know."

His speech was painfully slow and hard to understand. But Isaac heard him well enough.

"Who's been pulling your strings, Walkman? Who gave you these powers."

There was no answer. Walkman didn't even twitch. Isaac knew that Walkman even divulging the information about someone else was probably a mistake, and he knew that Walkman wasn't going to name the person or creature behind this. Still, he had hoped for some answers about Cynthia. He missed her every day and hated being without her. Isaac looked at Walkman a bit longer and he began to think about Jacob.

"Your son," Isaac said. "You put your son through all of that. I'm guessing now that you're struggling, you regret that."

Walkman nodded slowly.

"Your only son?" Isaac asked.

Walkman nodded again.

Isaac chuckled softly.

"Funny, how death can help bring much needed clarity in our lives. I sense your pain, Walkman. And not the obvious physical pain you're in right now."

Walkman looked up like a child who had just been scolded by their parent. He was intently listening to Isaac, even though he didn't have much of a choice.

"I don't pretend to know you. Where you come from, what you like, what you hate, etc. Actually, I try not to do that with anyone. You can get into dangerous territory, mentally, if you rely on prejudices. You've been in that territory for some time now though, haven't you?" Isaac asked.

Walkman nodded slowly. Both of his legs were gone now.

"Of course you have," Isaac said. "Something created you. Was it society? America? The Pinnacle? Or am I wrong? Have you always been the way you are?"

Walkman shook his head no.

"No? Well, that's good to hear. And on some level, I think I agree." Isaac held out his hand. It began to glow a light purple. Pretty soon, his hand a thick coat of energy around it. He didn't do anything though, he just let the energy build up.

"I think I can save you," Isaac said to Walkman. Walkman's eyes lit up. A dry smile crosses his face. Or at least Isaac thought it was a smile, some of Walkman's teeth had evaporated, along with half of his body.

"Maybe," Isaac said. "I sense a ton of dark energy within you. Living dark energy. Like a doctor extracting a bullet from a gunshot victim, I might be able to extract this dark energy from you. I also might be able to destroy it and restore your body to its full form."

"If I extract the dark energy," Isaac continued. "I might be able to track the person who's behind all of this. You live on and I get closer to finding Cynthia."

Walkman nodded his head in agreement.

"Do it," he said quietly. "Please, hurry."

Isaac moved his hand slowly towards Walkman. Almost instantly, part of Walkman's body became to come back. Just the mere presence of Isaac's energy was helping him. Surely then, Isaac could save this man's life, and maybe take the dark energy out of him.

"This is good," Isaac said. "Really good."

Walkman smiled.

Isaac closed his eyes. Once again, he thought about Imani, Jonas, and the people of Nigeria. Then, he allowed himself to break his consciousness into other parts of the world. Other galaxies, other universes. As Walkman died on the beach, each universe became whole again. Without his presence, whether he was a demon or a human, peace could be attained. Isaac's knowledge of his powers was lacking, there was no doubt about that. He couldn't explain the "science" behind it – if one could even call this science. But, in some way, he completely understood them. Understood what they were meant for, why he felt certain things, and why he could do certain things. Erasmus wanted him to save Earth. Said it was one of the most irredeemable planets in the multiverse. But, Isaac knew that just saving this Earth was never enough. No, he needed to help every planet, every universe, every galaxy. He understood that, and looking at Walkman, he understood that this man needed to die. Isaac lowered his hand, the purple glow went away, and so did Walkman's smile.

"I know that I can save you," Isaac said. "But I won't."

Walkman's deterioration wasn't going as fast now. But the pain seemed to be getting more intense.

"You---you stupid, moronic---," Walkman wanted to go on a tirade, but he winced in pain every other word.

"Your work for the Pinnacle has left millions to suffer. Not only do you profit off other's misfortune, you seem to relish in it. So much so, that you demonized your own son to get to me. Willing to kidnap people, torture them, and who knows what else."

Walkman was nearing the end. The child-like admiration that was in his eyes moments ago, was now rage. Anger, rage, and fear. The fear wasn't showing on his face, but Isaac could sense it. For maybe the first time in his life, Walkman was consumed by fear. The same fear that gave him power for years.

"I'm selfish as well," Isaac said. "Don't think I could ever get over the fact that you killed me daughter."

"That little bitch deserved every---" Isaac had heard enough. He extended his index finger and pointed it at Walkman. Slowly, purple electricity came from his finger. One sudden blast later and Walkman was gone. Isaac attempted to search for his energy but couldn't find him. He then took his mask off, sat on the beach and continued to meditate. When Mystic Man finally opened his eyes, it was nighttime, and Walkman's energy was still nowhere to be found.

CHAPTER 15

T itan had become Isaac's favorite place to think in the past
few weeks. Some others included Mercury, Iceland, and a
planet he discovered only a few days ago. Any time he didn't
spend on Earth was time well-spent. Mystic Man was the only thing
the world was talking about, ever since his encounter with
Walkman. Everyone in the world knew who he was now too. Isaac
was just happy that his superpower wasn't just super strength. He
wasn't sure he could push his way to privacy. Every now and then,
he'd let his mind float to his home in San Francisco. People
surrounded it every day hoping that their hero would show his face.
Except, a good chunk of people didn't think Isaac was a hero.
Conspiracy theorists were saying that he was a government
experiment. Others were saying that he was a pundit for political
organizations. The main one people mentioned was Black Lives
Matter. The craziest thing that Isaac heard was that he was a spy for
the President. That almost forced him to give a press conference,
but he didn't. Too much had happened recently.

Isaac wasn't big on vacations, he never saw the point of them.
But now, all he wanted to do was meditate and visit other planets.
One planet he visited was in his galaxy. He wasn't sure where, but
he just knew. Overall the planet was a nice one. Reminded him of
Earth. Humanoid creatures walked around the technologically
advanced planet. Sky scrapers Isaac never thought could exist were
in abundance here. The air was clean, and Isaac had never seen
such clear water before in his life. He didn't talk to anyone, he
didn't want to startle anybody. For all he knew, they knew nothing of
Earth or any other planet, although that was hard to believe given
the impressive society.

One day while walking along the outskirts of the city, Isaac
stopped to drink some water from a river. As he bent down and
cupped the water in his hands, he heard a noise. A little creature was
behind him. It was one of the humanoid creatures who lives on the

planet. Head resembled a basketball, six eyes, four arms, and light blue skin. The common look from what Isaac noticed. Isaac didn't really know what to do, so he slowly drank the water in his hands. While doing it, he made a loud slurping noise hoping to get the creature to laugh. It worked. The creature, who appeared to be young, let out a light giggle. Isaac grabbed more water and drank seriously this time. He couldn't believe how good the water tasted. After he was done, the creature was still standing there.

"Hello," Isaac said.

The creature bowed elegantly.

"How do you do?" it responded. It then let out another giggle.

"Just kidding," it said. "Imagine if we were that weird and formal. You humans wouldn't like us at all."

"You'd be surprised," Isaac said. "Some humans like that type of stuff."

"Mainly the bureaucrats though, right?"

Isaac didn't know what to say.

"I'm sorry. Where are my manners? I'm----well, I'm positive my native name would be too hard for you. Call me Loopy. Only human word I can think of that sounds like my name," Loopy said.

"You have some sort of communicator that translates what I'm saying?" Isaac asked.

Loopy pointed to a silver piece of metal attached to her weird head.

"You humans are the only ones who don't have this," she said.

Isaac laughed a bit.

"So, you know a lot about Earth?"

"Yeah, if you can't tell, we kind of take the whole better society thing pretty seriously. Almost everything here on Magnuss is perfect. I'm not complaining or anything, just can be off-putting to outsiders."

"Magnuss, huh?" Isaac turned around and looked at the city. Then at the sky. Two moons could be seen in the distance. One a light green, the other a purple.

"That green moon," Loopy said, "Is our biggest source of energy and food. It has a powerful element that we use to keep this entire place afloat. It's also very fertile. The richest people in our society live on that moon. Harvesting crops and what not. It's a solitary, quiet life, but they love it."

"You don't have to keep convincing me," Isaac said. "I get it, this place is pretty great."

"Not trying to convince you, but why else would Mystic Man be here? I figured you'd want to learn everything about us before you try and kill us all."

Isaac felt his heart almost burst through his chest. Loopy let out another giggle.

"Sorry, sorry," she said. "That was my poor attempt at human humor."

Isaac didn't say anything.

"I can see that I upset you," she said.

Still nothing. There was a long pause. Isaac wanted Loopy to leave. Thought that if he stood there long enough, she would. But she didn't.

"Why are you still here?" Isaac finally said.

"Why are you here? This is my planet," Loopy said.

"Fair point," Isaac started to fly away when Loopy yelled at him.

"Wait!" she said. Isaac flew back down to the surface. When he landed, he couldn't get over how soft the grass was.

This place is truly unbelievable, he thought.

"I'm sorry," she said. "We know about you. And by 'we' I mean pretty much the entire galaxy. Other galaxies too."

Isaac couldn't believe what he was hearing.

"Information travels fast between us. Another perk of that green moon up there. Scientists were able to use that element to build the galaxies only lightspeed message sender. The suits call it the Sender," Loopy said.

"Kind of redundant," Isaac said smiling.

"Ah! My attempt at getting you to stay has worked!"

"For the moment," Isaac said.

"So yeah, without that Moon, no more lightspeed communication between all the other worlds. So, for now, we know all about you and Earth."

"I see."

"Don't worry, Isaac," Loopy started to say. "The rest of the galaxy adores you. Some think you're a menace, but that happens. But trust me, the rest of us love you. The way people on Earth are treating you right now is---- um, help me out here."

"Terrible," Isaac said.

"Yes! That's it. Tell me Isaac, why did your people make such a mess of race and gender early in their society. The problems you find yourselves in today are almost unsolvable because they stem from people thousands of years dead. Me and my friends talk about it a lot you know. It's weird to me and I can't figure it out."

"I have my own theories," Isaac said. "But what you said is entirely correct. It's built into us. Created by men too insecure to do anything themselves. Thought I could help break that cycle."

"You're doing a good job. Inspired a bunch of people on Earth," Loopy said.

"Thanks," Isaac said.

Loopy told Isaac more about Magnuss. She also told him more about the rest of the galaxy. They were still on the outside of the city, but Loopy wanted to show Isaac one of her favorite parks. It was filled with more lush, blue grass and interesting architecture.

"Why are you here?" Loopy asked him.

"I like to see different worlds from time to time. This is one of the coolest I've ever seen," Isaac said.

"It's clear you don't want to be on Earth. Want to live here? My family and friends would love to meet you. Rest of the planet would too."

Isaac was seriously thinking about what Loopy had just said. When Walkman died, Isaac searched the multiverse for his energy, making sure he wasn't alive. An epiphany came to Isaac as he realized that maybe Earth isn't worth all the trouble. Racism, sexism, homophobia. Could it ever be cured? Could corruption truly be eradicated from Earth?

"Do you know about the multiverse?" Isaac asked Loopy.

She nodded. "Everyone does. No one is allowed to travel to other universes though. Plus, the only way anyone could do it is with a powerful machine that only citizens of Magnuss know about. I'm guessing you can travel between universes?"

"Yes, I can. I was just wondering, is this universe called anything different? Are there signifiers for each universe?"

"You mean like a system? Yeah, there's a system!" Loopy said.

"Well, what's this universe called, or my Earth?" Isaac asked.

"There's some debate about our universe, so it's funny you ask. The only ones allowed to roam universes freely are the scientists who constructed the system. This universe is the center of a debate because some think it's an older universe. Some believe it's newer," Loopy said.

"So, we know when and how these universes were created?"

"Not how, that's something they're working on. But when is pretty simple. Except this universe seems to have had some sort of change in energy recently. It's altered the 'age' of this universe. Before this alteration, I believe they said this was Earth-442, but now, they're saying Earth 244. Isn't that exciting?!"

"That new energy de-aged our universe. But only from an optic position, I'm guessing right? Surely, this energy didn't have any real effect on our universe," Isaac said.

"On the contrary, Mystic Man. Scientists say that this energy not only changed the age of this universe, but it also left us vulnerable. Have you heard of the outside? Where nothing, but everything exists?"

Isaac nodded.

"We've become vulnerable to attacks from outside," Loopy said. "There's a whole bunch of other stuff that it did too, but that's the main one. It's been the talk of the universe for quite some time now."

Isaac stood there for a second. His face was starting to itch, so he decided to take his mask off. Probably the best thing about the world, or rather multiverse, knowing his identity was the fact that he didn't have to wear his mask all the time. He just liked to wear it mainly for appearance. But he had lost track of time. He had no idea what month it was, how long he had been on Magnuss, or how long he'd been here, talking with Loopy. And it didn't matter. What Loopy had just told him sent his brain in different directions. A ripple in the universe? Vulnerable from the outside? Isaac knew why this was all happening. Apparently, his assuredness was written on his face.

"You know what that energy is, don't you?" she asked.

"I do," Isaac said.

"Is it how you got your powers?"

"Pretty positive," Isaac said.

"Fascinating," Loopy said looking at the ground intently. She did that a lot. Isaac assumed this was her thinking rather hard about something. From talking with her just now, he noticed it didn't take this alien long to come to correct conclusions. He wondered if that was a thing around here, or if she was special.

"Let's walk, Loopy" Isaac said.

"Where to?" she seemed excited.

"Anywhere. Preferably a library of sorts. Do you have one here? A place where I could look up information on different universes and stuff like that?" Isaac asked.

"But of course! It's not too far from here. I always take walks out this way when I get bored. Who knew I'd run into Mystic Man on a normal work day!"

The two of them headed towards the city.

"Tell me about yourself, Loopy. Where are you from? What do you like to do?"

Loopy started talking about her life, her family, and friends. Isaac was listening to every word his new friend was telling him, but he couldn't help but think of Erasmus and this change in the universe's structure. Sure, the first thing that came to mind was that

Erasmus' travelling caused this rift, but Isaac wasn't sure it was that simple. There was a good possibility that it was in fact himself, that was causing this change. Every day, Isaac felt himself growing stronger. Erasmus first mentioned his jealousy of it on Titan, but Isaac noticed his growth before that. It was possible that he was causing his universe, and possibly all of reality to change by using these powers. Honestly, he had no idea, so that's where Loopy came in. Right in front of him, was a resource he could use to gain some useful information. Her being such a delight to be around was just a plus.

As they walked through the enormous city, Isaac noticed that there were a bunch of different species here on Magnuss. Most looked like Loopy, it was clear that she was younger than most of the inhabitants on this planet, but there was diversity. Green, purple, red, and every other color Isaac could think of was represented in these aliens. Some didn't look like aliens at all. One alien Isaac saw looked exactly like a woman from Earth. Same proportions and everything, except her skin was a light yellow. She winked at Isaac as they passed each other.

"She likes you," Loopy said happily.

"I'm spoken for," Isaac said back.

"You should bring her here to Magnuss! I'm sure she'd love it," Loopy said.

"Maybe one day," Isaac said quietly.

They approached a building that was just as big as the ones Isaac had seen in this magnificent city.

"This is it," Loopy said. "Here you can learn all about the other universes. Maybe even find out why the universe is acting funny."

Isaac started walking up the steps, but he noticed that Loopy wasn't following him. She stood at the bottom of the steps, looking at the ground and twirling her feet like a child.

"I don't know what you're waiting for," Isaac said. "I'm going to need someone to help me do some research. If you want too, of course."

"Really? Oh, that's fantastic, Mystic Man!" Loopy ran up the stairs and hugged his leg as tight as she could.

"I like making new friends," Loopy said.

"Me too, Loopy. Me too."

CHAPTER 16

It had been a full two years since Isaac became Mystic Man. Overall, the world had become receptive ever since his battle with Walkman. Jacob, Walkman's son, revealed the truth about his father, and the world seemed to believe him. The Pinnacle was still a problem. Walkman was just a figurehead, and with him gone, they just got themselves a new puppet. But, they weren't bothering Isaac anymore, so he decided not to bother them. Not yet, anyways.

Isaac ended up staying on Magnuss for a full year. He worked as a laborer and hung out with Loopy and her family in his spare time. When he wasn't working, Isaac was learning. About the multiverse, about his own universe, and about every known planet. That year was the best Isaac felt since his time in Nigeria. Cynthia and Alisha didn't pop into his mind too much, and when they did, it tended to be happy thoughts. Isaac didn't focus on Earth too much in the time he was gone, and he didn't really need too. Nothing new was happening. Isaac loved Earth. It took him a while to admit it, but he did; it's hard to not love where you come from. Isaac was just tired of Earth. Tired with humanity in general. Same old stories day in and day out. But, Isaac had learned about the pride these other planets had. And it wasn't an arrogant pride. What made Earth so special, or maybe the better word was ignorant, was its pride. Its inability to see the things surrounding them, and its apathy in wanting to fix itself. Isaac was amazed at the number of planets he visited in the past year. Not many were better than Magnuss, but a few were. Even the planets involved in civil wars seemed to be having them for good reason. All that aside though, Earth was spectacular in some ways. Isaac, in some ways, was embarrassed with the knowledge he had acquired in his life. There were too many things he didn't know. Too many areas of science where he had failed and wasn't even close. It took him that full year to realize that maybe his frustrations with Earth weren't really with Earth, but rather himself.

Isaac wanted to show everyone from Earth everything he had learned. Loopy suggested to him that he does so slowly. First, show them how to purify their water, and run their societies on clean energy. If they didn't take to that, then maybe they didn't need the other knowledge. As it turned out, Loopy was right. When Isaac approached the American federal government as himself about implementing new energy and water procedures, they shut him down. Even the investors he met with didn't trust the idea. Stories began to circulate in the news cycle about Isaac potentially trying to harm Earth, after being gone for so long. People didn't trust his intentions. That was fine, he didn't expect them too. Instead of wallowing in hate and self-pity, Isaac decided to immerse himself in his job as a superhero again, helping wherever he could and helping whoever he could. Nigeria was his first destination. During his hiatus, he kept in contact with Imani. He helped her with some new ideas she was having regarding her book and career. He was happy when she told him about the new living quarters he demanded be built had been built. When he arrived, the Nigerian government took kindly to his proposals. Of course, they didn't understand the science behind them, but they were willing to try. Ever since Isaac helped them get rid of that terrorist organization, the country had been on the upswing. Time and effort were the main factors that were going to ultimately heal the country, but Isaac was pleased to see progress.

Some other countries accepted his proposal too. Denmark, Sweden, India, and even Russia. But America stayed firm on their stance. Isaac guessed it was because of the Pinnacle. Even with Walkman's death, the same hate and fear engulfed it daily. But Isaac didn't decide to wait around for America. He finally found a group of investors who liked the sound of clean water and clean energy. With some of the money he had left over from Nigeria, they began working. It involved a bunch of work from Isaac, some of the machines that Loopy had suggested needed parts that humans didn't have. But most of the parts could be built on Earth. Once they exited the preliminary stages, they settled on a city. There was only one option in Isaac's mind. Flint, Michigan. Not only had they not had clean water in over seven years, Isaac saw this as an opportunity to provide some much-needed life to a state that needed it. Sure enough, within three months, Flint had water as pure as Magnuss.

Most of the city ran on Solar energy now too. Loopy was positive that Magnuss wouldn't let Isaac take any of their precious element from their moon, and she was right. But, using the remainder of his Immobulum, Isaac was able to convert solar energy into physical solar cells that would never burn out. Loopy told him that some of the oldest buildings on Magnuss were still fueled by those solar cells. In Flint, they decided to build new factories and they used the cells to power them. People were able to get jobs and not worry about the factory being a hazardous environment. Isaac didn't tell anyone about how the solar cells were created. Immobulum was his little secret. And he was the only person on Earth who knew how to get any use out of it. If the Pinnacle had figured it out, they would have been bragging about their efforts by now.

After Flint, other cities wanted to be a part of this new movement. The countries who had signed on from the very beginning were starting to see major improvements. Still no word from the American government.

It had now been three years since Isaac became Mystic Man. Now, he was giving more speeches. Sometimes, he spoke about humanitarian crises happening around the world. Sometimes, if he was bored, he would walk around, as Mystic Man, to local homeless shelters. He would feed the homeless and would speak with them for as long as they would like. He did the same at prisons and schools. Someone had started a campaign for him to run for President. Originally, it was a joke, but now, with the election coming so soon, people were clamoring for their hero to become the President. But Isaac didn't take the bait. As always, he told everyone he represented Earth and all its people, not just America. He reminded them that being President meant involving himself in an "America First" mentality, and he was the farthest thing from that. This didn't win him any conservative fans, but Isaac figured most would understand, seeing as how his statement didn't deviate from anything he'd said before, regarding America.

It was Christmas Eve. Isaac's birthday. He never liked having his birthday on Christmas Eve, his mother would always mess with him, telling him that he'd get less gifts, but she never meant it. Isaac usually loved the holidays. In years past, that feeling had been slowly fading. This year was different. Isaac felt rejuvenated. And he spent

Christmas Eve doing what he loved to do most. Meditating. He hadn't carved out time to meditate for quite some while. It was all he could think about when he woke up that morning. He put on his suit and teleported on top of a skyscraper in New York City. Usually the noise of the city bothered Isaac, but not today. Snow was on the ground and there was a positive energy in the air. As Isaac closed his eyes, he could feel the energy in his body begin to surge. It was controlled though. The energy started in his stomach and extended to the rest of his body. A purple glow surrounded him. He was at peace.

That peace soon faded. The wind was starting to pick up. He was already up extremely high, so the wind had already been fierce. Isaac felt an energy he hadn't felt in at least a year. His eyes closed, he didn't need to look up or even move to know who was behind him.

"Hello, Isaac," Erasmus said.

Isaac didn't move.

Erasmus didn't say anything, either. He decided to sit down and assume his meditation pose. Isaac maintained his as well. Hours passed before Isaac opened his eyes and turned to face Erasmus. At first when he looked at his mentor, he expected to feel anger and rage. But he didn't. He just looked at Erasmus for a second, who's eyes were open now as well. He hardly recognized Erasmus. Erasmus had worn casual clothes before, but now, he looked like a homeless person. The clothes he was wearing reminded Isaac of something he would see in a Hollywood film about slavery. They were nothing more than rags, it reminded Isaac of potato sacks. Erasmus' face didn't do him any favors either. He had let his beard grow, as well as his hair. A good portion of his hair was gray as well. At first, Isaac was confused, but then he thought about the pressures that come with being the ruler of Earth for over a thousand years. Erasmus looked emaciated as well. In around two years, he went from king to peasant. Isaac wasn't too interested in the story behind this new appearance. He had other things on his mind.

"It's good to see you, Isaac," Erasmus said. The New York wind howled and brushed through his hair. Snow was starting to fall as well. It was light, and it made Erasmus' hair look even more gray.

His voice was soft, almost too soft. Isaac's hearing was enhanced, so he heard him perfectly, but he could still tell Erasmus was speaking quietly.

"I know you have questions, Isaac," Erasmus said.

"Later," Isaac put his hand up. "What do you think of everything I've done?" He extended his hand out towards the city. Obviously, he wasn't talking about New York. He knew that Erasmus had been watching him this entire time. He didn't sense his energy however, Isaac wasn't stupid.

"Amazing work," Erasmus said. "What you did in Flint will be talked about for years to come."

"That's good. Those people deserve it after everything they've been through."

"And your work in Nigeria seems to be progressing very nicely," Erasmus said.

Isaac nodded.

"Imani is special. The people of that country are special. They don't deserve to live in fear because of terrorists."

"And the universe knows who you are now. The planets sing songs of Mystic Man and everything he stands for," Erasmus said.

"Those language translators are a wonder," Isaac said. "But I want to learn some of them someday."

Erasmus still had his legs crossed. The snow had stopped falling too. Isaac turned his back to Erasmus and looked out at the city. He could sense the people scrambling for their Christmas presents and he could also sense the people who didn't have presents. People who didn't have anyone to come home too. That annoyed him. Isaac teleported to the street and began walking around. People began crowding him and asking questions. He didn't answer though. Isaac found the people he felt struggling the most. They appeared to be homeless. Their eyes lit up when he walked up next to them. Isaac teleported to the nearest restaurant and bought some food. When he returned, he gave it out to the homeless and they accepted it graciously. Some other people came up to Isaac, and they were asking questions about why he was doing this. One lady asked him why he didn't help the people down the street. Isaac looked at the lady. She was white with blonde hair and appeared to be wearing an expensive pair of sunglasses. Isaac found that weird seeing as how it wasn't bright outside.

"Because they're not done eating yet," Isaac said. "I want to make sure that these folks get their fill, and then I'll help them over there." It wasn't the answer the lady expected. She walked off mumbling something under her breath, but Isaac just shrugged. As promised, once they were done eating, Isaac went back to the restaurant and bought food for a group of people down the street. The more people he fed, the more he felt people who needed his help. After a couple of hours, he decided to announce that this block would be his last. Everyone was grateful. They thanked him and as he flew off, Isaac could sense that he had done some good. When he returned to the top of the building, Erasmus was still there. He wasn't meditating though. Just standing there. Smiling.

"Why'd you do that?" Erasmus asked.

Isaac looked at him with a confused look.

"Why not?" Isaac said. "I'm not doing anything else. No job, no other commitments. When I sense people in trouble, especially to the point that it's palpable, I have to help."

Erasmus smiled again.

Isaac sighed.

"You've been lying to me from the start," Isaac said.

Erasmus put his head down in shame.

"I'm not even too upset," Isaac said. "But I really want to know why. There are no rulers of the universe. No council that oversees anything that goes on between multiverses. Why lie to me about that?"

"I didn't think I'd get you to help me. I'm sorry," Erasmus said.

"That's another thing. I read your file. Your famous for your rule on Earth back in your other universe. Well documented. But nothing on why you left. Your Earth is a wasteland now, Erasmus. What happened?"

This must've been news to Erasmus because he looked up in shock. Tears filled his eyes and he dropped to his knees.

"Dammit! How?! Why?!" Erasmus screamed at the top of his lungs.

"You didn't know," Isaac said.

Erasmus shook his head.

"I didn't," he said. "How did it happen?"

"Doesn't say. Just says that life there has declined by almost ninety-five percent. Possibly more," Isaac said.

"Now, why did you leave in the first place?" Isaac asked. "No games."

"Isaac, I truly have grown tired. Tired of living. Before I decided to leave, I was contemplating suicide. The idea of death, something I never had to worry about, fascinated me. Bullets, swords, missiles, nothing hurt me. And as I grew in strength, I knew that suicide would be much harder. I came close to trying something. But instead, I decided to leave, and come to you."

"How could you leave your people like that?" Isaac asked.

"I thought I left them in good hands. I had advisors with me that were passed down from generation to generation. Good friends who were with me at the beginning. Their ancestors were there for me at the end. You're the only person who's tasted this power."

As Erasmus said the word power, he extended his hand out, his palm opened. Then, he looked down at his hand and slowly retreated it, until it was tightly placed against his side.

"You need to stop this," Isaac said. "Stop feeling sorry for yourself. You lied to me, and I can't be sure what else you've lied to me about. Or what else you haven't told me."

Erasmus didn't say anything.

"We still don't know how Walkman's son got those powers," Isaac said. "Erasmus, I can't take any more of your lies. I really can't. Did you have something to do with Walkman and his powers?"

"No, I swear I didn't. I don't have any enemies that have that type of power."

"Walkman didn't get those powers by accident. And I'm going to find out who did this." Isaac could feel his body starting to heat up, and fill with energy, but he calmed it instantly. He wasn't one hundred percent on Erasmus not being responsible for this, but he was sure about Erasmus not knowing how it happened.

"I can sense your anger," Erasmus said.

"Must be the anger of the lady who can't find her son that new Xbox," Isaac said. "Because I'm calm."

"You're right," Erasmus said. "I sensed it for a moment, but now it's gone."

Isaac smiled.

"How have you gotten so strong?" Erasmus asked.

"I told you to stop that," Isaac said.

"No, I mean it. I've been trying to figure it out in the past year or so, and it's puzzling me. You've become something I never thought you would."

"I have a theory. While I was on Magnuss, I spent a ton of time reading up on this universe de-aging problem that Loopy told me about. I wanted to question her on the council members and what they thought about this, but I figured you'd been lying about that, so I didn't. She said that about the same time myself and Walkman got our powers, the universe became vulnerable. Vulnerable to attacks from the outside, from other realms, but also other universes."

Erasmus nodded, showing that he was following along.

"All of the reports that I read said this event had to have been caused by some sort of machine. Not only by a machine, but a machine small enough and fast enough it rips through the fabric of the universe itself. No such machine exists. The best and brightest in all the universes can't figure that out. If they ever travel between universes, everyone knows, the effects are easy to see. Not a single scientist posed the question of someone causing this effect. Someone the size of a human," Isaac was looking directly at Erasmus now, who began to back away as if Isaac were going to attack.

"Calm down," Isaac said. "Although I don't know if I can fully trust you, most of what you've told me has been true. And you've helped me reinvigorate my life at a time where I wanted to die as well. When you first gave me powers, and all that crazy energy was flowing through me, I wanted nothing more than to die. But, you've kept your word and have helped me make something of this insane life I now live. I know you didn't intentionally do this to our universe. But you did do it."

"How do we fix it?" Erasmus asked.

"That's the thing," Isaac said. "You aren't the problem. I am."

Erasmus looked confused.

"While I've been doing my work around the world, this problem has been bothering me too. You're always asking how my powers have grown so much. I thought nothing of it. Maybe it's because I'm a different vessel and my powers react differently. No, I don't think it's that. You're from another universe, Erasmus. My theory is that you were never meant to give these powers to anyone, at least anyone from a different universe. By entering this universe with the speed, power, and velocity that you did, you created the ripple. The more I use my powers, I enhance it. I technically have powers from another universe. When you gave them to me, I think you unintentionally connected me with every known universe."

"Wow," Erasmus said.

"Wow is right," Isaac said laughing. "And I could be wrong, but I don't think so."

"What will happen if you continue to use your powers?" Erasmus said.

"I'm not sure, but I'm guessing it isn't good." Isaac said.

"How are you going to fix it?" Erasmus asked.

"Not sure right now. But, I've been throwing around some ideas. What I think I'm going to have to do though is pretty drastic. Until I, or someone can find a way to fix the holes within our own universe, that healing must be done by me."

"What do you mean?" Erasmus asked.

"I'm connected to every known universe. It's why my powers have been growing, and why I'm able to do stuff you can't. But, I'm sucking the life out of other universes, and maybe even neighboring galaxies, just by being here. The main problem is that I've only been here. Well, not always. On Magnuss, I could sense some of that energy being shifted, and I wasn't in a different galaxy. What I'm saying is, that I think I need to be in different galaxies and universes to maintain the whatever is holding us all together."

"Once again, I say wow," Erasmus said. "So that means---"

"It means I can never stay in one place too long. I'll have to figure out a way to measure exactly how long I can stay, but I'm guessing it won't be longer than six months."

"What if you never figure out a way to fix the universe?"

"No idea," Isaac said. "But the only option I see is me doing this for the rest of eternity."

Snow was starting to fall again. Heavier this time. Isaac walked to the edge of the rooftop and overlooked the city. He laughed quietly.

"It's funny," Isaac said. "I'm about as simple a person can get. When it comes to what I want, anyways. And for a brief moment in my life, I had exactly that. Thought it was never going to go away."

He took off his mask and dropped it on the ground. Erasmus gave Isaac a confused look.

"I got plenty at home," Isaac said. "Anyways, sometimes, I'm amazed that I can contemplate this stuff, Erasmus. As a human, over a hundred is hard to comprehend. As a scientist, I can imagine millions of years. It's hard to try and contemplate eternity."

"Are you sure you want to do this?" Erasmus asked. "You can always give up the powers. I could do it."

"Look at you," Isaac said. "I couldn't do that to you."

"How are you going to handle it?" Erasmus asked.

"Maybe there's some sweet spot, in between all of the universes. I could find it, and meditate there until the end of time, constantly releasing energy to heal the multiverse. In a way, that could be my death."

There was a long silence. It was at least ten minutes before Isaac said something.

"But I don't want that yet," Isaac said. "I want to keep helping people as long as possible."

"You're a good man, Isaac Eckspo," Erasmus said.

The day was almost over. It was getting dark. Isaac didn't have any plans for the night, so he just stood up there with Erasmus a while longer.

"You back for the long haul?" Isaac asked. "I think it's time for everyone to meet the man who helped me become a hero," he said smiling.

"I'm back," Erasmus said quietly. "I'm back."

Isaac extended his hand and Erasmus did the same. They shook hands firmly and smiled at each other for a moment. Then, Isaac decided it was time to go home. He didn't really need sleep nowadays with his powers, but he enjoyed sleeping. And he knew his body would enjoy it as well. He didn't teleport though. Isaac flew from the rooftop and glided through the air above New York City. As he felt the energy of the city, he smiled, knowing that what he had done earlier did help. Next, he teleported to Chicago. Then Seattle. Austin. Each city filled with life and love on Christmas Eve. Snow in most places, and some were dry, but each city reenergized him as he flew. Finally, Isaac was ready to go home. It was late by the time he teleported to San Francisco. When he teleported to the steps of his house, he just waited there for a moment. He was glad he waited, because just next to him, the jazz band he had heard those years ago was playing. Isaac couldn't remember the last time he had seen these men. Their instruments sounded livelier than ever. And as Isaac teleported on the steps, they acknowledged him. And he did the same.

He put his hand on the door.

Something was wrong. Something wasn't right. But he didn't know what it was. There was an energy surrounding the door that he wasn't familiar with. But at the same time, he felt as if he knew it like the back of his hand. It wasn't life-threatening or anything like that, but it wasn't good.

Someone's in my house, he thought.

Isaac looked around outside. The men were still playing their instruments and the rest of the city seemed to be calm. The rest of the world seemed to be calm. Isaac didn't want to deal with who was behind the door and in his home. What if Pinnacle workers were raiding his home? What if it was someone from another galaxy? What if Walkman was alive? There wasn't much he could do except face what was behind the door. Face whoever was in his home. Isaac looked down at his hands. He was still wearing his suit. He admired the design for a moment before closing his eyes. His hands began to glow purple along with his eyes. Isaac unlocked the door. Instantly though, those feelings of rage and paranoia ceased.

When Isaac opened his door, feelings began to rush over him. His body shivered a bit, because the feelings turned into energy. It was a feeling that he hadn't felt in a very long time. In fact, Isaac wasn't sure if he had felt this feeling before. Pure bliss. Pure happiness overcame him. The home was cleaned, and it smelled like it had been cleaned too. Isaac started in the living room. The carpet had been vacuumed thoroughly and with care. The television had been dusted. Any toys and junk that had been on the floor had been picked up. Isaac wanted to laugh out loud when he noticed that the couch cushions had been flipped and cleaned as well. As he continued through the house, this blissful feeling didn't end. It brought him to tears. Because he knew what it meant. He knew, but he just didn't want to believe it. He didn't want to believe that something like this was possible. For the past two years, he had been selfless. Caring about others and their needs. Thinking that his needs didn't matter. In Walkman's death, he found justice. It was something that would haunt Isaac for years to come, taking the life of another man, but he knew it had to be done. The universe spoke to him and begged him to do it. But now, in this moment, he couldn't believe this feeling. A feeling he had felt before he had his powers. Now with them, he could barely contain himself. It was a feeling that one person had ever given him before. And as Isaac walked into the kitchen, and let the aroma of spaghetti hit his nose, he saw her. Leg fixed from the accident. He saw the one person who could make him feel so nervous, but so confident. Scared, but courageous. Empowered, but weak. She turned around and Isaac barely found the strength to say her name.

"Cynthia," he said quietly. Isaac dropped to his knees and began to sob uncontrollably.

Cynthia looked at him for a moment and then walked over to her husband. She consoled him but didn't say anything as he cried.

She gestured for him to stand up and he did. Isaac could hardly look at his wife.

"I---I don't believe it," Isaac said. He was slurring his words. "I---I never thought I'd see you again."

Cynthia put a finger to Isaac's lips.

"We have a lot to talk about, Isaac," she said. Her eyes were filled with tears now too.

"Your friend Erasmus found me. Said it took him years to do it, but he did."

Isaac couldn't believe what he was hearing. He grabbed his wife and embraced her. They were both sobbing now, as Cynthia's food cooked on the stove.

"Alisha," Isaac started to say.

"No," Cynthia said. "Erasmus told me everything. You did your best. You did all you could."

Isaac could hardly breathe. They continued to hug.

"Happy birthday, Isaac," Erasmus said in Isaac's head. "This is the best present I could find. Hope it's good enough."

"Your sense of humor is terrible," Isaac said aloud. Cynthia looked at him and smiled.

"Oh, please," she said. "I've always been funnier than you, Isaac." She looked at his suit. Then, she hit his chest plate playfully.

"Or should I call you Mystic Man?" she asked.

"I love you," Isaac said. "So much."

"I love you too," she said. "Now, I did do some Christmas shopping, so we'll open gifts after dinner."

"Are we having spaghetti?" Isaac asked.

"Of course," Cynthia said. She gave Isaac a quick kiss and went back to the stove. She looked back at Isaac and smiled. He smiled back. When Cynthia brought the food to the table, Isaac couldn't remember the last time food had tasted this good.

"It was Alisha's favorite," he said.

Cynthia was fighting back tears. She looked up.

"It sure was," she said.

———— ·· —— ·· —— ·· —— ·· —— ·· —— ··

THE END

·

ABOUT THE AUTHOR

Toren Chenault was born and grew up in a small town just outside of Cincinnati. He attended college at Michigan State University and graduated with a bachelor's degree in Political Science – Prelaw. He currently lives in Michigan with his girlfriend.

Made in the USA
San Bernardino, CA
27 May 2018